MW00882103

35 Years Later

A Novel Inspired by True Events

Tania Heller & Izzy Heller

The book is a work of fiction.
Any references to real-life people, events, institutions or other places, are merely intended to lend the writing a sense of reality. All other events, incidents, names and characters, except a few well-known historical figures, are either products of the authors' imaginations or are used fictitiously.
Where real places appear, the characters and events concerning them are fictional.
Likewise, where real-life figures appear, the situations and dialogues concerning them are fictional.
In every other respect, any resemblance to actual persons, living or dead, places, or events, is entirely coincidental.

Copyright © 2018 Tania Heller and Izzy Heller

Cover image copyright © 2018 Zelda Heller

All rights reserved.

ISBN: 1985461242

ISBN-13: 978-1985461246

ACKNOWLEDGMENTS

We are indebted to several people who contributed to this book and allowed us to tell a better story.

The authors are especially grateful to Bill Cohen for giving of his valuable time and expertise.

Thank you to Nalini Natarajan, Ann Jones Stern, Gadi and Inbal Cohen and Cherian Verghese for support in reading and commenting on the manuscript.

Zelda, Leon, Gabriella and Benjamin Heller, Sam, Daniel and Ariel Messeca: we love you and your encouragement means a lot to us.

ONE

Silver Spring, Maryland, 1977

Hollow Oak Drive was dark, except for a single light emanating from number 1201, the three-level brick Colonial. The basement of Marc's host parents' home was a private enclave for the young lovers. Laura lifted a timeworn volume off the bookshelf. She opened its pages and read aloud from a sonnet by William Shakespeare.

"Shall I compare thee to a summer's day?

"Thou art more lovely and more temperate…"

She glanced up at Marc and frowned. "You're not paying attention!"

"I'm listening," said Marc. "It's beautiful. But it's the night before I return to South Africa. There're other things we could be doing."

Laura put the anthology aside. "You're right. I don't want to think about tomorrow. And I know you're worried about what's happening back home."

"Let's not talk about that now." Marc dimmed the lights and positioned himself on the sofa-bed. His shirt was partially unbuttoned, revealing his muscular frame.

He beckoned with outstretched arms. "Come over here," he said, coaxing Laura near.

Usually guarded, and inexperienced in matters of love, she was drawn to him in a way she could barely understand. A few months ago she didn't know this man, and now the thought of being separated from him filled her with dread.

His gentle touch sent a tingle through her body. She brought her mouth to his.

"You have the softest lips," he said.

Marc took off his shirt and reached under her sweater. For a few moments he fiddled with the hook of her lace bra, then it snapped open. If Laura was put off by his lack of manual dexterity, she didn't show it. She slipped out of her top and brought herself closer so that their skin touched. Marc felt her chest against his. He ran his fingers down the small of her back, then concerned he was moving too fast, he hesitated.

"It's okay," said Laura, as she undressed.

For Marc, this was uncharted territory. Yet in spite of his awkwardness, he felt a sense of urgency. As he held on to her, his breathing grew rapid and drops of perspiration trickled down his forehead.

Later, when he felt her body relax, he cradled her in his arms.

"I can't stand the thought of being thousands of miles away from you," said Marc, when he could finally speak.

He saw the sadness in her eyes. He knew that she trusted and respected him. She shared her deepest feelings with him. He would never violate that trust.

"You won't forget me, will you?" he asked.

"If I do," she teased, "I'll remind myself by looking at our prom photo."

"Very funny," he said. "I don't need a photo. I could never forget you." Then he grew somber. "As long as men can breathe, or eyes can see…"

Laura gasped. Shakespeare at its best. "So long lives this," she mouthed, "and this gives life to thee."

As they kissed, her hair fell in loose waves and brushed against his cheek.

Well after midnight, Laura rose. "I've got to get home," she said, glancing at her watch. "I'm sure my mother's worried."

Marc clung to her tightly.

She traced his lips with her fingers. "I can't stay. But I want to tell you something before I leave." He was silent as she continued, "I promise I'll love you always."

"It could be years before we're together again," cautioned Marc.

Laura nodded. "I'll wait."

On the drive home Laura tried to compose herself. She turned on the radio. The familiar sounds of 'Sweet Love' by The Commodores filled the car. She had time to contemplate her relationship with Marc. Her feelings were overwhelming. The relationship had reached emotional and physical heights she had never before experienced. Now, she wondered if she would ever see him again.

Halfway home, as she negotiated a turn in the road, she felt a stabbing pain in her abdomen. The car veered to the side and came to a screeching halt.

TWO

South Africa, 1975 (2 years earlier)

On a warm December afternoon after a long session at North Paarl Boys' High, Marc pedaled his bicycle over the bumpy gravel road toward home. Each bump caused his bruised shin to throb. He could think of only one thing: he and his friend, Aldo, were in deep shit. They could be expelled from school for what they did. Marc's lanky frame was sweating under the heavy woolen shorts and jacket that made up his school uniform, and he eagerly anticipated the cold lemonade that awaited him.

On the way home he passed Jacobi, the teenage son of the neighbor's maid, who slept in the outhouse behind the main home. From time to time, and unbeknownst to their parents, Marc and Jacobi snuck out to a small field to kick a soccer ball or play catch. Marc waved at his friend as he rode by.

As was Marc's custom, he stopped at the red mail-box at the front of his house to collect the mail. He removed the usual bills and pamphlets for his parents and to his surprise, a larger envelope with American postage stamps addressed to him, Mr. Marcus Sennet. He smiled. "Mister." Someone was treating him with respect.

He entered the Cape Dutch house via the garage, propped his bike against a wall and pushed open the kitchen door.

"Hi, mom."

His mother kissed him on the forehead. "Anything special at school today?" she asked.

"No," grunted Marc.

"Maybe this will interest you." She held out a book titled 'Adventures of Huckleberry Finn' by Mark Twain. As one of several librarians at the local library, Molly Sennet had a flexible schedule and chose the early shift to be home when her only child returned from school. She routinely shared with him the latest finds from the library shelves. One day it would be a mystery, other days it was a drama or biography.

Marc had read Twain's 'Tom Sawyer' and normally he would have been eager to delve into this novel. He loved reading about the adventures of the mischievous young boy growing up in a small American town. Today, however, he had other things on his mind. He'd get to Finn later.

He pulled off his striped blue and grey blazer with the embroidered shield surrounding the words 'Per Aspera ad Astra' and draped it over a yellowwood armchair in the kitchen. He sat down. Now, more than ever, he identified with the first part of the phrase, 'Through Difficulties'. The starry destination of the motto seemed more distant than ever. He took the lemonade his mother handed to him and downed it in three gulps. "How am I going to get out of this mess?" he wondered.

As Marc walked into the family room, trying to hide his limp, the front door swung open, and his father stepped through, shutting it loudly behind him. He came up to Marc.

"What're you doing?" Stan asked. He crushed a cigarette in an ashtray on the table. "Wasting time?"

Marc coughed. "No dad. Just came from school." He clutched the envelope. "Going through the mail, then I'll get to my homework."

"Excuses, excuses. You know how I feel about people who procrastinate."

"Yes, dad, you've told me many times."

His father cast him a disapproving glance. "Cheeky, aren't you?"

Marc felt a tightness in his stomach. He wished his father would quit nagging and quit smoking.

Because Marc was considering a career in healthcare, he had browsed through a couple of medical journals in the public library. The dangers of cigarettes were clear. To date, however, his attempt at educating his father about them had not yielded positive results. His dad kept smoking and he'd keep trying. There was nothing he could do about the nagging.

His mother entered the family room and Stan gave her a perfunctory kiss on the cheek.

"One of the factory workers, Tumelo, was completely out of line today," he said to her. "Came right out and demanded a pay increase. Said otherwise he would look for a second job. Sounded like a threat to me."

Molly shrugged her shoulders. "And so? You haven't given raises for years."

"So nothing. He should appreciate the fact we're hiring at all."

Marc cringed. "Dad, you're talking about people. People with families. They need to live."

Stan's lips stiffened and his face grew a shade darker. "Stay out of it," he said. Your generation thinks they have answers to everything."

He left the room and Marc was relieved to see him go.

"I understand how you feel, Marc," his mother said.

She claimed to be sympathetic to his stance on apartheid, but he was not convinced of her sincerity. If she felt as he did, why didn't she take a stronger stand against her husband's views?

She pulled open the curtains, letting in a stream of light, placed a few magazines in a neat pile and carried two dirty glasses to the kitchen.

Left alone now, the stack of mail sought Marc's attention. He opened the flap of the big envelope, removed the letter, and read to himself. *Dear Sir*, it began. He paused to savor that 'Sir.' More respect. Then he read the rest of the letter.

Upon the recommendation of your school principal, your name was submitted as a candidate for a one-year scholarship in the International Exchange Student Program. We have reviewed your grade transcripts as well as testimonials from your teachers and principal. On the basis of these reviews we hereby offer you free transportation, high school tuition and board and lodging in the Washington D.C. area for the 1976-77 academic year.

Should you accept this offer, we require your confirmation
with approval by your parents within thirty days of this
letter. We will forward details of your posting later.
Literature on the IESP is included for your consideration.
Congratulations on your selection.
Kindly respond at your earliest convenience.
Sincerely,
Stephen Q. Boyle, Director
IESP
World HQ, NYC
USA.

It took Marc several minutes of re-reading to absorb the
award letter and consider the ramifications. Although he knew of the
exchange program and was aware he had been nominated, he never
dreamed he would be chosen to participate. What an honor! Then he
thought of the challenge of being an alien in a foreign country and in
its capital city. In a recent issue of National Geographic magazine,
he had read about the different way of life, the superhighways, the
fast trains and the fast food. He saw pictures of the White House,
home to the President of the United States, and the majestic Lincoln
Memorial, built in honor of the great emancipator. He remembered
an image of a student body of all colors crowded together on a
university campus, peacefully advocating for a change in school
policy. No discrimination, and justice for all. What a contrast. North
Paarl, like most South African schools, was segregated as to sex and
race. Girls attended a block away. Non-whites had their separate and

inferior facilities in the neighboring township. Crossing either barrier was a major transgression, one that might cost him his trip to the United States.

Marc decided he would wait until that evening to tell his parents about the letter. He needed time to think. What on first read had seemed like the prospect of a fun adventure, now had turned into a nightmare. The scholarship offer amidst the doom of possible expulsion from school. He was in one helluva jam. And so too was Aldo Carbone, his buddy since preschool days. Aldo was captain of the school rugby team, touted as a future player for the South African International team, the Springboks, and the most popular guy in the class, but he could face serious punishment as well.

Marc leaned back in his favorite chair, a leather recliner, and reflected on the events of the past week. A lot had happened.

Marc had a girlfriend of sorts. Sofia was a year older, with long dark curls, shapely hips and a tiny waist. She was well-supervised by a strict mother, a member of the Dutch Reformed Church, who insisted on her daughter being chaperoned. From the day he met her at their joint high school social four months earlier, Marc had been enchanted by Sofia, and couldn't take his eyes off her budding figure. Both tall, they made a snug fit when they embraced on the dance floor. They loved to tease each other. He, about the way she twirled her hair in her fingers. She, how his eyes crinkled when he smiled. Marc admitted to Aldo his relationship with Sofia was based on lust. Merely a few months after their first meeting, Sofia devised a plan for Marc to pay her a private visit one night. Excited by the prospect of a liaison, he was a willing accomplice.

It had been the middle of the previous school week, under a moonlit sky. On the stroke of midnight, Marc, not yet licensed to drive, took the keys to his father's old Ford pick-up and snuck out on his mission. He slipped out of the house in the dark and met Aldo nearby, as arranged. They drove without headlights from the family carport to the girls' hostel two miles away. There, he and his friend slid an old ladder off the back of the vehicle, extended it to its full length, and leaned it against the brick wall, next to a second-level window that had been left slightly ajar. With Aldo steadying the ladder, Marc climbed, step-by-wobbly-step, to Sofia's bedroom, where she and her two roommates were impatiently waiting.

Her friends were as ecstatic as she when they heard the window sash slide. On cue, the understanding room-mates tip-toed out of the door as Marc crawled through the narrow opening. Once in the room he hurried into Sofia's arms. Whispering to each other, they hugged and kissed. Marc kicked off his shoes and climbed into her bed. She joined him. They cuddled, eagerly exploring each other's bodies in private bliss while Aldo waited impatiently down below alongside the getaway truck looking for the return signal.

After thirty minutes, reason prevailed. "Time's up," said Sofia, as she pried herself away from Marc.

With reluctance Marc slowly withdrew to the window and blew his girlfriend a farewell kiss. He leaned out of the opening, lifted his hand and gave a thumbs-up to Aldo. Slowly he backed and reversed his steps down the rungs in the dark.

Half-way down, Marc saw the lights of an oncoming vehicle. He was momentarily blinded, and when his vision returned, he saw Aldo running from the scene. The unstable ladder slid to the side, and Marc hit the ground hard, slamming his shin on a concrete slab. Bleeding profusely, he yelled for help. To his astonishment, his long-time friend was nowhere to be seen, leaving Marc to suffer without aid.

Hearing Marc's cries, a female student called for emergency assistance. While they waited she wrapped a bandage around his wound. The ambulance siren woke the hostel inmates, and many, excited by the drama, congregated outside.

Terrified someone would discover he had taken his dad's truck, Marc snuck away and hid until he heard the ambulance leave. Then, in pain, he made his way back to the Ford, drove home and replaced the keys without waking his parents.

At breakfast the next morning, when his parents noticed his injury, he told them a version of the story, leaving out any mention of the truck. His punishment included a month without allowance and two weeks of kitchen duty. He shuddered to think how angry they would be if they knew the full extent of what he had done.

That day both high schools were abuzz with the news of the daring escapade. "Hi Romeo," called one student as he passed Marc limping in the hallway.

Marc realized he was now a hero to his peers. Before he could enjoy his new standing, however, he discovered that Sofia's mother did not share the sentiment. Apparently when she heard the news in the morning, she had gone ballistic and rushed to the office of the seminary, screaming at the top of her lungs and demanding severe punishment for the perpetrators of this 'unspeakable crime.' The matron responded by calling for a special meeting of the joint Paarl school board and asked for expulsion of both boys.

Now Marc had one week to prepare for the school board hearing. He was certain his romantic dalliance had put his future plans in jeopardy. Holding the award letter from the U.S., he climbed the steps to his bedroom, wincing from the pain in his shin. His chance for an American scholarship was probably kaput. The academic opportunity of a lifetime was likely lost. But more than that, he would miss his chance to get away from the political situation and his controlling father. Yet there was a part of him that would not quit without a fight. He took out a pad of lined paper, tore off a sheet and wrote a letter to the secretary of the school board.

> *Dear Sir,"*
> *"re: Night-Time Incident*
> *It is with profound remorse that I assure you that my visit to the girls' seminary was an innocent teenage prank intended as a fun challenge and nothing more. I was dared to do this and I now regret it immensely.*
> *It was I who persuaded my friend Aldo Carbone to help me. He was an innocent bystander. He didn't enter the hostel at any time.*

I climbed up a ladder and surprised my friend Sofia Botha.
Nothing inappropriate happened between us. I stayed for a
short while only.
I am very sorry for what I did, and apologize to all
concerned. I have learned from the incident.
Please accept my apology, and excuse my stupid behavior.
Thank you for your understanding.
Yours sincerely,
Marc Sennet.

He edited it several times before copying it in his best handwriting one last time. Then he folded it and slid it into an envelope, which he addressed carefully. The following morning, he put it in a mailbox on his way to school.

THREE

Potomac, Maryland, 1972 (three years earlier)

Laura was already dressed in her pajamas when she kissed her mom
goodnight and went to her bedroom on the second floor. She waited
patiently until the house went dark, then carefully slid open the glass
window. It creaked. She held her breath, hoping her mother had not
heard the noise. Apart from a faint light coming from inside the
house next door, it was dark outside.

Laura had known Amber since kindergarten and now as
teenagers, they found their homes alongside each other, a mere
thirty foot apart. Although Amber was two years older than Laura,
the proximity cemented their friendship. Laura scribbled the
following words on notepaper, "Peter called and told me he likes
you." That said it all. She squeezed the message into a tiny box and
tied it to the cord attached to her window ledge. She reached for a
second cord, and gently pulled. As planned, the container inched its
way toward Amber's open bedroom window, close by in the next
building. After a few seconds, it was gone. All Laura could do was
wait for a response.

She went back to her bed and put an exercise book on her
lap. She enjoyed making notes. In pen she mapped out a tree of life
of various possibilities as she fantasized about her future. Lines
branched through graduations, a handsome husband, three children,
and a farm with horses. She wondered what last name she would
adopt when she married. Hightower. Laura Hightower. She

imagined walking into a room with her husband and being introduced as Lady and Lord Hightower. She resolved to do something important with her life, something that would change the world for the better and warrant the noble title.

After what seemed a long time, Laura heard a squeaky sound outside. To her delight the little container had made its way back. She reached in and read the note from Amber.

"Are you sure? I think he's sexy. Tell him to ask me out. Do your best! Now I'll unhook the string on my side. Don't forget to pull it in. My parents will kill me if they find out what we're up to."

The friends knew they were playing a risky game. That made it all the more exciting.

Laura knew that Amber's mother could become very angry. She often slapped her daughter for little reason. So different from Laura's mother, a part-time teacher, who, in her quiet way, had sacrificed so much for her. After Laura's dad died suddenly when she was only three, her mom was left a widow with a modest monthly income. It was she who attended every piano recital and drove Laura to ballet class and doctors' appointments. But as hard as it was to be a single parent, she was always kind and supportive.

Amber's mother was different, unpredictable. She reminded Laura of a witch with her straggly black hair streaked with grey and her high-pitched grating voice. For some reason she didn't like Laura, perhaps because she was a distraction from homework and chores. Laura was relieved they had gotten away with their deception one more time, if only sending notes back and forth, until she heard shouting from the house next door and a bright beam of light flashed in her eyes. She quickly turned her head away from the intrusion, but she recognized the angry voice.

"Leave my daughter alone," the witch yelled in Laura's direction.

Laura could hear Amber say, "We did nothing, mom. Shh, the neighbors can hear you shouting."

"Don't tell me what to do, Amber. You stay away from Laura. She's a bad influence."

"I'll tell dad you're mean!" cried Amber.

"Go ahead. You'll probably find him in the bar!"

Six weeks later Laura sat on a shaded patch of grass on the Potomac High School baseball field studying for a history test, while not far from her, Amber and Peter made out on the top bench of the wooden grandstand. After Laura set them up, the infatuated teens met whenever they could, and did everything possible to keep the relationship from Amber's suspicious mother. Frequently this involved fabrications by Amber such as "A student tripped over a step and a couple of us helped with ice and bandages. You should have seen the bleeding!" or "The school bus had a flat tire so we had to wait for hours while they put on a spare."

"Hey, Laura!" called Amber, after about an hour on the bleachers.

Laura looked up from her book to see Peter carrying her friend down the rungs. He was a stocky football player and she was petite, looking even smaller in his arms. She was a mess. Strands of her blonde hair had broken loose from its ponytail and her once crisp white shirt was now crumpled.

"Yes?" Laura replied.

"Good news," said Amber, as her boyfriend lowered her down onto the grass. "Peter said he has a friend he could fix you up with."

Peter nodded. "You helped us get together. Happy to return the favor."

"I'm not interested right now," said Laura.

"Why not?" asked Peter, staring at her. "He can probably have any girl he wants."

"I don't think so," said Laura, leading the way to the bus stop. She mumbled under her breath, "He can't have me."

It was late and she was ready to go home.

FOUR

Paarl, 1975

The special meeting of the five board members that comprised the supervising school committee, three men and two women, was called to order at the appointed time. Only one item was on the agenda: illegal trespassing.

The sparsely-furnished conference room was walled on one side with framed photographs in two rows. The upper row depicted Paarl Boys rugby teams going back twenty years, the players stern-faced with arms crossed. The lower row of pictures likewise featured school teams over two decades, the girls demurely portrayed in hockey outfits.

The three defendants were seated on a wooden bench below the image of the sports teams. Sofia, in her school uniform, with a cardigan buttoned all the way up to her neck, twisted a pencil round and round between her thumb and fingers. Aldo, looking down, avoided eye contact with the board members. Marc had entered the chamber with an accentuated limp. Now, in a navy suit, white shirt and tie, he remained outwardly composed, but his gut understood the gravity of the situation. His future and his opportunity to go abroad was at stake. The letter he had received seven days earlier was in his shirt pocket, a tangible reminder of what hung in the balance. And vengeance was in the air.

The Chairman tabled the facts of the matter as reconstructed from various accounts, then gave the students an opportunity to comment.

Aldo stood up first. "It was his idea," he said, pointing to Marc. He pressured me to go along with the plan."

Sofia raised her hand. When called upon she added, "I didn't know anything about it. I was shocked when he came into my room."

Marc squinted in their direction. His eyes burned with accusation and disappointment.

A motion was introduced to expel the two boys involved and to reprimand the girl. To Marc, the punishment seemed a foregone conclusion.

"Not so quick," said the Chairman. All were quiet as he read Marc's formal letter of apology and asked the members whether they thought it remorseful and sincere. Before they could reply, he reminded them of the forthcoming review. North Paarl was in the running to be chosen 'best country school of the year.' Two expulsions could have an adverse effect on the school's rating. If so agreed, his colleagues should reconsider.

The students were escorted out so that the committee members could debate the delicate matter. Waiting in the hallway, Marc could feel the tension build. Sofia paced up and down the narrow corridor. Her arm brushed against Aldo.

"Stop it," he said. "You're making it worse."

After about twenty minutes they were called back into the conference room. There was a long pause while Marc and the others waited for the verdict.

The Chairman appealed for a calm resolution of the matter with reprimands to the three teenagers.

"No expulsion," he suggested. He moved to amend. His colleagues were silent.

"Amendment adopted," the Chairman concluded, adjourning the meeting.

Marc, Aldo and Sofia were led out of the conference room. As soon as he was out in the hallway, Marc let out a deep, loud sigh.

The resolution of the school incident was bitter-sweet for him. He had succeeded in avoiding the severe penalty of expulsion but realized his comrades were not the loyal, devoted friends he had thought they were.

Marc woke when he heard the piercing 'ding dong' of the local church bell, signifying the noon hour. It had been two weeks since the hearing and he could finally put that behind him and look forward to his upcoming trip in July.

He had dozed off in the bentwood rocker in the living room while listening to an American radio show about the adventures of a taxi driver. In his dream he saw himself being driven around the bustling city of Manhattan. In contrast now, through the large window, he had a perfect view of the glistening mountains that graced one side of Paarl.

His stomach growled. Being the first day of summer vacation, his routine was off-schedule. He'd have an early lunch of the tomato stew his mom left for him in the fridge. Molly always made sure there were labeled Tupper-ware containers with leftovers in case Marc was hungry before she got home. He got up and walked to the kitchen. From there, he took in different, yet also breathtaking scenery on the other side of the house: flat agricultural land as far and wide as his eyes could see, dotted with famous vineyards and Cape Dutch homesteads. Marc was aware he was born in one of the most beautiful towns in the Cape Province. It was regularly mentioned in tourist magazines, 'situated in a picturesque and fertile area, the wine-producing Napa Valley of South Africa, rich with facilities in the arts, education and recreation fields.' Yet he knew that hidden underneath all this beauty was pain, poverty and neglect.

The next day, the family was scheduled to go to Cape Town, to a Sea Point home they leased every summer. When it was time to leave, Marc helped his mother pack the Volvo. They took ample clothes, bedding, food, and recreation equipment. They attached Marc's 3-speed bike to a roof rack.

"I'll let dad know we're ready," Marc said, after cramming one last pillow into the car.

Molly held out her hand to stop him. "Let me call him. Your dad's been moodier than usual. Yesterday he fired a worker for no good reason. He felt guilty about what he'd done, but it was too late."

Marc felt sickened but not surprised.

"Has a wife and three small children," said Molly. "They live in District Six. Doubt he'll find another job soon." She paused. "Your dad has a lot of stress at work. He does much better when he takes time off."

Stan was indeed calmer on vacation, but Marc knew to tread cautiously. The wrong topic, such as equal rights or subsidized housing, could get his father riled up.

They drove along the N1 highway in awkward silence. Marc distracted himself by counting trees and bushes along the side of the road. Soon he would be traveling on his own. He wondered what the highways were like in America, and how it felt to drive on the wrong side of the street. He'd soon find out. Upon arriving at their vacation home, they unloaded the vehicle. Stan threw a half-smoked, lit cigarette onto the sidewalk. Marc got to it just before it rolled away and stamped on it until he was certain the flame had died.

After they unpacked, ate lunch and settled in, Marc climbed the outside steps holding a tin of freshly baked chocolate-chip cookies for the landlord, who lived above. A retired pathologist and widower with a shock of white hair and a cane, Dr. Roscoe Murray seldom had company. He greeted Marc enthusiastically.

"Hmm," Murray said, as he helped himself to a cookie and took a bite. "Your mom's a good baker. Marc, come in for a while. You're interested in the sciences, I heard. I'm in the process of analyzing a series of slides for a lecture. Would you like to take a look?"

Marc nodded, following as Murray hobbled to the other side of the room.

The doctor leaned his cane against a desk topped with various pieces of equipment.

"I was given this Bausch and Lomb when I started medical school," he said as he lifted the cover off the microscope. "Probably what got me interested in pathology."

He inserted a slide on the stage, adjusted the focus, and motioned to Marc to look through the eyepiece. Marc was unsure at first, but he soon mastered the machine, viewing slide after slide, as Dr. Murray patiently explained what he was looking at.

"Tell me what you see, Marc."

"Umm, I see round objects clustered together. They look like bunches of grapes."

Murray laughed. "They sure do. Those are bacteria. You're looking at Staph. Aureus." Then reaching for something on the shelf, he said, "Hold on. Take a look at this histology book." He showed Marc enlarged, colorful pictures of microscopic organisms, and taught him about gram positive and gram negative bacteria and how to differentiate Staphylococcus from E. Coli.

"One more," said Marc over and over, until his teacher pushed the machine aside. "Enough for one day," he said, after they had looked at a stack of slides about six inches high. "Let's have tea."

Marc's preference was soda, but he graciously accepted the offer. As they sipped on Five Roses Ceylon, the doctor eagerly shared his professional experiences and explained how pathologists analyzed lab data and tissue samples to help diagnose the cause and development of disease.

"Have you ever been to America?" Marc asked, noticing a travel manual on the bookshelf.

The old man's tired eyes stretched open. "A long time ago, with my sweetheart," he said, his voice breaking.

Not knowing what to say, Marc waited till Murray continued. "My wife of fifty-two years. She passed away a year ago."

Marc lowered his head. "I heard. I'm so sorry." He didn't pursue his line of questioning about America. There was enough said.

"Don't be a stranger," called Dr. Murray, as Marc left, with a gift of an old anatomy book in hand. "That is," he added, "if you can spare time away from the beach. The weather's been terrific."

It certainly was. Marc loved to walk the two blocks down Graham, then Worcester Road toward the Sea Point beachfront. As always, he took note of the carving on the apartment block on the corner – three monkeys portraying 'see no evil, hear no evil, say no evil'. A political statement, he thought. Did they not mean 'pretend you see and hear no evil, and don't dare say anything?'

But breathing in the salty air of the ocean and listening to the squawking of the seagulls, he was quickly distracted. The warmth buoyed him and gave a bounce to his step. As the beach came into view, Marc watched the waves hit the rocks and spray white bubbles and sea water high into the air. He strolled to the Ambrosia outdoor café, and watched a game of chess being played

with pieces two feet tall. Life was easy. Life was good. But not for
everyone.

The next day Marc woke early and took the bus to Clifton, a favorite
teenage hang-out. The beach area was divided by giant granite
boulders and he spent most of the time on Fourth Beach, which
bustled with beauty and youth. He lay in the sun, watching as surfers
rode the waves, families strolled alongside the water, and pretty girls
in scanty swimsuits confirmed the maxim 'less is more'.

Marc buried his toes in the soft white sand. Now and again,
the sound of the surf was interrupted by a barking dog or a vendor
calling 'ice-cream, popsicles!' From his vantage point he could see
Lion's Head, the mountain he had climbed with his pals a few
months before. He shuddered at the memory of the chains toward
the top, accessible only to those brave enough to climb all the way
to its peak. He would miss all this when he left for the U.S. As an
exchange student in a big city, he doubted he would get the
opportunity to visit a beach or go mountain climbing.

Lazing under a multicolored umbrella drinking a fizzy
orange soda and reading the Cape Times, Marc couldn't imagine
anything more peaceful, until he heard a voice bellowing, "Get off
our beach, bastard! You don't belong here!" He turned around, and
in the midst of the all-white beachgoers, near a metal sign that read
'Blankes Alleen', he saw a man of mixed race, a Cape Coloured
man, sitting on the sand with a large container next to him.

Earlier Marc had seen him patrolling the beach in the hot
sun, carrying the portable cooler. Marc imagined he was now

resting, tired from carrying his load. Nearby, a group of rowdy teenagers began to chant, "Get off our beach," over and over. One boy stood up and shouted, "I'll call the police! They'll lock you up!" The ice cream vendor hesitated at first, then rose slowly, lifted his box and began to walk away. Two boys ran after him, shoving him down and emptying dozens of frozen treats onto the sand. The man betrayed no emotion. He stood up, retrieved his empty container and continued to retreat. But the bully leader was apparently unsatisfied. As his accomplices laughed and egged him on, he picked up a stone and hurled it.

The stone flew through the air like a missile and hit the hawker on his head, causing him to fall over and wince in pain.

Marc, horrified, ran to him instinctively.

"Let me help," he said to the man whose scalp was dripping blood down his arm and onto the beach, forming red spatters on the white sand. Marc held out his beach towel. "Take this. You're bleeding. I'll get someone to phone for an ambulance."

The man pulled away. "Don't!" he shouted. "I don't want your help." Grabbing the bottom of his stained T-shirt, he wiped at the fresh blood. Ignoring his empty container, he rose to his feet with difficulty, and hobbled away, leaving Marc wondering how he could have handled the situation differently and admonishing himself for not stepping up sooner and stopping the attack. He turned around and noticed the bullies huddled, the leader with a smirk on his face.

A winding cobbled path led upwards to a large house on the beachfront. Marc ran to the front door and rang the bell. A blonde-haired woman wearing a sarong and lots of gold jewelry appeared.

"What is it?" she asked. "I can't have you kids using my facilities all the time. This is a private home."

"No, someone's been injured," said Marc. I've got to call for help."

Soon he was on the phone to emergency medical services requesting an ambulance.

"What type of emergency are you reporting?" asked the man on the line.

"A man was attacked on Clifton Beach," said Marc, panting. "He's bleeding. He's climbing up toward Glengariff Road above Fourth."

Within minutes of his phone call, he heard the shrill sirens. From the open front window, Marc had a good vantage point of the ocean as well as the ambulance as it approached the victim. When the injured man saw the vehicle, he held up his arm to signal for help. Marc was shocked at what transpired next.

The driver of the emergency medical van got out and shook his head at the pleading patient. Marc heard him say, "Sorry, this is a white's-only ambulance."

Despite protests from several bystanders, the best chance of help drove away. Marc, in disbelief, ran from the house to the spot where the man had been standing. He was gone. Marc looked in all directions and, in the distance, saw him walking off. He went after him and called loudly for him to wait. But the man kept on going. Disheartened, Marc returned to the beach to retrieve his belongings.

For a long time he sat in contemplation, rubbing the grains of sand between his fingers. He thought of the vendor, suffering without aid, and probably having to reimburse his boss for the loss of the icebox and its contents. He felt many emotions, but mostly he felt ashamed of his race and the laws and that he had not been able to help. When the sun began to set, he headed back home. He waited till his mother was alone to recount the traumatic events. He knew his father would not be empathetic.

"There's nothing you can do," she said. "Just be thankful for what you have." She handed Marc a handkerchief to wipe his eyes.

"It's just so unfair," he said.

She put her arm around him. "I know."

The following day Marc was restless. He didn't return to Clifton Beach that summer, but he was haunted by the young Coloured man's eyes, the way he looked at Marc, pleading, even as he rejected his offer of help.

Before the Sennets ended their vacation in the summer rental, Dr. Murray invited Marc to visit again. This time they spoke about Marc's anticipated trip to America, and Murray opened up about his own travels in the U.S. and described the numerous cities he had visited. Marc enquired about the doctor's medical career.

"A long time before you were born," he said, "I trained in Cape Town, and later became chief of pathology at Paarl Memorial."

Marc was surprised to learn that the doctor had practiced in Marc's home town. "What made you decide on medicine?"

"Our family doctor made house calls," said Murray. "I was a curious boy, intrigued by his black bag filled with medical equipment, and he indulged me by allowing me to hold and examine the instruments. When he retired, he gave me his microscope."

They shook hands and Marc thanked him for having him over, before heading for the door.

"Wait a sec," said Murray. "It's been fun getting to know you, Marc. I don't have any family, so, from an old retired physician to a future doctor, please accept this gift." He pointed to a large box on his desk. Marc opened the box and saw, to his delight, the Bausch & Lomb.

FIVE

Potomac, Maryland, 1975

It was a cold December Friday afternoon when Laura entered the school library for her appointment. When the opportunity presented itself for high school students to apply for an after-school mentorship program, Laura had signed up immediately. Her weekly duty was to help a disadvantaged teenager with reading and writing, and after ten days of training she was ready to begin.

Fifteen-year old Tharisa Bryan was her first mentee. She had seen a photograph of the student and recognized her slight build, wavy black hair, dark complexion and high cheekbones. She was sitting alone at a desk.

"Good afternoon, Tharisa. I'm Laura Atkin. I'll be your mentor for the next six months."

"Hello," answered the student, her voice barely a whisper. She remained seated and avoided direct eye contact.

"This is my first time doing this, so take it easy on me," Laura said, trying to break the ice.

Tharisa didn't smile. "I need help with writing," she said. "My grammar isn't good."

"How about taking off your coat?" Laura suggested. "Make yourself comfortable and we can get started right away. Let's see what you have over there."

Tharisa reluctantly took off her jacket. From a back-pack she pulled out a big binder. Tucked in the cover, Laura noticed a faded photograph of a man and a woman. The woman was wearing a wedding dress.

"That's a beautiful photo," said Laura.

"Yes."

"Who are they?"

"My mother and father."

"They look very happy."

Tharisa looked away. "They're not living," she said, so quietly Laura could barely hear her. She glanced at Laura before continuing. "My mother died when she was birthing me, and my father was in a car crash when I was ten."

Laura picked up a pen. "I'm really sorry," she said, wishing she could take back her words.

She wasn't sure how to proceed, but decided it was best to focus on the task at hand. She opened the binder and found pages of short stories and poems. Laura scanned a few excerpts. The grammar was poor in places, but the writing was heartfelt. One of the poems related to Tharisa's upbringing as an orphan. In it, she addressed her biological mom and dad.

"I wish I did know you better. I promise I'll do everything so I make you proud........"

As Laura read aloud, she felt as if she were talking directly to her own father.

She cleared her throat, hoping she had not betrayed her emotions. "Let's work on the first two today," she suggested. "You read. Don't be shy."

Tharisa read slowly. Toward the end of the poem Laura stopped her. "Take a look at this section, this stanza. I think it really gets to the heart of the theme and how you feel about your loss. Is that right?"

"Yes."

"Let's think about introducing that earlier."

Tharisa nodded, as Laura circled, commented and underlined in pencil.

They spent an intense afternoon reading and analyzing the writing. It triggered strong emotions in Laura, but she was glad to see how motivated her student was. She was also surprised to find how much she enjoyed teaching. At the end of the session, she felt Tharisa warming to her and Laura looked forward to their next meeting a week later.

It had been snowing for three long days. No big surprise for December. The temperature had dropped precipitously overnight, which made for slippery roads and side-walks in the morning. Laura, bundled up in layers of clothing, and wearing rain boots, tried to avoid the icy patches as she walked toward the neighborhood bus-stop. It had been an eventful week and she was keen to meet Amber so they could catch up on each other's news. The moment Laura saw her, she knew there was a problem. Amber was sitting on a wooden bench at the side of the road, her head cupped in her hands, lost in thought. It took several moments before she realized that Laura was standing right beside her.

"Amber," whispered Laura. "Hey, what's wrong? Are you okay?"

"Not really, Laura. No, I'm not okay."

"What happened? You're shivering."

No answer.

"Is anyone hurt? Are you sick?" Laura prodded. "Here. Take my scarf. You must be freezing."

"I didn't get......."

"Didn't get what?"

"I mean... I'm... I'm late," Amber sobbed. Her eyes were red and swollen.

"Late for what? We're not late. What are you talking about?"

"Laura, I didn't get my period this month. You know Peter and I have been together. I'm sure I'm pregnant. I'm so scared." Tears streamed down her face. "I can't tell my parents. You know how mad they would be."

It took a while for Laura to absorb the news. With a calm, steady voice, she tried as best she could to console her friend.

"It'll be alright, Amber," she said. "You don't know yet if you are pregnant, but either way, things will work out."

"What'll happen?" asked Amber. "Can anyone help?"

"Stay calm," advised Laura. "I promise we'll come up with a solution. Let's meet at break and we'll talk more."

They were so absorbed in the probability of an unwanted pregnancy, they had been oblivious to the approaching school bus, which pulled up close, splashing water from the gutter on both of them.

"Yuck!" Laura wiped her cheek with her sleeve.

Amber let out another sob, and the two reluctantly climbed into the crowded vehicle. They sat together in silence all the way to school, avoiding eye contact with their friends, afraid someone could read the truth from their eyes.

Throughout her morning classes, Laura's mind was elsewhere.

"Laura, what is the capital of Iceland?"

Laura startled and looked up to see Mrs. Roth peering down at her through her tortoise-shell spectacles. Why were they always at the tip of her nose? They looked so ridiculous.

"Laura!" Mrs. Roth said.

"Um, could you please repeat the question?"

"This is most unlike you, Laura. Try to focus now."

Laura stared blankly. She felt sad for Amber, yet frustrated that her friend had not taken precaution. Laura would never let that happen. Thankfully, Mrs. Roth shifted her attention to another student.

"Rob, tell the class. What's the capital?"

As soon as the bell rang for recess, Laura and Amber got together.

"I've been thinking," Laura said. "I know you won't like this, but you've got to talk to your parents. Your dad's probably too busy to get involved. We both know your mom can be tough, but better you're honest now than have her discover the truth later."

"I'm scared," said Amber.

"If you keep the baby," said Laura, "she'll find out soon enough, and if you have an abortion – what if something goes wrong? She'll be mad when you tell her, but you'll be okay. I'm here to support you. I can even ask my mom to help."

"I know you're right, Laura, but I just don't have the courage."

"You'll be okay." Laura gave her a reassuring hug. "If she tries to hurt you, I'll call the police."

"I know, Laura. I trust you."

The next Saturday morning Amber met up with Laura at a nearby park. They sat on adjacent swings. "I told my mother," said Amber.

"And?"

"She was really angry."

"We knew she would be. How about Peter?"

"After talking to my mom, I called and asked Peter to come over. I guess I was hoping for some understanding from him. When I told him I was keeping the baby, he said he didn't want to be involved." Amber raised her voice. "That's what some men do, Laura. Instead of taking responsibility, they leave."

"Luckily not all men," said Laura, as she wrapped her arms around her friend. She thought of her own responsible father who had been taken from her too soon. "Oh Amber, it's not fair. I'm so sorry about what happened."

After sitting in silence for a while, Laura said, "I'm here for you and your baby if you ever need me." As she uttered those words and thought of her own fatherless childhood, her stomach twisted in a knot.

SIX

Cape Town, March 1976

Marc sat in the spacious, empty auditorium of the University of Cape Town Medical School, paging through his high school chemistry textbook and running his fingers along the crisp edge of his starched white lab coat while he waited for the next presentation. He had been counting the days till he left to become an exchange student. Time was moving too slowly. In the meanwhile he filled the hours with academic and other distractions.

Intrigued by the career of internationally famous cardiac surgeon Christiaan Barnard, who had performed the first successful human-to-human heart transplant at Groote Schuur Hospital, Marc had jumped at the chance when offered a high school internship at the same institution. Now he watched as medical students filtered slowly into the class. A short stocky student with ginger hair dropped his backpack on the floor and pulled up a chair next to him.

"Hi," he said, extending his hand. "Ben Murphy. Mind if I sit here?"

Marc introduced himself and explained that he was here on a special high school program.

"You planning to go to med school?" asked Ben, leaning back in his chair.

"I was considering it before," said Marc. "Now, after shadowing a couple of doctors and speaking to students, I'm more convinced."

"I myself thought I would end up in politics," said Ben.

"How so?"

"Runs in the family," he said. "My dad's Sam Murphy, political activist."

Marc vaguely recalled reading about him in the papers.

As they waited for the classroom to fill, Ben opened up about his frustration with the government policies. He seemed pleasantly surprised that Marc shared his views. Just before the lecture began, Ben pulled a flyer out of his backpack and handed it to Marc. "If you know of anyone interested," he said quietly, "there's a planned march to be held in Cape Town to protest apartheid policies. For safety reasons it hasn't been widely publicized."

Marc read on the flyer that the march was on a day he was scheduled to be in Cape Town. After his mother dropped him off for his internship, he could easily bus to the event without her knowledge.

"I'll try to make it," said Marc. He tucked the pamphlet in his pocket.

The following day Marc lifted a large white plastic board off the garage shelf. From his schoolbag he pulled out red and black permanent markers and a pair of scissors. Then he hunted around until he found a long piece of string. He carried his supplies to a corner of the garage, where he sat on a sturdy cardboard box and began constructing a sign for the protest.

As he punctured holes into the board, and threaded and fastened the string, he thought about his own experiences with apartheid. He couldn't get away from the signs mandating separation, at parks, outside public restrooms and as he saw recently, on the beach. He thought back to the Coloured maid who worked for his grandparents when he was little. He had seen how she came to be subservient, how she called him Master. Nobody spoke to him about it, but he noticed. To his grandparents, who both died before he was twelve, segregation was a fact of life.

Beads of sweat formed on his forehead and he wiped them off with the back of his hand, then he picked up a black marker and began writing. He got as far as the word Apartheid, when the door leading from the house into the garage swung open, and he saw his father looking down at him. Marc turned the sign over, but it was too late.

"What the hell are you doing?" Stan demanded to know.

"Just working on a project," said Marc, holding onto his hands to stop them from shaking. He had not yet seen the full wrath of his father and he didn't want to now.

Stan approached him and swiped the board from his hands. "Apartheid? Apartheid? What is this? You a protestor or something?" He threw it down on the wet concrete floor and stepped on it before going back into the house and slamming the door.

Marc sat frozen for a few minutes, then picked up the damp sign. The letters were smudged. He fixed them carefully, and continued writing.

As announced, students gathered on De Waal Drive below the university rugby field at 3:00 p.m. on the nineteenth of May. The chairman of the Student Representative Council was there with a megaphone, instructing his following to march peacefully ten across, to police headquarters, three miles down the mountain road.

Dressed in the long pants, white shirt and blazer prescribed for his internship, Marc felt conspicuous, but he held up his large board with the words "Apartheid is Hate." The word 'Hate' was written in bright red.

An angry crowd surrounded Marc and his fellow protesters, intent on disrupting the protest. It was clear to him that there were few supporters of the march.

"Do you want your daughter to marry a black man?" someone shouted at them.

"I don't want our country partitioned into separate black and white areas," replied a woman wearing a black sash. "No more discrimination," she chanted.

One man pushed into the line and tried to pull the sign from Marc. Marc held on tightly and continued walking, proud that he was standing up for what was right, but also afraid of the consequences. What would his father do if he knew? He shuddered to imagine. Anti-government protests could be met with violence. He wished he hadn't come alone. He looked around to see if he recognized anyone. Toward the back he spotted Ben Murphy and approached him. "Recognized you by your hair," said Marc.

"Oh hello Marc. I didn't expect you to come."

"Decided to take a stand against the crimes of our society. You know."

"You must be the youngest marcher," said Ben. "You came alone? This can be pretty dangerous."

"So I've been told."

They marched together. Slowly with determination, the group took over one traffic lane and walked to certain confrontation.

After about a mile, Marc and twelve other protestors, including Ben, were grabbed by angry white uniformed security officials. The rest of the marchers escaped and ran off in different directions. Marc's first thought was that he would never see his family again. His wrists ached as they were pressed into steel handcuffs. He was led by foot to a nearby police station, and into a cold, windowless room where he was interrogated about his family, his faith and his political affiliation. Cautious with his answers, he stated he had no particular affiliation, but simply believed in fairness. When his answers displeased, the policeman squeezed the back of his neck and Marc, refusing to give the cop satisfaction, tried to hide any sign that he was in pain.

He was allowed one brief phone call and a five-minute visit. He called his mother, but it was his father who arrived at the jail, irate and demanding his son's immediate release. The request was denied in spite of a cash offer to provide bail. Marc heard loud arguing and foul language as his father finally left.

He spent eighteen long hours in an uncomfortable holding area, with primitive toilets and very little food and water. His head throbbed and it felt as if the room was spinning. He sat down on the cold floor and put his head down in his hands. He tried to focus on better things, such as what life would be like in America, but now that dream seemed too distant. His stomach ached and he threw up into the toilet.

Finally, Marc and the other prisoners were brought before a magistrate. Exhausted, he thought back to the time he sat before the school committee. This court appearance was far more sinister – he'd heard stories of people being jailed for years, without due process. Perhaps, in a small way, the previous event prepared him for this. As before, he was outwardly composed, even as he could hear the loud beat of his heart in his ears.

After a biased hearing, the prisoners given no opportunity to plead their cases, he was released with a stern order not to engage in 'disorderly conduct against the State.' As he left the prison in the rain and the custody of his parents, a guard tapped him firmly on the arm with a baton. "We'll be watching you," he warned. Marc trembled. In the distance he recognized a few of the released protestors. Ben Murphy was not among them.

"Get in the car," ordered his father. As they drove, the silence made Marc feel even more uneasy.

Back home, he felt he had wasted two days. In spite of marching and protesting, nothing seemed to change. It was time to leave, to get out.

SEVEN

Potomac, USA, 1976

Backstage, in the wings of the school hall, Laura paced up and down, hands clammy, as she rehearsed her arguments for the end-of-year junior debate. She peeked through a gap in the curtains. The stage was bare except for three chairs, and the auditorium was filling up quickly. Some of her teachers sat in the front row, and behind them, her mother and a group of her classmates. She took a deep breath and reminded herself to be confident. She was a good debater. However persuasive Diane was, Laura had the better case.

A bell signified it was time to start. Their English teacher was the moderator of the debate, and Diane and Laura were her two top students. The three of them walked onto the stage and took their seats.

The controversial topic was the 1973 Supreme Court decision Roe v. Wade. Laura was arguing 'for' the legalization of abortion, Diane against. There was a coin toss. Diane would speak first. She straightened her blouse, clasped her hands together and threw a look at Laura as if she were launching a psychological war.

Diane began her remarks by stating that unborn babies are human beings and have a right to live. She asserted that a woman faced with an unwanted pregnancy should opt for adoption rather than abortion. There was no shortage of women seeking to adopt. She covered various other points and ended by stating she strongly disagreed with the Supreme Court's decision and felt it was a mistake. The audience cheered.

It was Laura's turn. She stood up and walked to the middle of the stage where she faced the crowd and established eye contact. She stated her case with vehemence, despite knowing that she was facing a conservative audience.

"Abortion," she said, "falls within the sphere of the basic entitlement to privacy which is and should always continue to be a woman's fundamental right." She went on to make the case that women should be given control over their own bodies and able to make their own decisions about their reproductive lives. She cited statistics which proved that legalizing abortion would reduce the number of deaths from illegal and dangerous procedures. "My position in no way implies that I would personally choose to abort," she said, as an image of Amber at the bus stop crossed her mind fleetingly. "However, I do not feel that you or I should make that decision for someone else."

The audience stood up and clapped. Laura and Diane shook hands formally, then retreated backstage for the votes to be tallied. It felt like hours till they heard a bell and then the announcement. Laura's knees wobbled when she learned she had lost the debate by two votes.

EIGHT

Over the next few months, Marc prepared for his trip to the United States. Together with his mother, he shopped for winter clothes that would befit a trip to Antarctica.

"You've got to take long thermal underwear," his mother said, to his horror. "The winters are harsh. People freeze to death." To avoid this calamity, she bought two sets, as well as thick socks, a hat, leather gloves and a heavy coat.

Marc took out library books on American history and culture and studied them eagerly in anticipation of his new home and school curriculum. He read 'All the President's Men' by journalists Bernstein and Woodward, which dealt with the investigation of the Watergate scandal. He also read books on pop culture, and a spy novel by an American author.

He met with friends to say farewell and give them his overseas address so that they could keep in touch. Although he wrestled with the decision, he didn't say goodbye to Sofia or Aldo, the friends who had disappointed him and been disloyal at a time of crisis. Loyalty, he reasoned, was the basis of true friendship.

On the morning of July tenth, the day of Marc's departure, the entire family was up before dawn. Molly shifted in her seat and made small talk as she and her husband drove their only child to D.F. Malan airport near Cape Town to take the first leg of his flights to a far-away place. Marc felt a little sad as he looked up at Table

Mountain with its misty "cloth" and cable car, knowing it would be some time before he saw that familiar landmark again.

As the sun rose, they drove past a non-white township called Guguletu, where poor families lived in tin shanties. Undernourished, barefooted children roamed the narrow gravel streets. There was no real future for them. Marc's heart sank as he considered how these children had done nothing to deserve such a fate. The stark contrast between the haves and the have-nots wasn't lost on him. He pictured America where nobody would be homeless and no child would starve.

When Stan said farewell to his son, he gave him advice.

"Be a good ambassador of your country. Don't make waves."

Marc understood the message – 'Accept the status quo.' He rejected it in silence. An argument with his father would get him nowhere.

Marc remembered the most recent unpleasant conversation with his father.

"Blacks don't have any desire to be educated," said Stan. "They are not ambitious."

"That's just not true," protested Marc. "They haven't been given a fair chance."

Stan had thumped his fist on the table as if to make a definitive point. "Well I think society does better with its money by spending it on whites."

Now, at the airport, Marc vowed to himself he would be a better person, a better father. He would not become a product of prejudice. He felt ready to leave, ready to get away.

Marc hugged his parents and then walked out to the tarmac to board. He took a deep breath as he embarked on his first trip out of the country and his chance at a better way of life.

NINE

Pennsylvania, 1976

Laura arrived with her mother at the Allentown motel just after noon. They had made an early start and she yawned as she carried the small suitcase they shared for the overnight trip. It had been a year since she had seen her late father's sister Beth and her husband Vic. They rarely traveled, but hosted an annual family barbecue. This year it occurred a week after the July Fourth holiday.

Aunt Beth was one of the smartest people Laura knew. According to Laura's mom, Beth had forfeited a promising career in journalism to marry and have children, both grown now. Back then, her mother had explained, married women were discouraged from working outside of the home, so Beth had become a stay-at-home mom. She never complained, but Laura could tell she bore a grudge.

When they arrived at the cottage later that afternoon they were greeted with hugs and kisses by Aunt Beth and Uncle Vic and cousins, Evan and Matt, all preparing food on the back porch. Vic was wearing shorts and a green and orange island shirt, and was grilling chicken and hot dogs. Others carried drinks, salads and buns from the kitchen. Laura offered to help.

"You can bring out the ketchup and mustard if you don't mind," said Beth. "They're in the fridge."

Laura followed her aunt through the cluttered hallway into the kitchen. On the fridge were a couple of magnets and several photographs. Laura stared at a black and white picture of a young man carrying an infant. She recognized her father.

He must have been only a few years older than she was now. He was wearing a cardigan sweater, his hair slicked back. He and the baby were looking at each other as if they were having a conversation.

"That's you," said Beth. "On your first birthday. He loved to show you off."

Laura had seen only a few photographs of her father. Her mother kept shoeboxes filled with photos but never invited her to look. Laura, afraid of stirring up emotion, didn't ask.

"What was he like?" asked Laura tentatively.

Beth put down her tray, took the photograph off the fridge door and examined it closely. "There was nobody like him," she said. "He was brilliant, as you probably know. An aerospace engineer. But more than that, he was the best brother one could wish for. I'll tell you a story. I hadn't been driving that long and my car broke down in a rural area about an hour from the city. I called him, because I was afraid our parents would be angry. He drove out to pick me up, and arranged and paid for the repair. No questions asked. He was like that. Always ready to help someone in need."

They joined the others outside and Vic made Laura a 'hotdog with the works', which included mustard, ketchup, sauerkraut and pickles.

On their way back to Maryland the following day, Laura dreamed what it would have been like to have her father here now. She wished her mother would tell her more about him, but as before, she was too afraid to ask. She wondered whether she took after him in any way and whether she would have made him proud.

TEN

South Africa, 1976

The two-hour bumpy plane-trip to Johannesburg felt like an eternity. The situation was aggravated by the rude passenger in the adjacent seat.

"So, where are you off to?" asked the woman sharply. She reeked of smoke.

"United States," Marc answered, as turbulence caused him to lurch forward in his chair. He felt nauseous and kept his eyes on the paper bag in the seat pocket in front of him.

"You still in school?" she persisted.

"Yes, I'll finish my matric in America."

"I hear they have mixed-race classes. You may be sitting next to a non-white. You okay with that?"

Marc didn't dignify her with an answer. Instead, from his window seat, he raised the shade, and focused on the wing of the aircraft and the cloud formation below. Soon he heard her snoring loudly. At least he was saved from further interrogation.

He was pleased to get out of the confined space and stretch his long legs at Jan Smuts Airport. He also used the time to purchase souvenirs for his host parents. At passport control, prior to boarding the inter-continental flight, a uniformed man greeted him in Afrikaans, one of the country's two official languages, the one forced onto the curriculum of every black school, causing resentment and boycotts.

"Goeie more, Meneer. Hoe gaan dit met jou?"

"Goed, dankie," answered Marc. He realized he would not hear the language, unique to South Africa, for a long time.

"Alles van die beste."

Marc nodded a thank you. "All the best to you too."

Soon he was back in the sky en route northwards to a rocky outpost called Il de Sol, a Portuguese possession off the coast of West Africa where South African Airways refueled its planes. Apart from a bare-bones airport, the island boasted little else. Marc felt uneasy. It irked him to be reminded of apartheid's cost. His country's planes were barred from flying directly over the bulge of Africa. Hence this inconvenient stop.

The final leg of his trip was an uncomfortable eight-hour flight west over the Atlantic Ocean to New York City's Idlewild terminal. Marc had trouble falling asleep in a sitting position. He stretched his legs as often as he could by walking up and down the aisle.

The trip became more tolerable once he struck up a conversation with a middle-aged American sitting alongside him by the name of Brent Barlow, who disclosed that he was the Medical Director of pediatrics at Mount Sinai Hospital. Brent was a native New Yorker, who readily answered Marc's many questions.

"Why is New York repeated in addresses?"

"Because there are many New Yorks in the U.S. The second in the address refers to one of the fifty states."

"What is The Bronx?" asked Marc.

"One of five boroughs that make up New York City. The others are Queens, Staten Island, Brooklyn and the one with the skyscrapers, Manhattan."

Brent was a talker. He switched the subject to South Africa. He too had questions galore.

"Is it true that eighty-five percent of your population is denied the vote? Are Blacks forced to live in poor rural areas? I heard that nine times more is spent on educating a white kid compared to a black one. Is that so? Are you comfortable living in a society that discriminates on such a cruel basis?"

Marc tried as best he could to address Brent's valid issues. Well-versed in the propaganda machine back home which sought to make the doctrine of race separation palatable to foreigners, he found the arguments of the minority government misleading.

"There are no good answers," said Marc. "As much as some may try, one can't justify these policies."

There was no defense for apartheid. As a member of the privileged class, he felt guiltier than ever. He also felt relieved that he was about to leave it all behind, if only for a year.

When Dr. Barlow learned of Marc's work at the renowned Groote Schuur Hospital, he spoke with pride about Mount Sinai's achievements and his senior position there.

"It's one of the biggest teaching hospitals in the States," he said. "Here's my card. Call me tomorrow afternoon and I'll show you the facility and what I do."

Marc was excited about this new connection and possible future prospects. He tucked Brent's business card into his wallet. Approaching their destination at dusk, Marc caught a quick view of the Hudson and East Rivers from his window seat.

He was physically exhausted when he finally set foot on American soil. New York City was hot and humid. He was relieved his trip called for a two-night stay in Manhattan before going on to his final destination, Washington, District of Columbia. On the cramped bus ride from the airport to the city center, he was taken aback by the throngs in the street and the sight of policemen carrying guns. The neon signs, the skyscrapers and the deafening noise were all too much to absorb. He couldn't wait to rest at the YMCA hostel mid-town on East 47th Street where he had a reservation.

Upon arrival, he checked in, dragged his suitcase into the rickety elevator, and proceeded up to the thirty-fifth floor where his room was located. The Y was more run-down than he had imagined, although he didn't expect the Ritz for five dollars a night. He dumped his case, flopped on the bed, clothes and all, and was soon in a deep sleep.

In the early hours of the morning, when even Manhattan's revelers had turned in, a pounding on the door awakened Marc.

"Phone call! Phone call for you," a strange voice shouted.

Marc jumped out of bed and still in his ruffled clothes from the flight, made for the only phone on the floor, centrally positioned in the elevator hallway. The connection was poor but he could make out a woman's voice.

"Is this Helene?" he asked.

When she responded yes, he, believing the woman at the other end of the line was his host mother for the year, provided detailed information about his accommodation and flights.

After a lengthy conversation, he went back to his room. As soon as he opened the door, he saw the mess. Someone had been there. He searched for his wallet - gone; his new camera and the wrist watch from his grandfather - gone. Fortunately his South African passport was left with the front desk staff at check-in, and he had fifty dollars in the pocket of the pants he was wearing.

He sat on his bed and analyzed the events leading up to the scam. He was obviously vulnerable to being conned. A target, an alien in a new environment. Welcome to America! Maybe the country wasn't all he had imagined it to be. Crime was international after all.

Marc was tempted to get some much-needed sleep but determination got the better of him. Prioritize, he was taught. His first instinct was to call home, but that wasn't feasible. Instead, he wrote down a to-do list for the next day, which included a police report and a visit to American Express to replace lost checks. He'd talk to his parents later. If he needed assistance, he was sure Brent Barlow would help. Soon he was again horizontal, eyes closed, out to the world.

To reach his destination the following morning, Marc took the subway. Although a first, he mastered the procedure and traveled quickly downtown to the bank on Wall Street, where his businesslike approach to his problem yielded positive results. He presented his passport and the counterfoil numbers of his stolen traveler's checks, and they were quickly replaced.

The clerk smiled. "Given your indecipherable signature, our company has never been safer. You'll make a good doctor."

Marc was back in business, none the worse for his introduction to America. He bought a fake Rolex from a persuasive street vendor and decided he'd take care of a camera later.

Punctually, Marc entered the glass doors of Mount Sinai Hospital and was welcomed by the Medical Director.

As they walked through the busy neonatal intensive care unit, Marc was struck by the rows of incubators, isolettes as referred to by his guide. Each had a premature infant hiding under various pieces of apparatus - intravenous lines, nasogastric tubes and respirators. Next to one incubator was a woman in gown, gloves and mask, gently caressing a baby's arm through a small opening in the life-saving unit. Two nurses in rocking chairs were bottle-feeding newborns. In the corner several white-coated individuals crowded around a small examining table. Dr. Barlow explained that an intern was inserting a needle into an infant's chest to remove excess air pushing on the lung, while medical students were observing.

Marc was fascinated by all the activity. He and Barlow continued on to the pediatric ward. In one room a young girl with bacterial meningitis was hooked up to an IV dripping antibiotics into her veins. Two family members in surgical face masks were sitting by her bedside. In the next room was a patient with tuberculosis. There were children recovering from surgery. Others were being treated for dehydration. Physicians and medical students in lab coats seemed to be everywhere. A group of them congregated around a bed discussing the occupant's case. Another was sitting at the nurse's station writing notes. Overhead Marc heard announcements over the public address system. He found the activity exciting and invigorating.

His experience at the hospital this day, witnessing the impact of the dedicated doctors on the well-being of the sickest young patients of all skin colors, cemented his decision. With a degree in medicine he would have the ability to improve people's lives significantly.

ELEVEN

Potomac, Maryland, 1976

After the visit with Aunt Beth and the conversation about her father, Laura was curious to see the photographs her mother kept stored in a closet in her bedroom.

One afternoon when her mother was filling in as a substitute teacher, Laura went into her bedroom closet, pulled out two heavy shoeboxes and placed them on the bed. She opened the first box, picked up a handful of pictures and lay them out on the bedspread.

One by one she scrutinized each photo, before moving on to the next group. The photographs were not dated, nor were they arranged in any order. She found one of her parents standing in a garden. Her mother looked radiant in a yellow sundress. Her long hair covered her shoulders. Her father had his arm around her. Laura could tell he was happy. Possibly the day they became engaged, Laura thought. Then she found a picture of her father playing golf. And one of him accepting an award at a university. There were numerous photographs of the three of them, on a picnic, at a swimming pool and in a park.

As she went through photo after photo, Laura felt as if she was completing a puzzle. Before, she didn't really know her dad. Now at least she had a better picture.

She had just packed away the last box of photographs when the phone rang. It was Amber, who had been accepted to a trade school in Boston after her daughter was born. Laura was overjoyed to hear the voice of her childhood friend whom she had not seen for over a year. It felt like yesterday when she had lived right next door and they had gotten up to all sorts of childish mischief together. Now her friend sounded like a grown-up.

"They provide child care and support which I would never have received at home," said Amber. "My daughter's doing really well."

"I'm happy for you," said Laura. "How are things going at school?"

"I'm taking part-time college courses, mostly at night. It's not easy as a single mom, but I'm doing okay."

They caught up on the events of the past year and Amber told Laura about the shame she had felt when she became pregnant and had to leave school.

"I was sure everyone was talking about me," she said. "I hated myself, but I'm getting over that now."

"I didn't know it was that bad," said Laura. "I'm sorry."

"It's okay."

"Are you dating at all? Do you have time?"

"There's someone," said Amber, "but I'm taking it slowly. Don't want to get burned again. How about you? Seeing anyone?"

"No," said Laura. "You'd be the first I'd tell."

TWELVE

Washington DC, July 1976

Upon arrival at Washington's National Airport, Marc caught sight of a cardboard welcome sign bearing his name. It was held up by a tall, grey-haired man, standing next to a petite woman with matching hair color. Marc, with his back-pack slung over one shoulder and both arms filled with African curios, walked toward his hosts.

He blushed as each gave him a tight hug, so unlike the formality of personal space he was accustomed to back home. They introduced themselves as his foster parents, Sid and Helene Drake. She was smiling and soft-spoken and he was casual and untucked. Marc quickly felt at ease. He handed his hosts gifts, including a hand-painted ostrich egg and a carved wooden giraffe. The three spoke about the theft from his room as they waited alongside the carousel for Marc's baggage. He felt embarrassed that he had been so gullible. He would know better next time. His two cases came on the belt and the men carried them to a Buick station wagon in the short-term parking lot.

On the drive from the airport to the Drake's home in Silver Spring, Marc felt the cold, uncomfortable blast from the vehicle's air-conditioning, something he had not experienced. He was accustomed to cars being driven with open windows and fresh, untreated air. Not an option here, he realized, knowing this was only one of many more differences to come in his new world.

As Sid drove, Helene explained the city's three jurisdictions. "You landed in Virginia, we are now driving through the District of Columbia and will soon be in Maryland. Each jurisdiction in the city has its own laws."

From the back seat Marc stared at the scenery, taking in the Potomac River and the interesting landscape with its dense greenery, so different from the southern tip of Africa. For a moment he felt homesick. He missed Cape Town, home territory that lay so safely tucked between the mountain and the ocean. Sid pointed to Georgetown across the water and as they neared their destination they passed through different residential neighborhoods, none of them resembling the tin shanties he had seen on the way to the Cape Town airport.

It was close to dusk when the Drakes pulled up to the three-level Colonial brick house, yet the air was still muggy. Strange that it was winter in South Africa. With pride, Sid took him on a tour of their home, the three bedrooms, newly-painted kitchen overlooking a small herb garden, and den with an impressive library and comfortable-looking leather couches. The outside of the house was lit up, the garden was colorful with yellow sunflowers and pink peonies, the lawn carefully manicured. They ended up in the kitchen. Hungry now, Marc enjoyed a bowl of granola with milk and thereafter a 'turkey melt', a sandwich that was new to him.

He said goodnight, unpacked in the guest room on the upper floor and went to bed. Within minutes he was asleep.

He found himself running along Riebeek Street, Cape Town. It was night, but spots of light from streetlamps paved his way. He moved as fast as he could, but he could feel them gaining ground. He glanced back.

One of four armed policemen chasing him held up a South African flag. "Traitor!" he called out. "Traitor!"

Faster and faster Marc ran, till exhaustion took over and his legs buckled. Officers stood over him with rifles pointed. His heart beat so loudly that he was deafened by its noise. The streetlamps dimmed and everything went dark.

Marc awakened, sweating, to find Helene smiling at him.

"You slept for thirteen hours," she said. "You surely needed the rest. I have scrambled eggs and fruit waiting for you downstairs. Afterwards we'll explore the city. You okay?"

Marc nodded. Having difficulty shaking off the nightmare, he forced himself to get out of bed and shower. As he dressed for breakfast, he began to feel the thrill of being in a different country. New scenery, new people, new accents, new food. Someone had mentioned Armand's deep dish pizza. He made a mental note to add that to his list.

"Three of our landmarks are named after early presidents," said Helene. "Washington, Jefferson and Lincoln." She shared information readily as she drove through Rock Creek Park to downtown D.C.

Marc marveled at the elegant simplicity of the White House, home to the president of the United States. They crossed the Potomac and the Anacostia rivers. So much water everywhere. If only South Africa could have a stream of fresh water in its hinterland, the Karoo desert would bloom. The 35 mm Leica, borrowed from the Drakes, worked overtime as he captured photo after photo and changed reels of film frequently. He envisioned the excitement of sharing the images in a slide show with his parents and friends, most of who had never been out of South Africa. The Tidal Basin and the Japanese cherry trees were beautiful backdrops to a dozen shots. They took a short walk on Maine Avenue along the waterfront, then on to Georgetown for shopping. Marc bought a T-shirt emblazed with the words 'D.C. – taxation without representation.'

It was much hotter and more humid than he had expected. He was glad he had dressed in shorts. Helene pointed to the site of the historic Kennedy Center and informed Marc it had opened just a few years before, in 1971.

As they walked along the side streets of the city, Marc heard someone call 'Spare some change?' A wrinkled woman in tattered clothing was sitting on the sidewalk near an alley. Next to her was a jam tin with a few coins. She held a hand-written cardboard sign that read 'Help. Must feed 4 children.' Further in the alley, Marc noticed a man sleeping curled up on the gravel, with paper bags for a pillow. Rotted food nearby gave off a strong stench. Helene placed a dollar bill in the container. The woman nodded. "Bless you ma'am."

"Where do these people live?" asked Marc.

"Sadly this is where they live, Marc," explained Helene. "They're homeless. Some of the men and women on the streets used to have jobs and money, but for one reason or another, whether illness, substance abuse or lack of support, they do not make it, and this is where they end up."

Marc felt sick to his stomach. "Isn't there any help?"

"There are government programs," said Helene. "Shelters, food banks and kitchens. There is assistance, but we need more. They need housing, medical care, medications."

Marc was stunned. He hadn't expected this in the United States. Where was the American Dream?

"Want to see the Espionage Center?" asked Helene, changing the subject.

"Of course." Marc was excited. In South Africa he had read about the downtown D.C. museum with the adjacent shop featuring the latest spy gadgets. He was eager to visit.

The museum was only a few blocks away, so they had time till closure at six. They decided to stop at a deli for a sandwich. Marc took a seat next to Helene at the bar, and studied the huge menu which featured many delicious choices. There was chicken salad, egg salad, pastrami, roast beef, turkey and more. What would it be? The song 'Yesterday' by The Beatles played on the jukebox. As Marc hummed along in his mind he thought how different his life had been yesterday. Right now, though, he had to make a decision.

"I suggest the pastrami," said the waitress, coming to Marc's rescue. "It's our specialty."

"We'll take two," said Helene.

Marc was stunned when the double-deckers arrived. Too much to eat in one go, he thought, knowing that even untouched left food was trashed. So much waste. He finished half the sandwich, wrapped the rest, and put it in his back-pack to take home. Walking on the way to the museum, he marveled at the shops, cafes, and parks, until he felt the drops of water.

"Uh oh, "said Helene. "It's starting to rain. We'd better get inside."

Washington's fickle weather was true to form. The sky darkened and it began to storm. They hadn't prepared for the soaking rain. Their hair and clothes got drenched. They darted inside and dried off with paper towels before they took in the museum. There were photographs and stories of infamous spies, glass cases of recording devices and other state-of-the-art gadgets.

"Look at this, Mrs. Drake." Marc pointed to a pair of high definition goggles.

"Those could come in handy," she said, "especially if you're following someone at night. By the way, call me Helene."

Marc knew of the extensive police activity in South Africa which monitored citizens in their private lives. Tapping phone calls, especially international ones, was routine. B.O.S.S., the Bureau of State Security, was everywhere to protect the apartheid regime from being overthrown by the blacks. The South African Embassy on Massachusetts Avenue was only a few blocks away. Perhaps they got some of their ideas from these sophisticated products. By the time they left the center, the sun had re-appeared. Marc felt his mood lighten.

The following afternoon, Sid took him shopping for school supplies. After stocking up on notebooks, folders, pencils and paper, they stopped at an ice cream parlor. Marc had never seen so many flavors. Choices galore. Bubblegum, lavender, ginger-beer! He and Sid chatted while enjoying their cold treats and got home at dusk.

Marc entered the house and was taken aback to find Helene holding a huge cluster of multi-colored helium balloons surrounded by a group of people – young and old, singing happy birthday to him. Marc, who had recently turned seventeen, was embarrassed at first, but soon became more comfortable with the attention and enjoyed meeting his neighbors, a few of whom would be his classmates. Over a buffet dinner, the guests presented him with an assortment of gifts. A scarf –'in the winter it gets much colder than Cape Town,' said one card. A calendar, a phone book and a photo album. A little notebook – 'for the names of all the girls you'll meet'.

He thought back to Sofia and decided he had to do better in the new world.

Late that evening, after they had cleaned up, Marc thanked the Drakes for going to so much trouble. Helene gave him a hug. "Are you looking forward to starting school next week?"

"I'm very excited," said Marc.

"Good," she said. "We want you to be happy here. This is your home now."

THIRTEEN

U.S.A. October 1976

Marc took out pen and paper.

> *Dear Ben,*
>
> *I'm enjoying my stay in the U.S. but I miss my family and friends in South Africa. I also dream about the mild weather and the beaches and the food! What I wouldn't do for some 'bobotie'. Of course I don't miss everything there. You know what I mean. America is very different. Everything's bigger. And one feels less afraid to speak one's mind. School is good. Lots of homework, but less formal. The way students talk in class and question teachers – back home we would be sent to detention. Here it's acceptable to be informal. My foster parents don't have children of their own, so they treat me as their kid.*
>
> *Sid is an owner of a plumbing business and Helene is a freelance journalist, but they take lots of time off to be with me. We spend weekends on their houseboat outside Annapolis. Sid bought me a wet-suit and with some practice I've turned out to be quite a good water-skier. I have even mastered slalom. Hope you're impressed! Sometimes we play chess. Sid was a champion at his school. Because they both work, we go out to restaurants a lot and I've learned to like pizza and Chinese food. There were definitely things that*

surprised me here. I saw homeless people begging for
money. So sad that in this great country there is such poverty
right before our eyes. As for girls, I haven't met anyone
serious, but I've made a few friends.
Have you attended any more rallies? Hope you're safe.
Please write.
Your friend,
Marc."

Weekly Marc wrote to friends in South Africa and eagerly awaited replies. He was glad when his parents sent a gift package filled with his favorite treats – peppermint crisp, licorice allsorts and guava rolls. Late one evening he called to thank them and he could hear his mom choking back tears.

His father came to the phone.

"The big news here is that things are changing fast and the changes are not good," he growled. "The blacks are getting more uppity by the day."

Marc changed the subject. "Here it's going pretty well. I'm enjoying school, especially science. The lecturer was a professor at MIT. How are you and mom?"

"Your mother has been very depressed lately," said his dad. "We don't know what the future will hold. We're increasing security, preparing for more riots. It's not the same country as when you left."

The government had made the Afrikaans language compulsory in all schools. Marc had read about the resultant anger and clashes with police. Nonwhites viewed the language as that of the oppressor and expressed their outrage in protests which turned violent.

He did not want to continue the conversation with his father. He pointed out that international phone calls were expensive. His mother came back on the line. They chatted about school and the weather. Molly seemed reluctant to end the conversation. Only when Marc reminded her that the Drakes were footing the bill, did she say goodbye.

FOURTEEN

Lincoln Secondary was six street blocks from the Silver Spring house. When weather permitted, Marc walked to and from school, which to his surprise and delight did not prescribe uniforms. The students welcomed him and within days he had a string of acquaintances. Stacy, wide-eyed with a catchy laugh, was enamored by the South African accent. Jason, a fitness enthusiast, offered to show Marc the ropes and teach him about American sports. Cory, a wannabe comedian, kept him and others amused at lunchtime and in class. He showed Marc a couple of magic tricks – the disappearing handkerchief and the metal ring trick. Marc begged Cory to teach him, but Cory declined with 'A magician never discloses his secrets.'

On the way to school, Marc bumped into Jason and discovered he lived a block away from the Drake's home. They walked together and found they had a lot to talk about.

The next day, Jason was waiting. "Hey," he said. "I was thinking we could go biking together sometime? There's a bike path down the street."

"I rode a lot in South Africa, so yes, definitely. I'm sure Mr. Drake will let me use his bike."

"Otherwise you can ride my brother's. He's away at college. He won't care."

They spoke about sports and school, then the conversation turned to politics and Jason didn't hold back.

"If I lived in South Africa, we'd never be friends, isn't that so?" Jason asked.

"You're probably right," said Marc. "It's shocking. Under the country's rules, we would attend different schools and live in separate neighborhoods – just because we don't have the same skin color." He winced as he thought of his own father's views. "It's very different here."

"But not perfect," said Jason. We may have come a long way in this country, but we still have far to go."

Marc nodded. "I realize that now."

After Marc settled in to his new school, he was asked to give a brief talk about South Africa to the students in his history class. Before he began his presentation, the teacher handed back the weekly graded homework assignments. He glanced at his. He was satisfied with the A, but vowed to get an A plus the next time.

After everyone was given their papers, Marc was called to the front of the classroom. He talked informally about his South African upbringing. To make it more interesting he circulated several photographs of Cape Town and Paarl, including Table Mountain and the Wine Route. He spoke about his country as being the powerhouse of the African Continent with its abundance of coal, gold, diamonds and grain. The response was mainly indifference. Until he mentioned the a-word, apartheid. Marc's audience pelted him with questions.

"What are you doing in the battle against the system? Do you have any black friends there? Are movie theaters segregated? Do you ever think of leaving South Africa permanently?"

Although Marc answered their questions, he felt embarrassed and tried to change the subject when he could.

"South Africa does have a serious problem with its political system," he agreed. "But it's also a beautiful country. Cape Town, at the tip of Africa, has the ocean and beaches on one side and the mountains on the other. The weather's really good." He informed them that it was a surfing haven and told them about the annual Cape to Rio yacht race.

After Marc's presentation Jason came up to him.

"Interesting talk," he said. "I learned a lot. Now you probably don't know much about American football. Want to go to a game next Sunday?"

FIFTEEN

Marc and Jason climbed the many steps to their lofty seats at RFK stadium. Jason was wearing his team colors, burgundy and white.

"Remember, we're cheering for the Redskins," he said.

"Oh, I thought you were a Dallas Cowboys fan," said Marc. "Only kidding," he added, when he saw the expression on his friend's face.

The pretty cheerleaders in their short shorts, the food vendors, the booming sounds, the gigantic projected images – all were new to Marc. He was familiar with the shape of a football and the poles of the goalpost, but little else. He stared as one by one the tall muscular players trotted out from the tunnel. The crowd cheered wildly. He was impressed by the athletes' protective wear, especially their helmets and shoulder pads, and wished rugby would mandate similar precaution. He'd witnessed many serious injuries that could have been prevented.

He and Jason stood as the National Anthem played, and then the action started. After the kick-off the players moved with lightning speed. As the game got underway, Jason explained the play on the field. He also taught Marc about two rival teams, the Giants based in New York and the Eagles in Philadelphia. He could cite the winning teams and game stats dating far back. Marc tried to absorb as much as he could.

At half-time, after waiting in a long line, they carried hotdogs, pretzels and sodas back to their seats.

En route, two girls brushed past them. "Sorry," said one, as she spilled some soda onto Jason's pants. She was tall, with strawberry blonde hair pulled back into a high ponytail.

"Any time," said Jason.

To Marc, after the girls had moved out of ear-shot, Jason said, "Wow, not bad looking. Wouldn't mind going out with her. That reminds me, how's your dating life?"

"Not great," said Marc. "But I guess there's hope. A counselor friend of Helene asked whether I'd like to go to prom with this student, Laura. She figured it would be an experience."

"Who's this girl?"

"A high school senior. Goes to a nearby school."

"So, you going with her?"

"If she agrees," said Marc. "I miss having a girlfriend. Not that keen on a blind date, though. Who knows what she's like?"

Jason pressed for more information. "What are you looking for?"

"Someone different from the girl I dated in South Africa. I want to be with someone intelligent and classy. And loyal. She must be loyal."

"Good luck with that," said Jason.

The girl with the ponytail walked past them again. Jason smiled at her. "Care to join me during half-time?" he asked, pointing to the empty seat next to him.

"You're not my type," she said. Then she turned to Marc and winked at him. Marc looked down and then at Jason, who was silent.

Marc was restless during the second part of the game. He couldn't help wondering if they had experienced a racial snub. He refrained from discussing it with his friend.

As Marc watched the game half-heartedly, he thought back to the recent chess game with the school counselor.

He was engrossed when out of the blue Edith suggested he go to the prom. He did not want his attention drawn away from his strategy on the board. After previously losing to Edith, he was determined to redeem himself. He did not answer immediately. Only a few pieces remained. He moved his knight. She responded by shifting a pawn.

Marc saw an opportunity. "Check," he said, as he slid his queen diagonally in line with Edith's king.

"Oops, missed that. I'm in trouble now. Oh my...well, would you like to meet her? Laura's a lovely girl." Edith moved a pawn to shield her king, than held up a photograph.

Marc studied the picture of a tall girl with chestnut hair and striking features. "Yes, I guess that would be okay." Then he grinned and firmly planted his castle in a dominant fork position. "Check mate!"

"You're a focused young man, a force to be reckoned with," said Edith, as she lay down her king horizontally, conceding the match.

SIXTEEN

Potomac Maryland, April 1977

Laura was proud of the significant strides her mentee, Tharisa, had made and hoped that by meeting with her weekly for the past year she had contributed in some way to her student's betterment. The original commitment was only six months, but because of their good chemistry, it was decided that Laura would continue longer. Tharisa now wrote and spoke with confidence and didn't shy away from speaking her mind. Sometimes Laura was taken aback by her candor such as when she asked, "Laura, who cut your hair? I liked it better the other way."

She shared with Laura the positive comments from her teachers.

"Remember our first meeting?" Laura asked after they completed their final session. "You barely made eye contact with me. Look at you now."

"I guess I've overcome my shyness," Tharisa agreed.

"I would say so," said Laura. "But more than that, you're a good writer. I hope you keep it up."

"I will. I was invited to enter the school's poetry contest. I've started working on the poem."

Laura held up her thumb in approval. "You've worked so hard. I'm really proud of you."

After they said goodbye, Tharisa turned to walk away. Laura stopped her. "One more thing," she said. "Keep studying hard. No-one can take an education away from you."

After they parted, Laura surprised herself by how emotional she felt. Although she had sacrificed her free time, she felt she had gained a lot from the experience and was disappointed that her mentorship commitment had come to an end. Perhaps it was more than seeing her tutoring pay off. She felt a kinship with the student who had also suffered parental loss at such a young age.

At home after school Laura decided to take a break to clear her mind before starting on her homework. She was lying on the living room couch reading the Travel Section of 'The Washington Post' when she heard her mother's voice from the kitchen.

"Edith Thomas called this morning."

"Who's Edith?" asked Laura.

Her mother came into the living room. "She's the guidance counselor at Lincoln. There's a young man, Marc, here from South Africa on an exchange program. She thought it would be fun and a good experience for him to attend a senior prom. She was hoping you would be available to go with him."

Laura put down the magazine and sat up. "No way. We've been learning about South Africa and the sanctions. What if he's a racist?"

"I'm sure he's not, Laura. Just think about it. It could be a good experience for both of you. And you can learn something about Africa."

Laura was not impressed with the sudden appearance of an alien on her horizon. "I don't know anything about him," she said. "I don't know what he looks like. And Eric will be upset if I go with someone else."

"Who's Eric?" asked her mother.

"He's someone I've been seeing," said Laura.

She had chatted with a senior student Eric a few times, but that was as far as it went. At this moment, however, he was a convenient excuse.

"Laura," said her mother, calmly. "I have not responded to Edith. You decide. Tell me what you want and I'll speak to her. Either way is fine with me. It's your call."

Laura didn't have time to give much thought to a relationship now. Apart from school and homework, she was the editor of the school newspaper and on the debating team. She also remembered vividly what had happened with Amber.

That night, however, she gave it more thought. She was wrong to pre-judge. Perhaps she could learn something about another country. Soon Laura was on the phone to a friend at Lincoln Secondary asking about the student from Africa.

"He's tall, dark-haired and good-looking. His name is Marc Sennet. Nice guy."

Laura decided to take the initiative. She didn't really care to go with an unknown, even if he was a heartbreaker. At best, it was a short-term relationship. But, she was interested in geography and fascinated by politics. She called the counselor and responded with a 'yes.'

SEVENTEEN

The shiny limo with the five excited teenagers pulled up outside Laura's modest house. Marc, in a well-fitting rented tuxedo, climbed out and went to meet his prom date. Mrs. Atkin opened the door and introduced herself and her daughter. Laura, tall and slender, wore a full-length halter-dress in the color of a Columbian emerald, accentuating her green eyes. Her golden-brown hair draped in soft curls onto her tanned, athletic shoulders.

For an instant, Marc's eyes locked onto Laura's. So struck by her fascinating beauty, he tried not to embarrass himself by revealing his vulnerability. He moved his gaze to the left. Then to the right. He tried to resist staring at her. He failed. He simply could not take his eyes off her.

He thought, "This is my blind date. How lucky can I get?"

She greeted him with a demure smile accentuating the dimples on her cheek. "So pleased to meet you."

Marc was smitten. He loved her voice. He composed himself sufficiently to give her a formal hug.

"It'll be fun tonight," he said.

She nodded.

He helped her into the limo and presented her with a yellow orchid corsage while they made their way to the school hall. Marc sat in the back seat wedged between Laura and a fellow student. Marc could feel Laura's thigh against his. She tried to inch away. He gave no indication that he noticed. Instead, he made small talk, introducing her to the other passengers and asking about her school. He noticed she seemed more relaxed. They had only just met, but Marc already had a good feeling about her.

The party room was decorated in an outer-space theme with ultra-violet light which showed up the white lamps and fixtures. Laura burst into laughter when she saw how Marc's teeth and shirt glowed. On the stage, a DJ played 'You Should be Dancing'. They joined a crowd of noisy partygoers and received admiring glances. Marc sought out a quiet spot, pulled up two chairs and the two spent an hour getting to know each other. They had plenty to talk about. Laura learned that Marc had strong opinions on issues relating to equality and justice. On a number of occasions he had put himself at risk in Cape Town as he stood up for the rights of others.

Marc noticed Laura looking at him intently. "What are you thinking?" he asked.

"When I first heard of you," she said, "as a white South African, I was worried you might be a racist. I read a lot about South African policies and boycotts. I'm happy to find you're not."

"Not all white South Africans are," said Marc.

Laura admitted she knew little about race in South Africa, but as he informed her, she shared his views.

"Aren't you scared of being locked up?" she asked.

"That's par for the course, as we say in South Africa."

Marc changed the subject. "Do you have a boyfriend?"

"I'm not really interested in having a boyfriend."

"So you don't have one right now?" Marc wanted to be sure. She shook her head. He was relieved.

Laura asked about Marc's high school in Paarl and in the course of the conversation she learned that he was bilingual. She patted him on the arm playfully. "Say something in Afrikaans. Please."

"Alright," he said. "Goeie naand."

"What does that mean?"

"It means 'good evening'.

"Teach me more."

Marc held out his hand. "Laat ons dans."

"Let us dance?"

"Yes." With that he led her to the middle of the room, where young couples were swinging and rocking to the loud beat. As the night went on and the music slowed, Marc held Laura close, and she lay her head on his shoulder. She breathed in his scent as they danced, and she lost count of time.

"We're taking a short break," announced the DJ, interrupting her trance.

Face flushed, Laura followed Marc to the outside terrace to cool down, away from the crowd.

"How do you pronounce s-c-h-e-d-u-l-e?" she spelled, smiling naughtily.

"Shedule," replied Marc.

"I like the way you talk."

"I love your accent too."

"I didn't think I had one." Laura blushed. "Do I?"

She introduced Marc to several other students at the dance. She noticed how comfortable he appeared with strangers and how easily he communicated with her friends. Her girlfriends oohed and aahed over him. "He's so good looking," said one. "You'd better make sure nobody snatches him." Laura wasn't concerned. She saw the admiring way Marc looked at her. Everyone at the party seemed to be in a joyous mood but Laura remained cautious about 'letting go' with Marc. She did not want to allow herself to become vulnerable.

In the middle of a slow dance near the end of the function, a large hand grabbed Marc's shoulder and shoved him to the side of the dance floor. He turned around to look into the chest of a tall, muscular black man.

"You're not welcome here, whitey! Go back to South Africa, where you racists belong," the man shouted. Before Marc could respond, Laura punched the assailant on his arm, and positioned herself between the men. A teacher intervened and an escalation of the confrontation was averted.

"I'm so sorry about that," said Laura. "I know him. He's a brute."

"I am glad I didn't cause a bigger scene." Marc attempted a smile. "Especially at my first prom."

After the incident, Laura noticed a change in Marc's demeanor. Whereas earlier he had been carefree and outgoing, he was now subdued. When the limo dropped her off back home, he walked her to the front door and gave her a formal hug. After he left, she waited inside, standing at the door for several minutes, hoping he had second thoughts and returned. He didn't.

She stayed up late into the night, thinking about Marc and the physical altercation at the dance and the effect it had. She wondered whether he would contact her again. He hadn't kissed her goodnight. Perhaps that was South African etiquette. Or maybe he wasn't interested in her. On the other hand, she had definitely felt a mutual attraction on the dance floor. Certainly up to the time of the incident. She was drawn to the way he spoke and to his smile that was shy with a hint of flirtatiousness. She was attracted to his tall strong physique and the way he held her. No, this was ridiculous. They had just met. She didn't need a boyfriend in her life right now. Especially one who was going to leave. And yet, this one magical night together had been worth it even if it were the last.

Longing to see him again, she put aside her pride and decided to call him the next morning.

Immediately after breakfast she dialed his number. The phone rang twice, then second-guessing herself she quickly replaced the receiver. Now, worried he would know it was she who called, she rang again. She took a deep breath.

When she heard his voice she said, "My mom gave me two tickets for a new movie. Would you like to go tomorrow night?" She realized she was speaking way too fast.

To her relief, Marc accepted the offer anyway.

Laura surprised herself as she anticipated her date. She had not experienced this nervous excitement with Eric.

Walking side by side, Marc said to Laura, "I haven't been to a bioscope for a while."

"What did you say?" she asked. "Bioscope?"

"Oh sorry," said Marc. "I forgot. You would use the word cinema."

Laura was amused. She knew if they got together it would be unlike any relationship she had experienced before. She liked the idea.

The preview of 'Saturday Night Fever' was sold out. Fortunately they had obtained tickets before. The lead actor, John Travolta, was making a name for himself. They were met with a large crowd at the cinema, and took their reserved seats in the back row. When the lights went down, Marc reached for Laura's hand. As the film progressed, they found themselves pressed together. He kissed Laura on the neck and then on her lips, open-mouthed. She felt a tingling sensation move from her head all the way to her feet. She hadn't wanted it to go this far, but she couldn't help herself. She was very attracted to him.

As they left for home after the show, Laura was aware that her blouse was crumpled and her hair was unruly. She blushed as she tried to smooth her clothes. It was not lost on Marc and he reassured her with a comforting hug.

Back in the den of her house after the movie, Laura lay curled up on the sofa with her head resting on Marc's lap.

"I like the Bee Gees music," she said, "especially the song 'How Deep is your Love'.

"That's my favorite number," said Marc, as he ran his fingers through her hair.

"What if one doesn't fall in love? Some people never find partners."

"That's sad."

"On the other hand, who knows what love is, really?"

"When you want what's best for the other person," said Marc. "When you try never to do anything that would make them unhappy. I think that's true love."

The following Saturday, the weather was mild and the sky pale blue. Marc called Laura to make plans for another date. She suggested they take a walk alongside the Potomac River.

En route to the water, they came to a flower boutique which was closed for the weekend. They peered through the shopfront.

"Look, that's protea, our national flower." Marc pointed to a display of pink and white blooms. "Those are called 'blushing brides'. They grow wild on our mountainside."

Laura joined him at the glass. "They're magnificent. I've never seen them before. So delicate."

Marc winked at her. "Ideal for a wedding," he said.

Laura looked away.

"What is it?" he asked.

"Nothing. I was just thinking of my parents. Their marriage didn't last long."

"Want to tell me about it?" Marc took her hand in his.

"Dad died when I was only…." Laura's eyes welled with tears. "I'm sorry. I don't know why I'm telling you this now.

"You can talk to me," said Marc. "Tell me about your dad."

"Everyone says my father was the kindest man. He always wanted to help. Sometimes people took advantage, but it didn't stop him. He was also very well-read. Carried a book wherever he went."

"What did he do?"

"He was an engineer and also taught at the university twice a week," said Laura. "My parents grew up in the same neighborhood and then reconnected in college when they began dating. He passed away when I was little. I basically grew up with a single mother. She did everything for me."

"She did a good job."

Laura wiped her face. "Tell me about your parents."

Marc hesitated. "I'm very close to my mom. My dad, not so much. We disagree on major issues."

"Like what?"

"Politics mostly. He tends to sympathize with the government. For instance, he agrees with the plan to evacuate blacks from designated white areas."

Marc noticed Laura stiffen, and she asked, "How do you deal with that, as your father?"

"It's hard for me to believe I'm his son," he said. "Some of us students went on strike outside the university a few months back. We were protesting school segregation. It really angered my dad. I thought he was going to hit me."

"I'm so sorry," said Laura.

"Don't be. I can take care of myself."

"It's sad," she said. "You don't get along with your dad, and I didn't get the chance to know mine."

Hand in hand, they walked for about a mile until they came to a Haagen Dazs shop. Soon they were staring into its freezer case.

"May I try the butter pecan?" Laura asked the attendant. She was handed a teaspoonful and sampled the ice cream. She was non-committal. "And the mint chocolate?" She paused and repeated a taste. "No, I'll have the raspberry, please. In a cone."

"And you, young man. What will you have?"

Sid had educated Marc on American ice cream.

He was decisive. "Chocolate in a sugar cone, please."

They took seats outside under a bright umbrella and enjoyed their ice cream as they watched the world go by.

"What do you want to do with your life?" asked Laura. "Professionally, I mean."

"Practice medicine," said Marc. "What about you?"

"I've always wanted to teach. Perhaps that's my way of contributing." Laura added, "That's my dream."

A young woman walked to the entrance of the ice cream shop pushing a double-seated stroller with twins. With her hands full she struggled to open the door. Marc stood up to help.

"I'm sure those two keep her busy," Laura said when Marc sat down. "Do you think about having kids one day?"

"I do see myself married with kids," he said. "There's the saying 'children are the continuity of life'. In fact some believe that without children, there is no true marriage."

"I've always wanted children too," said Laura. "When I was younger, I used to dream about what my future would look like. I imagined three children. And horses, and a castle, and a fortune."

She laughed. "Only kidding. Being an only child, I'd be happy to have a big family, though."

"We have something in common then."

"Do you think you'll stay in South Africa?" asked Laura. "I'll probably be living in Potomac forever. I've never traveled overseas."

"This is my first time out of Africa," said Marc. "I don't know where I'll end up."

Laura's eyes widened. "I'd really love to visit South Africa. You've told me so much about the Sea Point beachfront, I feel I know it."

"I'll take you there one day," said Marc.

Laura laughed. "And I'll ask my mom if she'll take us to Bethany Beach, which is a little closer and a bit more realistic. It's not Sea Point, but it's also beautiful."

EIGHTEEN

Laura sat at a table opposite Marc inside the Potomac public library near the Drake's home. She was reading a book on sociology in preparation for a class discussion the following day. The author hypothesized that subsidizing poor people with financial aid would promote a welfare state. Laura strongly disagreed. Holding the book, she walked over to where Marc was sitting and whispered, "Read this paragraph. Tell me what you think."

Marc scanned the section. "That's not right," he said. "I believe most people want to be financially independent. They don't want to rely on handouts. And I wonder if one can really support a family on a welfare check?"

"Exactly," said Laura. "I knew you'd agree. I think I'll write to the author."

"Do that," he said. "You should speak out." Then he pointed to the door. "Let's go outside. What do you say?"

As soon as they had left the quiet zone, Marc wrapped his arms around Laura, leaned her against the library wall and gave her a long kiss on the mouth. Only when they felt someone's presence and heard a loud "ahem", did they withdraw and return to their studies.

Compared with the rigorous bilingual curriculum at North Paarl Boys' High, Marc found his senior academic year in the U.S. to be relatively easy. Whereas Laura's forte was English, he excelled in the sciences. It was a good match. They both delivered with excellent grades in their interims and approached the final exams with confidence.

A few weeks before graduation, Laura made good on her promise to take Marc to the Delaware shore. Her mother agreed to drive them to the town of Bethany for the day.

As they crossed the Chesapeake Bay Bridge and drove toward the ocean, Marc breathed the fresh sea air. It reminded him of the anticipation he felt when traveling from Paarl to Cape Town. They broke the journey for a quick omelet breakfast at a local diner, packed with hungry patrons. Marc observed diners of various races and cultures speaking more than one language. He peeked at the plates on the nearby tables. Several of the dishes were unfamiliar to him.

"What are they having?" he asked, pointing.

"Those are hash browns," said Naomi. "Potatoes."

Marc looked at the menu. "Looks like they also serve scones," he said, pointing to an illustration. "At home we eat them with jam and cream."

"Well here they're called biscuits," explained Laura. "They're similar, but not quite the same."

After waiting too long for a waiter, Marc revealed his mischievous side by donning a napkin over his arm, picking up an adjacent coffee pot and going from table to table refilling empty mugs. He sat down without being confronted. The three broke into laughter.

"By the time they bring the food," said Naomi, "anything will taste good."

When they pulled into Bethany, she said, "I can see you're bursting to get to the beach. You two go, and I'll meet you back here in two hours."

They needed no encouragement. They rushed to the sand, pulled off their sandals and sprinted to the water. Marc watched as Laura pranced along the shoreline in her flowing teal summer dress. Her long wavy hair bounced in the breeze. He admired the beautiful picture she created.

"Come and feel the surf," she called. "It's quite warm."

He ran to join her and together they strolled along the water's edge, feet squishing in the wet sand, occasionally stopping to collect colored sea glass or point out a unique sandcastle. Then they perched on a boulder with a view of sea, sand and birds.

"I'll miss you very much when I leave," said Marc.

"We live on different continents," she said. "Do you think we'll ever be together again?"

Marc tried to keep it positive. "I think so. You never know when our paths could cross." He kissed her and she giggled as she tasted the salty water on his lips.

He knew he would remember this day for a long time.

On the morning of his high school graduation, Marc, dressed in a suit, cap and gown, sat in the assembly room between the Drakes and Laura. After a brief welcome introduction by a teacher, they stood with the rest of the attendees in deference as the band played the National Anthem, followed by the school theme song. The principal gave an inspirational speech about journeying into the adult world. He stressed the importance of continually expanding one's knowledge and using one's talents to help others. Marc felt Laura's hand tighten on his, as she listened intently.

Soon it was time for presentation of the diplomas. When Marc's name was called, he walked with pride to the stage to receive his certificate, as Sid took numerous photographs to document the event. Afterwards the excited graduates threw their caps high into the air, as family and friends cheered.

That afternoon a large crowd, including Laura, her mother and Jason, attended a celebratory function at the Drake's home. Sid and Helene had obviously gone to a lot of trouble. Above the dining room table hung a nylon line attached to which were numerous photographs of Marc and his U.S. friends. On the table were various desserts as well as popcorn in individual bags decorated with the words 'Class of '77'. Sid made a congratulatory speech and Marc responded with a few words of thanks.

After the festivities died down, he and Laura walked to a nearby park.

"I need fresh air," she said. "It's been a chaotic two weeks."

She sat in a swing and Marc pushed gently. "Faster," she said, "faster," as she swung higher and higher.

"You're reckless," said Marc. "Careful, you'll fly off."

Laura felt exuberant. "A little more. It's such fun." Like a freed child she ran around the playground.

"What's next?" Laura asked rhetorically. She climbed up to the top of the slide and slid down fast, landing in the hard sand with a bump. She laughed. "Amber and I spent lots of time here on weekends."

"Who's Amber?"

"She was a close friend. Still is, but I don't get to see her anymore. Became pregnant during high school and had to leave with the baby. Her parents weren't supportive. It was very sad."

Laura stepped onto a red and yellow merry-go-round and held on as Marc pushed.

As it spun around and around, she shouted out in delight. Within seconds, children had gathered, waiting their turn. She climbed off, dizzy, and clung to Marc. "I'll miss doing crazy things with you," she said.

His attention was elsewhere. A toddler had wandered toward the edge of the playground and was making her way toward the busy street. With lightning speed, Marc ran to her, picked her up and carried her to the mother, who was caring for two other children, unaware of the one child's disappearance.

The woman was shaking when Marc handed her the child.

Laura looked at Marc and shook her head. "You're amazing."

He shrugged. "I'm sure anyone who saw what happened would have done the same."

They stayed in the park until the sun went down. Laura realized her feelings for Marc had reached a new high.

The following week Marc reciprocated by attending Laura's graduation party, held on the USS Sequoia, a meticulously restored motor yacht referred to as an important piece of Americana. Laura was excited because she had read that prominent people had sailed on that boat, including JFK who celebrated his 46th birthday with a dinner cruise.

When Laura and Marc entered the cabin for the graduation event, she noticed a fancy leather-bound guest book and ink pen on a small table near the door. She paged through the book and found that it was filled with comments and personal anecdotes, some signed by names she recognized. A teacher must have noticed her interest, because right then he made an announcement to the group, "We encourage you all to sign the guest book by the end of the evening."

"Write something," said Laura to Marc. She handed him the pen. "You'll be in the company of greatness. Go ahead. Anything you want."

Marc took the pen, dated his entry and wrote, "*We hope the future will bring success to you and to us and bless our lives with many children.*

Marc and Laura."

"Oops, I hope that wasn't too forward," said Marc, realizing this was ink, and trying to read Laura's expression.

"Probably," she said, "but I'm okay with it. You're quite a romantic."

Everyone was called inside and seated on chairs or cushions as they participated in games, including one in which someone pretended to be a famous person and the others guessed the name of the celebrity. After dinner there were speeches and several students, including Laura, were honored for their academic achievements.

Before the evening ended, Marc, his arm around Laura, walked with her onto the deck outside. They leaned against the railing, hypnotized by the waves and the gentle movement of the boat.

NINETEEN

July 1977

The neighborhood streets were closed to traffic for the
Independence Day holiday, and families with young children of all
ages were hanging out in anticipation of fun games and the
inevitable barbecue bash. Marc and Laura appeared, each wearing
cut-off jeans and a bright red Paarl school cap. Marc carried a three-
foot long flat-faced wooden bat brought all the way from Cape
Town. He asked a small group of kids if they were ready to join in a
game. There was a chorus of 'yeses.'

"Who will get us a tennis ball?"

"I will," volunteered a seven-year-old boy in an over-sized
T-shirt and baseball cap.

"Who can get us a big box?" Marc held his hand as high as
the bat. "And a smaller one."

Soon he had a bat, a ball and a wicket, the essential pieces of
equipment for the informal game. The smaller box would be used as
a marker to define the end of the so-called pitch.

"Let's gather onto the field near the dead-end and there we
will play cricket."

Marc had learned that the game of cricket, so popular in
South Africa and elsewhere, with over 150 million people enjoying
the sport, was hardly known in America. He thought back to his
time at Newlands, home to the famous cricket grounds in South
Africa, where international games were played. At Newlands,

everyone relaxed, including the barmen charged with restricting under-age consumption of alcohol. It was there that Marc and his friends were introduced to beer, the brew that was bottled a mere stone's throw from the sports field. The grain silos of Castle Breweries loomed across the horizon, hugging their precious barley.

"Years ago I was at Newlands with friends when the Lions played the Springboks," Marc said to Laura, as they walked across the field in Silver Spring. "That was some contest. Kobus, Brian and I were known as the 'three musketeers'. I remember us hanging out on the sloping grass turf under the grandstand, in shorts and sleeveless shirts."

"Looks like today brings back a lot of memories," said Laura.

"Yes, I can still picture that day. It was as hot as it is now, but the tall oaks gave us shade. From where we sat we had a view of Rhodes Memorial above the University near Kirstenbosch Gardens."

"Oh yes, you told me about Kirstenbosch. That's where they have the good scones."

Marc laughed. "You mean that's where they have the botanical gardens and flowers. They happen to also have a café with good scones. Anyway, I remember the three of us sipping cold beer and watching the batsman from England, Denis Compton, as he attacked a cricket ball hurled at him, one after another, scoring for the Lions."

"Our baseball's quite different," said Laura.

"Sadly what's also different with the day at Newlands is that two players, Nunes and Singh, from West Indies and India, needed special passes from the Minister of Apartheid."

"No," she said, in disbelief.

Marc nodded. "Oh yes."

"Go on, tell me more about Newlands," urged Laura.

"Well, sitting above us on the grandstand, the members of the Newlands Cricket Club, mostly Europeans, were seated in comfort and dressed to the hilt, unlike the three of us."

"What did they wear?"

"The men wore a uniform of white trousers, open-necked white shirts and royal blue blazers, most with a coat of arms in a shield on the breast pocket. The women wore mid-length colorful dresses and big hats. Black waiters in formal uniforms served snacks."

"It sounds like an all-day event."

"Even longer," said Marc. He did not regard cricket as slow, despite the fact that strangers to the game could not understand a match lasting over several days.

Now in the United States on his first Fourth of July holiday, when families got together to celebrate Independence Day, he had volunteered to introduce this activity to the nearby children. Intrigued by his idea, Laura had agreed to partner him. Parents signed their kids up and looked forward to the novel recreation.

About a dozen active youngsters ranging in age from six to twelve followed the young couple eagerly to the turn in the road where there was a large flat area covered by short grass. Marc measured out a pitch twelve paces long, placing the big box at one end and the small box at the other.

"Cricket's a bat and ball game," he explained. "Here's the bat. It's a little big for some of you. One person bats and tries to score runs, while everyone else tries to get him out. With a straight arm, the bowler throws the ball to the batter who tries to hit far from the fielders so he can run between the boxes and score a run. He keeps on batting until he is out."

"When is the batter out?" asked Laura.

Marc simplified the rules to accommodate the large number of young children who had gathered. "Good question. A batter is out when the ball hits the big box, or when a fielder catches the ball before it hits the ground." He threw the ball into the air and caught it. "The highest score wins a prize. Let's get started."

Marc moved to the small box, preparing to bowl to Laura, now facing him in front of the big box wicket, ready to bat. The game began with Marc taking a few strides and hurling the ball down the pitch to Laura. She was ready. She swiped at the ball, but missed. The ball hit the box, overturning it with a big thud.

Led by a mischievous Marc, a chorus erupted, "Out, Out, Out."

Laura laughed loudly as she handed the bat to a boy who was next in line. One after the other, the boys and girls batted against Marc's bowling – some scoring a run or two, others vanquished. All were smiling.

Then a ten-year-old freckle-faced kid with a bushy head of red hair took the bat. He seemed at ease. He moved to the ball when it approached and with a big swing sent it far beyond all the fielders, the equivalent of a home run. He was the obvious winner and with much fanfare was given the prize, a Paarl school cap.

His father walked up to Marc and Laura and with an English accent said, "I am so happy that you've re-introduced my son to cricket. We came from Manchester two years ago and I assumed he'd forget the game."

Boisterous fun and laughter continued on the field until everyone was called to eat. Hungry after all the activity, the children abandoned their equipment, and charged off the field in the direction of the food. Marc hoped all the participants would remember July 1977 as the 201st birthday of the United States and as a fun day when they were introduced by the guy in the Paarl cap to the strange game of cricket.

Laura spent the evening of July 24th, her eighteenth birthday, at home, celebrating with Marc, her mother and a few close friends. They shared stories and jokes, laughed, listened to music and ate a lot of chocolate cake. After Naomi retired to bed and all except Marc had left, Laura unwrapped the presents from her guests. Marc waited till she was done, then handed her one more.

He had searched to find a gift he thought most appropriate. He settled on a small framed oil painting of a young couple on a beach walking barefoot toward the water holding hands. She had long golden hair and wore a blue-green dress.

"She reminds me of you," he said.

"A memory of our day at Bethany," said Laura. "I'll treasure it."

Laura told Marc about a television documentary on railway travel in South Africa to be aired that night. She asked him to stay a little longer and he, needing no encouragement to be with her, and intrigued, was happy to oblige.

Watching the travelogue got them talking.

"I imagine it's quite an experience to ride the Blue Train," she said.

"Yes, it travels about a thousand miles from Pretoria in the North down to Cape Town," said Marc. "I've never ridden it, but I've heard it's a great experience, mostly for rich tourists and white locals. It's a luxury most people can't afford."

"What can one do," she asked, "to help change the situation back home? I know you try."

"Race has been an issue in Africa for centuries. It will take a long time to overcome generations of discrimination. But I know for sure that the minority can't control one hundred percent of the country forever."

Marc looked at Laura. "And you? I know you're very committed to certain causes here."

Laura nodded. "I believe that every child, no matter what their background, should be able to get a good education. I'll fight for that."

TWENTY

The day before Marc's departure to South Africa, Laura agonized over how she would deal with saying goodbye. She wanted to spend every possible moment with him. She arranged to come to the Drake's home so they could share his last evening in Maryland together. When she arrived after dinner, he took her hand and led her downstairs to the comfort and privacy of the basement.

His uncharacteristic silence brought home to Laura the finality of their current relationship. Unexpectedly, she had fallen deeply in love with a stranger from another part of the world. Tomorrow he would be gone. She had known this day would come, but nothing had prepared her for the heartbreak she felt now. Yet she would do it all over again if this was the price she had to pay. She wanted so much to tell Marc how she felt but couldn't find the words. Instead she walked over to the wooden bookcase and ran her fingers along the dusty spines of the books until she settled on the volume she wanted. She opened it to page forty, and read aloud from a Shakespeare sonnet. As she read, she wondered if her own love story would endure, or whether there was no promise of a future.

She looked up and saw Marc pacing the room. She chided him for not paying attention.

"I'm listening," he replied. "It's beautiful. But it's the night before I return to South Africa. There're other things we could be doing."

He dimmed the lights, got onto the sofa-bed and beckoned her to join him. Laura hesitated, knowing where this would lead. Although she was taking birth control pills, they had been prescribed because of her irregular periods and not because she intended to have intercourse anytime soon. Now Laura wanted desperately to be with Marc and to make love with him, but to do so would make herself vulnerable and she didn't want to get hurt. Their eyes met. She was mesmerized by the hazel color with the tiny flecks of amber, attracted to his sensual mouth and his muscular body. She put down the book and walked over to where he was sitting. "I will miss you," she said.

He drew her to him. "I haven't left yet."

He kissed her on the side of her neck, then brought her mouth to his. Laura wanted to remember this feeling forever.

"You have the softest lips," he said.

Marc took off his shirt and reached under Laura's sweater. Her heart beat so fast that she was afraid she would faint. He felt for the hook of her bra and with shaky hands, struggled with it until it snapped open. She slipped out of her bra and sweater and tossed them onto a chair, then self-conscious, leaned over to switch off the lamp. In the dark she brought herself so close that she could feel his whole body against hers. She felt his fingers trace the small of her back and send a shiver down her spine. Then he stopped and looked at her for reassurance.

"It's okay," said Laura, as she undressed fully. She had never before gone all the way. She had never wanted to. As soon as a relationship went beyond kissing and touching, she retreated. This time was different.

She knew for Marc, too, this was uncharted territory, but as they clung to each other, she lost all count of time.

When they finally relaxed, he held her close to him and they lay together. His warm body and the movement of his chest as he breathed in and out was calming.

Laura thought about how they met. At the time she certainly wasn't looking for a serious relationship, yet she had found one more meaningful than she could ever have imagined.

When it was time to leave, she tried to be strong. Holding his hands in hers she said, "I promise I'll love you always."

"It could be years before we're together again," cautioned Marc.

She nodded. "I'll wait."

Fighting back tears, Laura embarked on the drive home. She turned on the radio. As the familiar sound of The Commodores filled the car, she reflected upon her relationship with Marc. She wondered if she would ever see him again.

Halfway home, as she negotiated a turn in the road, Laura felt a stabbing pain in her abdomen. The car veered to the side, and came to a screeching halt just off the main road. She bent over the steering wheel, gripping it with both hands.

Time passed excruciatingly slowly, but at last the pain eased. With great difficulty she made it home, where her mother was asleep. Laura felt lightheaded, but attributed it to dehydration. She hadn't had anything to drink since before she visited Marc.

She had a few sips of water in the kitchen, then tip-toed into the bathroom and looked in the mirror. She hardly recognized herself. Her eyes were bloodshot and her cheeks were smudged with mascara. As she stared at the unfamiliar image, her reflection became blurred. She wiped a tissue across the glass in an attempt to see more clearly. Then her head felt fuzzy and her legs gave way.

When she opened her eyes, she had no idea how long she had been lying on the cold bathroom floor, nor how she had come to be there. She saw a bruise on her arm. Through the window she learned it was almost dawn. Grabbing onto the sink, she tried to get up, and found she was too weak to stand without support. She could no longer keep this from her mother. She called out for help.

Less than an hour later, Laura's apprehensive mother drove her to a clinic, for evaluation by Dr. O'Rourke, their family physician. Martin O'Rourke was a doctor of the old school. He had a good bedside manner and Laura found it easy to talk to him.

"Laura," he said, after examining her. "With your recent history of abnormal bleeding and dizziness, I must ask if there's any chance you could be pregnant."

Laura shook her head, but confided in him that she had been sexually active with a recent partner. She reassured him that she was taking the pill regularly. After counseling her on additional precautions, the doctor ran a few tests, including a pregnancy test.

Laura spent the following day resting in bed. Dr. O'Rourke called with test results. "You're not pregnant," he said, but you are slightly anemic. I've gone over instructions with your mother. Let's be conservative and just monitor your symptoms for now."

After the call, Laura tried to stand up, but felt the blood drain to her feet. She lay down quickly. She contemplated letting Marc know, but decided against it. Their last evening together had been perfect. She wanted him to remember her that way.

After going through security at Dulles International Airport, Marc sat near Gate 16, facing the window and a parked 747, and waited for his flight back home. The Drakes had dropped him off at the terminal and helped him check in. They would have gladly waited with him longer, but were not allowed to enter the passenger section. Helene had become very emotional. As Marc thought about it, it made sense. They had no children of their own, so to some extent, he had become their son. And how lucky he was. He couldn't have wished for better host parents, and better friends. He thought about his goodbye visit with Jason in the park that morning.

"I hope we see each other again," Jason had said. "But I don't imagine myself ever traveling to South Africa. You've got to come here."

Marc had responded that he'd like to, but didn't know how feasible it would be. He was starting college soon. Still, they promised to keep in touch, and Marc left, knowing he had made a special friend in Jason, and bitter that he would never have been allowed to experience such an attachment in South Africa.

Sitting at the terminal and reflecting on his time in the U.S., Marc tried to push any thoughts of Laura from his mind. It didn't work. Now, staring outside, he pondered her commitment of loyalty. The love he felt for her included an intense physical desire, but it went far beyond that. It pleased him to be in her presence, to hear her voice, to see her eyes, to appreciate her insights. He wanted her. He would miss Laura Atkin.

To add to the difficulty of separation, he had mixed feelings about going back home. He liked the luxuries he had become accustomed to there, but was constantly reminded that not everyone enjoyed the same freedoms and privileges. Living abroad for the year gave him a greater perspective on the problems in his homeland and made him feel uneasy about returning to South Africa.

TWENTY-ONE

August 1977

Marc's last flight home landed in Cape Town, a full thirty-two hours after leaving Washington. The Cape temperature was comfortable and the air felt fresh, different from the humidity he had experienced before he left.

He walked off the plane wearing a Texan cowboy hat, and met with a welcoming group of excited parents and friends. Holding multi-colored balloons and flowers, they enveloped him with love, kisses, and dozens of questions. His mother, with a huge smile, presented him with a replacement camera.

The festivity did not prevent jetlag from taking its toll. Marc's muscles hurt and his legs felt heavy as he walked with effort to the family car in the airport's parking lot.

For the sixty minute drive to Paarl over du Toit's Kloof Mountain, Marc dozed.

"Wakey, wakey," called his mother. "We're back."

Marc opened his eyes and thought he was dreaming. He did not recognize their house. Whereas before, one could walk from the street onto the front garden, now a high fence topped with barbed wire surrounded the residence. They made their way through the metal gate which shut and locked noisily after they passed through. His father was waiting inside.

"What's going on?" Marc asked, pointing outside.

"Security, my boy, security," said his father. "This is the new South Africa. They're breaking into homes and stealing. Home-owners have been beaten up and even killed. I've always said the police have got to get tougher. They steal one time, I say lock them up for good."

"Oh no," Marc murmured. "I'm not used to this kind of talk anymore."

"You're in my house now," said his father. "If you prefer to live in the States, you do that."

Marc had just come home, and already he felt sick.

Dearest Laura,

I have only been here for a few hours and I realize I left a big part of my universe in Washington. I wish more than anything that you were with me now. Things have changed in South Africa. There is violence and fear. People don't feel safe.

The relationship with my dad is more strained. He has become even harsher. Perhaps he was always this way and I'm seeing it more clearly. It's not the same without you. When will we be together?

Fatigue overcame Marc. He had difficulty concentrating and his head drooped. He wakened momentarily, knew he could not continue and fell on his bed. The letter would have to wait until dawn to be finished. He woke early, well before sunrise and completed his declaration of love to Laura before joining his parents for breakfast.

Later that day Marc answered the front door to find Ben Murphy, soon to enter his fifth year of medical school. He looked thinner and older than when Marc had last seen him.

"Welcome home," said Ben, giving Marc a slap on the back.

"What a surprise," said Marc. "I'm glad to see you're safe." He led Ben into the kitchen where they sat down at the table. "Last time I saw you was at the protest."

"They can't knock me down." Ben flexed his arm to show his biceps. "Believe me they have tried. They even had my phone tapped."

"How do you know?" Marc asked.

"There's a tell-tale clicking sound. Not very high-tech."

"What happened to you after the arrest?"

"They didn't release me with the others," explained. Ben. "When they discovered my father had a connection to the ANC, that's the African National Congress…"

"I know about the ANC."

Ben continued. "Although my dad was only involved in peaceful protests, the authorities had been watching him and recording his phone calls, as you can imagine. On the day of our march, they brought him in for interrogation."

"I'm so sorry," said Marc. "What happened then?"

"I was held for three days. I didn't know what they would do to my father, although they taunted me by letting me know they had him in custody. It was terrible. Eventually they let us both go. Too little evidence they said to detain us longer."

"I had no idea," said Marc. He poured a glass of Coca-Cola for Ben. "Tell me more about your mom and dad."

Ben told Marc that his parents had been civil activists for many years. When Ben was a child his father helped him craft a letter of support to Helen Suzman, an outspoken liberal of the anti-apartheid Progressive Party.

"I was excited to be involved in some way," he said. "But Marc, tell me more about living in the States. You didn't say much in your letters. "Did you go to any concerts or games? What surprised you most about the culture?"

"I went to a Bruce Springsteen concert which was wild," said Marc. "I thought I'd be crushed by the crowd! I was also taken to a football game, totally different from rugby or soccer. I've become quite a fan."

Marc refilled Ben's glass. "I think what surprised me most was the waste in some communities, and at the same time the large number of people in those same communities who are struggling. For example, I ordered a sandwich in a deli. It was massive, and came with a big bowl of pickles, and several packets of ketchup and mustard. I couldn't finish the sandwich or the pickles and I left the condiments unopened. The waiter cleared the table and threw away the sandwich as well as the unopened packets. They bring more than anyone can finish. Not far from there, people were begging for food. We have huge problems in our country. I just wasn't expecting to see that kind of waste there."

Ben shook his head reflecting on what Marc had said. Then he stood up and made his way to the door. "There's a lot to talk about," he said, "about politics and medical school. You have some time off in the next few days?"

Marc explained he had a couple of weeks respite before classes began at the University of Cape Town, where he had enrolled into the combined undergraduate-graduate medical program. "I signed up for a three-month chemistry prep course before beginning medical school," he said.

"Let's follow up soon," said Ben.

Before stepping outside he asked, "By the way, did you meet anyone?" Marc blushed, and Ben added. "I can tell you did."

Marc nodded. "Let's just say it was the best year of my life."

Within a few days of familiar routine, Marc became re-accustomed to the local scene. He felt he had never left South Africa. He filled out forms for U.C.T., completed reading assignments, played rugby, went swimming at Muizenberg beach, and relaxed in the mirage of sunny South Africa.

Correspondence between the young lovers over the span of the Atlantic Ocean initially continued unabated. Marc shared with Laura every detail of his life on paper, and she reciprocated to a point. She left out any mention of her fainting spell and occasional episodes of dizziness. The months flew by and Marc became more and more absorbed in his studies. With the passage of time, the frequency of communication with Laura lessened. Marc was now compelled to focus on the important goal of becoming a doctor.

TWENTY-TWO

February 1978

"Go to sleep ba-by, go to sleep ba-by," Laura whispered softly. She held the infant close to her as she gently rocked back and forth.

Twice weekly she took time off from college to volunteer at Mercy General neonatal unit in Rockville, Maryland. Her own doctor had made her aware of this volunteer opportunity, believing Laura would be a good fit. He was right. And the local college where Laura was pursuing a career in education was not far from the hospital.

Laura remembered how she and Amber used to play 'school'. Laura always volunteered to be the teacher. She loved creating assignments, making lists and checking the homework she had given Amber. Now she was following the first step of her dream of becoming a teacher to disadvantaged children, but it was no smooth ride. Having grown up with a single mother, finances were always a challenge. She had watched her frugal mom save by using grocery coupons and rarely going out. Naomi would do anything for her daughter, but Laura could never burden her mom with hefty college costs. She made an appointment with the school financial aid officer, and they discussed her options. After submitting several applications, a scholarship and reduced tuition solved the problem.

As a volunteer at Mercy, Laura assisted with bottle-feeding babies and new parent educational activities. One infant really got to her inner being. The boy had been born prematurely to a single eighteen-year-old mother. The identity of the father was unknown. Holding the infant now, she felt his little feet kick the blanket and she saw his eyes open.

"Go to sleep ba-by, such a sweet ba-by," Laura whispered, as she wrapped him neatly.

She watched his face as they swayed back and forth together and his eyes slowly closed. Because of his gestational age, baby Adam faced enormous challenges initially in terms of respiratory distress and later on, infection and feeding difficulty. In the neonatal intensive care and thereafter in the regular nursery, he required attention almost around the clock.

"Want me to take over, Laura?" asked a nurse who was making unit rounds. "Your shift was over twenty minutes ago."

"I'll stay a little longer," said Laura.

Laura had heard that the child's young, inexperienced mother was overwhelmed. The hospital social workers had tried to arrange for family support so that the biological mother could raise her baby. It was not forthcoming. The boy was transferred to the nursery and his mother relinquished her parental rights. Laura was heart-broken at the prospect of the separation of mother and child. She signed up for more frequent shifts and when she had the opportunity she held the baby a little longer and a little closer.

"Did you hear," asked the nurse one afternoon, "that Adam's going to a foster home next week? There's no grandparent or other family member who is willing to care for him."

"Can't we take care of him here till he finds an adoptive family? I'll help out whenever I can." Even as she said the words Laura knew that could never happen.

"Sometimes it takes a long time for a baby to be adopted," explained the nurse. "And baby Adam has physical and developmental problems. It will be a challenge for anyone looking after him."

Laura felt sad. She hugged Adam, but couldn't find the strength to say goodbye. She knew she would never see him again. That night she dreamed a young woman holding a swaddled baby came to her front door. The woman tried to hand the baby to her. Laura hesitated. She saw the pleading in the woman's eyes. When she woke, the image was still there.

The idea that any child was left without a parent pained Laura. She thought of Amber and the difficult decision she had to make. She put her feelings on paper, as she often did.

Dear Amber,

"I think about you a lot. I hope you and your daughter are doing well. I met someone really amazing. Told you I'd let you know. He's different from anyone I've dated before. An exchange student. It was exciting and totally unexpected. The problem is he's from South Africa, believe it or not, and has returned home already. There's no guarantee I'll see him again. I've fallen in love, Amber. Life has a way of playing tricks on us, doesn't it?

Please write soon.

Your friend,

Laura.

TWENTY-THREE

University Residence, Cape Town

There was a knock on Marc's dorm room door. He opened it to find a well-groomed young man in beige pants and jacket.

"You must be Marc," he said in a soft-spoken voice. "I saw your name on the door. I'm Dieter, your neighbor."

Marc opened the door wider. "Come in. Nice to meet you."

It was Marc's first day at the University of Cape Town as a resident of the men-only elite Stanton Hall located alongside Jameson Hall, the steps of which sited many romantic encounters. Marc took a seat on the single bed, and pointed to the only chair in the small room. "What are you studying?"

Dieter sat down. "Economics. You?"

"Medicine."

"I should have guessed when I saw 'Gray's Anatomy' on your desk," said Dieter. He was about five foot nine, a few inches shorter than Marc and had fair hair and blue-grey eyes.

"I hear a slight accent," said Marc.

"German. Dieter's my last name, but I answer to that. Our family moved here from Frankfurt when I was a teenager. I'm surprised you could tell."

"I've become sensitive to accents. I spent a year in the States and wherever I went, people asked about mine."

"Are you a Capetonian?"

"No, from Paarl."

"The wine valley. Nice."

Marc worried he wasn't being a good host. Dieter was sitting on a hard rickety chair and he hadn't offered him anything to eat or drink. From the bedside table drawer, he pulled out a package of trail-mix and opened it, then set out two bottles of water. "Help yourself," he said. "Do you have other family here?"

Dieter put a pretzel into his mouth. "Not here, Port Elizabeth." He finished chewing and swallowing. "I have a younger brother, a tennis player. Won several championships. As far as my parents are concerned, he can do nothing wrong."

Marc noticed Dieter's voice become forced as he told of his brother and he sensed there were problems between them.

"We don't speak," said Dieter, confirming Marc's suspicions.

Days after his meeting with Marc, Dieter was reminded that although the Second World War had ended decades earlier, the hatred for the Third Reich still lingered among many South Africans. After all, family members had given their lives to fight the Nazis in North Africa and Italy. It befell Dieter, soon after his enrollment at UCT, to be a target for anti-German sentiment in the hazing ritual of Stanton Hall. He was singled out to perform humiliating tasks by bigots in the name of 'initiation.'

'Line-Up' was the roll call of freshmen each morning at seven in the central quad. A senior student, Bliks, called out the names alphabetically and the juniors responded with 'present.' "Agar, Arnold, Atkinson, Barr, Battiste, Botha, Carrington, Christopher", shouted Bliks, and when he reached the letter 'D', his voice changed to a gutteral rasp as he slowly accented "Dieter." The following week he prefixed 'Dieter' with 'Herr.'

Marc was disgusted by the bullying rite and psychological warfare, but felt powerless to stand up to the tradition of almost a century. He was offended by the insulting, painful treatment his friend had to endure. At many morning line-ups, there was a call for volunteers. Silence usually followed. It didn't matter. Bliks selected volunteers and summoned them, one by one, to the front of the group.

"You, Kruger," commanded Bliks, "will volunteer to make the beds and clean the bathrooms and toilets for the gentlemen of tier 'D' every day next week. And you, Rothstein, will wash and polish the cars of the six gentlemen who parked in garage level B-3." He concluded with an abrupt "I thank you all for giving your valuable time."

Marc hated the sarcasm.

Stanton Hall celebrated Arbor Day with a gathering of all residents around the huge palm tree in the quad. There, after a ceremonial dinner, the men would chant 'Under the tree we gather to pee,' and empty their bladders at the base of the palm. The urine would nourish the roots and ensure everlasting life, they were told. The ridiculous ritual was viewed by Marc as childish and unseemly.

Finally, when a swastika appeared on Dieter's door, Marc could take no more of hazing. He reached out to several students and together they founded a campus group to end the barbaric discriminating practice. "No More Hazing" became the popular refrain and forerunner to the "Do No Harm" of Marc's medical

Hippocratic Oath. Within a few weeks, the slogan, the abbreviation NMH with a diagonal line through the letters, signifying its desirable end, was seen all over campus on posters. Stanton Hall did end its hazing practice. However, for Dieter, who was found in his dorm room having committed suicide, it was too late. Marc felt bitter that a tragedy like this had to occur before any change was made.

The first year of medical school was challenging, a giant step up from high school. Marc was aware it would be when he applied to enter graduate school directly, instead of enrolling in a bachelor's degree program before making the transition. He had a new schedule which included waking at six a.m. to attend early lectures and returning home late in the evening to his books. Although he enjoyed the physics and chemistry courses, he could not wait to delve into real medicine - anatomy, physiology and hands-on practice.

He took advantage of every opportunity to meet with Ben, ostensibly to discuss medical topics, but actually to pick his brain about the secret activity of the African National Congress. They met for lunch just off campus one day. Ben came directly from the cardiology lab and was still wearing his white coat and stethoscope. He was flustered.

"Sorry I'm late," he said.

"How's everything been going?" Marc asked. "Only one more year till you become Dr. Murphy. Hope you'll still have time for me."

Ben didn't have time for idle chatter. His face was dead serious. "The ANC got wind of the poor facilities on Robben Island," he said. "They've got something in the works."

"What do you mean by 'something'?" asked Marc. Ben was often vague and Marc was never sure how he got his information or whether he was personally involved in any of these activities.

"I can't say much yet. I have my sources and I don't want anyone to get hurt."

"I hope you won't get hurt," said Marc. "It sounds dangerous."

A waitress interrupted to take their order. After she left, Marc fiddled with the menu as he contemplated whether he should ask his friend more questions or stay as far away from the topic as possible.

"Hey," said Ben, "did you hear from that girl in the States?"

"It's been a while," said Marc. "Still think about her, though."

He should have added 'all the time', for when he strolled along the beach front by himself, he always pictured the girl on the other side of the ocean. He imagined her in the cold stormy weather of the American east coast. By contrast, Bantry Bay was mild and beautiful all year round, even in the midst of winter. He wished he could walk with her and show her how the playful waves splashed onto the boardwalk railings. He wished she could be here now.

"I think about her all the time," he muttered to himself.

The first year of medical school ended uneventfully, just as it began, but year two was life-changing. It began well enough. Marc moved into a comfortable studio apartment not far from campus and was happy to live on his own. Anatomy was more fascinating than he had imagined. Days were spent studying the bones of a skeleton, dissecting a human cadaver and performing post-mortems. The lingering smell on his lab coat of dogfish entrails and frog vessels was nauseating. Perhaps not by co-incidence, that was the year Marc became a vegetarian.

TWENTY-FOUR

After a particularly challenging afternoon in the lab, Marc returned to his apartment to find an envelope from Western Union. Another one of those marketing ploys, he thought. He tossed it aside for later reading, then went to the fridge to see what leftovers he had for dinner. He would have liked one of his mother's homemade Tupperware meals, but for now he settled on a cheese sandwich, which he ate in the kitchen while scanning the Cape Times. After supper he picked up the envelope and other papers on the entrance table for sorting. He tore open the Western Union wire and stared at the words in disbelief.

> *Dear Marc,*
>
> *Not been easy trying to get over you. Can't pretend nothing happened between us. Sorry to have to share this news, but I haven't been doing well for a few months. Had abdominal pain and heavy bleeding. Tests showed uterine tumor. Not sure if cancer. Discussing treatment options. Really scared. Miss you. Wish you were here.*
>
> *Love, Laura.*

Marc re-read the last few lines several times. He felt his legs get weak. For a few moments, he stared into space, picturing the last time he had seen Laura. So beautiful and healthy. No hint of illness. Had he missed a symptom? Was there something he could have done? Consumed by fear, he picked up the phone and asked the international operator for emergency assistance.

"Would you please help me call a number in the U.S.? It's in Maryland. I'm trying to reach a Ms. Laura Atkin."

Marc gave the number and repeated it slowly. He listened as the operator tried to place the call. He heard several rings and then silence.

"I'll try your call again," said the operator.

Marc tapped his fingers on the table as he waited.

"Sorry," she said. "Same problem. I'm not getting a connection."

After three unsuccessful attempts, Marc became frustrated and moved to return the handset to its cradle. Then he heard a ring tone, and her familiar 'hello'.

"Laura! Are you okay?"

Her voice was barely audible. "So happy to hear you, Marc. There's good news and bad news. It's not cancer, but medications haven't helped, so they're planning to operate next week. The surgeon's still not sure whether or not I'll need a hysterectomy."

"I'm so sorry," said Marc. "I wish I could be there for you."

"Me too. I think about you all the time."

"Love you."

"Always."

As soon as he got off the phone, Marc tried to process what he had heard. He was aware that a hysterectomy involved major surgery. He referred to his pocket medical dictionary and confirmed that it meant removal of the uterus, resulting in the inability to have children.

He called his father and told him of Laura's forthcoming operation. "Her surgery's planned for next Wednesday. I'd like to be there for her."

"Who's Laura? That the prom girl?"

"Yes, dad. I have to fly to the United States. I can't let her down." When Stan didn't speak he added, "I'll use my savings."

"I'm glad you don't look to me to pay for the trip," said his father. "But I think it's crazy. You're not a millionaire. And you can't help her anyway."

Marc regretted having contacted his dad. "That's all right," he said. "I'll manage by myself."

He waited till the following morning to call his mother. He told her about the conversation with his father and she gave him different advice.

"I heard it all," she said. "Follow your heart, son."

Marc obtained permission to miss the week of classes prior to the spring vacation. He withdrew a sizeable percentage of money from his savings account and with help from his mother, bought a return ticket to the United States. He decided not to let Laura know. It was to be a surprise visit.

The overseas flight seemed longer and even more uncomfortable than previously. Marc was tense and restless. He barely slept. He began doubting his decision to visit Laura unannounced. There was one plus, however. He had made a reservation to stay at the Marriott

Hotel in Bethesda. No YMCA in New York this time. He had learned his lesson.

The cab dropped him off at the hotel and after he checked in, he took a short nap, showered and changed his clothes. Then with his heart racing, he dialed Laura's number.

"Hello," she answered sleepily.

"Hello Laura."

"Who is this? Marc, is that you?"

"It's me," he said. "Would you like a visitor?"

"I don't know when we'll see each other again, Marc. My surgery's scheduled for tomorrow."

"I'll be at your home within the hour."

He heard the surprise in her voice and "You're kidding!"

He hung up the phone and called for a taxi. Soon he was embracing a sobbing Laura.

"They're tears of joy," she reassured him.

He handed her a small, neatly wrapped box tied with a red ribbon. Laura opened it to find a gold chain with a pendant in the shape of a protea flower.

"So that you'll always remember your friend from South Africa," said Marc.

"As if I could ever forget."

She removed the necklace and held her hair up in a makeshift knot while he helped her fasten the chain around her neck. He felt the smoothness of her skin and the silkiness of her hair as it glided back gently onto her shoulders. She was wearing a white mid-length eyelet dress and no make-up except for a touch of coral gloss accentuating her enticing lips. She was as beautiful as he remembered.

"It's been too long," he said, studying every inch of her face.

Her cheeks became rose-colored. Laura tilted her head. Their lips touched and as they kissed, it felt as exhilarating as it did the very first time, and she forgot what day it was and where she was standing.

The shrill ring of the telephone brought Laura back to reality. It was her mother, checking in with her and letting her know she'd be home soon. Laura straightened her clothes, then paced up and down the small room as she told Marc about the dizziness and the pain that had led her to visit the doctor. As she spoke, Marc noticed the blue-grey shadows under her eyes.

"You've been through a lot," he said. "I'm sure you haven't been sleeping much."

She sat down next to him. "True, but I'm not afraid anymore." She shifted in her seat till she found a comfortable position. "Tell me about you, now," she said. "Fill me in on the last year-and-a-half."

"Where do I start?" Marc asked. "I've missed you terribly, as I'm sure you know."

Laura nodded.

"Besides that," he continued, "I'm really enjoying medical school. It was the right decision, although there's a ton of work."

Marc went on to describe some of his experiences. She brought tissues as he informed her about the tragedy with Dieter and the group he founded as a result. Laura in turn told him about her volunteer experience at Mercy General, how she loved working with the newborns and how attached she had become to one baby in particular.

"He was so vulnerable," she said. "It was hard to say goodbye."

Early the following morning Marc accompanied Laura and her mother to Georgetown University Hospital in Washington D.C. He waited in the crowded visitor's room while the surgeon and the anesthesiologist did their pre-op assessments and the nurse obtained Laura's vital signs and drew blood. Whenever allowed, he went inside to comfort her. He noticed that she was wearing the pendant.

"For luck," said Laura, weakly. She forced a smile.

Marc, having enough medical knowledge to worry, asked the staff lots of questions. When it was time for the surgery to take place, Laura's mother sat next to him in the waiting room.

"You've made all the difference," she said solemnly. "I don't know what to say."

"There's nothing to say," said Marc. "I care about Laura a lot. I want to be here."

They sat together in silence and waited impatiently. Marc brought two hot teas from the cafeteria, but they remained untouched. He watched as patients and families checked in at the front desk.

"Put your name in the column right here," instructed the receptionist to one after the other. "Keep this assigned number."

"Have you been looking for us?" asked a family member of an earlier patient. "We stepped out for a moment to make a call."

The receptionist checked the long list of names. "No sir. Have a seat. We'll call you by the number when it's time for you to see the patient. You can also check for updates on the board in the back."

The room became even more crowded and noisy, except when a clerk walked to the board, signaling an update with one of the patients. Then there was an empty silence.

After what seemed like hours, Marc heard someone call out, "Mrs. Atkin, please come to the front."

Marc went along instinctively. The receptionist was on the phone, apparently trying to make sense of what the person on the other side was saying. The call went on too long. Marc became agitated.

"Tell us what's happening," he interrupted, trying to get her attention. "We've waited for hours. What's going on?"

He looked at Naomi and saw how pale she had become. He tried to console her. "I'm sure it's fine." They both knew it was not.

At last, the receptionist put down the phone. "One of the nurses will come out to talk to you," she said.

That's not a good sign, thought Marc, as Naomi began to shake. Feeling helpless, they returned to their seats. Marc felt as if he were going to faint. This was taking far longer than the anticipated surgery and recovery room time. He looked up to see a nurse in gown, cap and booties looking down at them.

"I'm sorry this is happening," she said.

"What? What is happening?" asked Marc.

"There was a lot of bleeding. They're trying to control it now. There's still a good chance everything will be okay."

When she left, Marc and Naomi sat together, barely moving. Tears flowed freely from her as Marc tried to contain his emotion. Through Marc's mind flashed images of his first meeting with Laura and their romantic experiences together. He loved her so much and now there was a chance he could lose her.

The door to the operating area swung open. The surgeon, still gowned, appeared and entered the lounge. Laura's mother squeezed Marc's hand.

"She's quite stable now and doing as well as can be expected," said the doctor matter-of-factly.

Marc sighed with relief, as the surgeon continued. "Unfortunately, we did have to remove her uterus, but the bleeding has stopped, and she'll probably be able to go home in a week or so."

There was a chilling silence as the two tried to absorb the news and process the implications. Laura would be infertile. Laura, someone who would make a wonderful mother, could never bear children of her own.

Much later, as they gathered in the recovery room, Marc sat close to her and kept the conversation light. She still seemed dazed from the anesthesia.

"Everything will be alright," Marc whispered, trying to convince both Laura and himself.

When her eyes closed, a nurse in a starched uniform with a concerned look, escorted Naomi and Marc to the hallway. "You two must have questions." They nodded. "I'm Mavis and I'll be here till tonight. If you think of anything at any time, here's my number." She handed them each a card. "Also, I have to mention something. Apart from the physical ramifications, there are often psychological consequences following this type of surgery. You know, Laura is young. This will probably hit her hard later. I'm just saying, prepare for possible mood fluctuations."

Sid and Helene Drake insisted Marc move out of the hotel and in with them, which he gratefully did. Over the next few days, he shared time between the Drakes and the Atkins. Laura's post-op recovery in the hospital went as well as could be expected. On the surface, she seemed to handle the news about her condition with equanimity, but Marc knew that she was deeply affected by the prospect of infertility. When he felt she was well enough to talk about it, he decided to broach the subject. Alone with her, he sat on the edge of the hospital bed and took her hand in his. "How are you doing, really?" he asked.

"I'm fine," she said, withdrawing her hand and looking away from him.

"Laura," said Marc, "I know you. We've always been open with each other. I can tell you're not fine."

She cleared her throat. "I can't explain," she said.

"Try."

"I feel damaged, broken."

"What do you mean?" Marc asked.

"I can never ever have my own children. Don't you understand that?"

Marc was overcome by the pain she bore and the closeness he felt for her. He tried to reassure her. "No diagnosis will stand in the way of my love for you," he said, "even if it's long-distance."

When he left for the return trip to Africa a few days later, he vowed to keep in close contact.

TWENTY-FIVE

Two days after Marc left back to South Africa, Laura was officially discharged from the hospital.

"Got all your belongings?" asked the nurse, as she wheeled Laura through the dark and narrow hospital corridors.

The halls reeked of antiseptic. Outside the patient rooms were bags of laundry and bins marked hazardous waste. A stretcher, carrying a young girl with shaven hair and an intravenous line squeezed by, bumping into Laura.

"Sorry," called the porter.

At the hospital entrance, Laura's mother was waiting. She helped Laura out of the wheelchair and into the car. "Ready to go home?" she asked.

"I am," said Laura. Her body hurt when she moved and she felt exhausted from little sleep. But it was the depression of the verdict that got to her inner self more than mere physical pain.

"Tell me what you're thinking," said Naomi. She could read her daughter well. "I'm worried about you."

Laura shrugged. The physician's words after the surgery, "you will not be able to bear children", were like a life sentence. Marc had declared to her that he wanted to be a father. 'Without children, there is no true marriage.' In her mind, she had visualized having a large family with him.

Laura sat in the back seat as her mother drove home. Naomi tried to distract her, but Laura remembered the long philosophical conversations with Marc. What future was there for her as a barren wife? She was like a plant without water. She could not live with herself if she could not give him what he so wanted and deserved – his own children. The unselfish thing would be to give him an 'out', free to choose someone else as a partner.

For the next several days Laura wrestled with the only option she could see as viable. Heartbroken, she made up her mind that she would leave town quietly without a forwarding address. She would apply to be a transfer student at a school in Pennsylvania. Her mother would be sad, but she'd understand. It was only a few hours away whenever she wanted to visit.

Laura felt a gnawing pain in her stomach. No, she could never abandon the woman who had done so much for her. There was no other family. Who would be there if her mother needed help, if she became ill? Laura spent that night in a restless state between sleep and wakefulness until she got up feeling as if her head was going to burst. She would try to persuade her mother to join her in the move and undertake a vow of silence.

Naomi didn't take it well. She shook her head repeatedly. "No," she said. "You're not thinking this through clearly. Marc's an adult. You have no right to decide his future."

"I've made my decision, mom," said Laura. "I know how he feels."

Her mother left the room, shutting the door loudly. Laura had not seen her react this way before. Laura was in the same spot when she returned. "I'll do it because I love you," said Naomi. "But promise me you'll think about it for another day."

The life-changing decision that Laura made required a major plan of action. As she considered her strategy, she realized that it was no simple matter to change abodes secretly. But complexity never stood in her way in the past and she was not going to succumb to these challenges. She had to make this move to free Marc from an unproductive woman.

Back in Cape Town, Marc wrote to Laura at the very first opportunity. He was lying in bed unable to fall asleep, thinking about the surgery and its implications, and imagining how terrible she must feel. He got up to retrieve pen and paper, then, sitting in his bed, propped up with three pillows, he began to write. He chose his words carefully, knowing she was sensitive about the topic of parenthood.

> *Dear Laura,*
>
> *Spending time with you last week only reinforced the strong feelings I have for you. I wish I could have stayed longer. I was worried about some of the things you said before I left. I promise you I will adore you always, no matter what.*
> *With all my love,*
> *Marc.*

He mailed the note and waited for her response. Days went by, then weeks. He panicked. In the past, Laura was always quick to answer his letters. He called her home and was surprised when he heard the words "…number no longer in service." He tried again, sure he had misdialed the first time. But no, the same message.

Convinced Laura was ill and unable to respond, Marc mailed a postcard to her mother, with a message to have Laura contact him as soon as possible. He checked the mailbox every day until he finally accepted the fact that he was not going to hear from either one of them. He was stunned. The fact that he didn't know where she was and had no logical explanation for her disappearance left him feeling perplexed, anxious, and above all, powerless.

Desperate to find Laura's whereabouts, Marc wrote to the Drakes as well as to Edith. They responded with regrets that they were unable to help. The hospital where she was treated confirmed her discharge in good health. Speaking to Mavis, the nurse who had warned about possible depression, only made him more worried.

He called Ben Murphy, and told him what had happened. They arranged to meet at the Ambrosia beachfront café. Ben looked surprised when he saw Marc, eyes puffy and hair uncharacteristically untidy. The advice Marc got was not what he wanted to hear.

"If you have done everything possible, you have to get on with your life," said Ben. "Maybe she wanted to end whatever you had. Perhaps she realized she could not fulfill her commitment. Face it and accept it."

Marc had imagined various possibilities, none of them good. Laura had succumbed to her illness. Laura had redefined her life to exclude Marc. Laura had fallen in love with someone else.

Short of hiring a detective agency, something he could hardly afford, there seemed to be no way of tracking her down. Ben's suggestion was probably the only avenue open to Marc. But it was difficult to write off whatever they had between them to only 'an experience.' The relationship, and now the loss, was far greater. For a long time Marc agonized over what more he could do, until eventually, hard as it was, he found the mantra 'accept' to be his fate.

TWENTY-SIX

Philadelphia, 1979

"This week, here from our classroom, we will visit Italy," said Laura Atkin to a group of twenty middle-school students.

In an attempt to look professional she was wearing a pencil skirt, blouse, blazer and heels, the latter being a mistake, she soon discovered. Her feet ached. She'd know better tomorrow. She pointed to a colorful travel poster in front of the classroom.

"Who can tell me something about Rome? Anything?"

There were blank stares. A pencil flew from the back of the room and landed at Laura's feet. There was an outbreak of laughter. Laura waited for silence, then continued. "We were talking about Rome. No more flying pencils, okay?"

She thought about how she got to be in this position. Soon after her major surgery, she received her acceptance letter to Muhlenberg College in Allentown, Pennsylvania. There was a problem, however. She could only enroll in August, at which time she would be considered to be a third year transfer student. She had a void of three months. She decided to put the time gap to good use and experience education in the raw, at a public school in Philadelphia. During week one, things were not going as well as she had planned.

Finally a student raised her hand. "The Vatican is in Rome."

"Good," said Laura, relieved. "What else?"

Her temporary assignment as a geography substitute involved teaching students about places outside of America. Neither she nor any of these students, as far as she knew, had traveled beyond U.S. borders. Few of them had left the city. She decided to choose a country in each of the continents and focus on a city there for a weekly class discussion.

"Okay, no problem," said Laura, to break the silence. "Let me tell you about Rome. It's a very exciting place and the capital of Italy. It's an ancient city, home of an enormous amphitheater, the Colosseum. Have you heard of it?" She held up several photographs. "Come up to my desk and take a look at these."

The students gathered around Laura as she passed out images of the city and its historical landmarks. Now curious, they began to communicate. With patience she entertained all their questions and encouraged dialogue. Then Laura pulled out a small insulated bag with two Tupperware containers.

"I brought you a taste of Italy," she said. "Would you like to try some Italian pasta and biscotti?"

Soon the students, initially skeptical, were enjoying the food, and talking and giggling so loudly that Laura had to remind them they were in school and required to keep the noise down.

With little training, Laura embraced the challenge of substitute and was determined to make her mark. She was aware that few teachers were eager to accept this job in a public school in the South East quadrant, where the students were predominantly black and on the poverty line, often with a single parent. There were minimal resources available to teachers. It was no great hurdle to be appointed. All that was needed was a high school diploma and a clean criminal record. The pay was a mere thirty dollars per day. If she subtracted what she had to pay for her temporary rental apartment, she made next to nothing. It was regarded as a menial position with no future. But Laura disagreed. She felt it was a good stepping stone for a wonderful cause.

She took a sincere interest in the home life of her charges. Some had night jobs, others had two-hour commutes. Several lived in dysfunctional households. Her caring and patience seemed to pay off. The students became more engaged, completed assignments and shared their stories. She believed they had learned a lot from her.

A student raised his hand. "Yes, Anton," said Laura. "Go ahead."

The student stood up. Laura knew him as a bright child who frequently stayed after class to ask questions. He was significantly taller than his peers and regularly teased for being different.

"I've been to Italy," he said. There was a disbelieving gasp from the class. "My mother's boss took her and me to Rome when I was three."

"Tell us what you remember," said Laura.

As soon as Anton opened his mouth, students in the back row started banging their fists on the desks, drowning out his voice.

Laura walked toward the back. "You obviously have something you need to say," she said to them. "Whoever was making the noise, come to the front, and tell us all. We'll decide if it's important."

Nobody stood up.

"Nothing more to say?" she asked. "Okay, Anton will continue. If there's any more disruption, we'll stay after class."

There was silence as the boy described what he could remember.

"Can you say anything in Italian?" Laura asked.

When he spoke two sentences in a believable Italian accent, Laura clapped, and the students clapped along. Anton sat down, leaned back in his chair and looked around the room at his new admirers.

By the time her three-month contract was up, Laura had also learned. She knew how to control an unruly class, plan interesting lessons, advocate for better books and teaching materials, and deal with the bureaucracy of the education system. She discovered that with motivation and adequate resources, these children could achieve all their more advantaged brothers and sisters down the street could. Laura also found what her own role would be in life. She was ready to continue her undergraduate training in education.

On move-in day at Muhlenberg, Laura's mother rented a van and they packed it with a mini-fridge, a fan, blankets, pillows, clothes, storage containers and food items. Laura was happy to make the formal move away from the memories that were still raw.

Although several of her friends were interested in attending schools with larger campuses, Laura preferred the smaller school, where students could get to know one another better. Muhlenberg College had a long history of fine teaching. It was also close to New York City. Laura remembered with fondness her mother, Naomi, performing songs from 'The King and I' and 'Sound of Music' to an audience of one. Perhaps now they could take in a live Broadway show or two.

After a three-hour drive, Laura and her mother pulled up to the front of the dorm building behind a long row of cars and mini-vans. The side-walk was bustling with nervous freshmen and worried parents. Laura began unpacking the vehicle. It was a hot, humid day and she was sweating. As she tried to lift the fridge, she heard an unfamiliar voice call out to her. "Would you like some help with that? It looks heavy and there's no elevator in this building."

She hesitated, and then gratefully accepted. The young man lifted one side of the large appliance and together they made their way up the two flights of steps, while Naomi waited in the car.

"We can put it in the hallway for now," said Laura. "I haven't decided where this will go yet."

"No problem, I'll leave it here. By the way, I'm Robert. Hope to meet you again, Laura."

"Surprised you know my name," she said. "Anyway, I appreciate the help. Good luck with your move-in."

The rest of the day was hectic. Laura's room-mate arrived with her loud, extended family. Two people could barely fit into the tiny space, filled with boxes and equipment. Once the others left, the students began to get acquainted and found they were quite compatible. Gradually the room took shape. Each occupant had a bed, a desk and a closet. They shared a fridge. That was everything they needed.

Over the next few weeks Laura ran into Robert in the cafeteria, in the dorm hallway, and in the library. She noticed his blue eyes and his friendly smile. "Don't go there," she thought. It had taken a long time to recover from the painful separation from Marc. Better to concentrate on school right now. Yet Laura was not allowed to get Robert out of her mind. From across a room, their eyes would meet, and she would look away, embarrassed. One day she found a note in her locker. "How about we meet at Java tonight at eight?" She was curious, so she agreed to the date.

When Laura entered the coffee house, Robert was waiting.

"Thanks for coming," he said. "I've been dying to ask you out since we first met."

Laura blushed.

"What would you like?" Robert asked.

"I'm not hungry. Just a small coffee."

"Two small coffees, please." Robert returned the menus to the waiter. "Nothing to eat right now."

"Robert, thanks again for your help on move-in day."

"No problem. And call me Rob. By the way, I hear you have Prof Lewis for English. I have him next semester. How are his classes?"

"He's great. Makes lectures interesting and fun. Have you declared a major?"

"Not yet. I'm considering finance. I heard you're in education." Laura nodded.

As Laura began to relax she found herself opening up about her life. She told him about Marc.

"Sounds like you still have feelings for him. Should I be jealous?"

"Of course not," Laura responded. "He's far away and pretty much out of my life."

"How about Saturday night then, movie?"

"Sure."

In the small-town, half-empty theater, Laura sat next to Rob, sharing a bag of buttered popcorn as they watched an action-packed film rife with speeding cars, shooting, and spilled blood. She shut her eyes for much of the movie, but feigned enjoyment when he nudged her and asked, "A bit gory, but exciting, isn't it?"

She couldn't help thinking about 'Saturday Night Fever' and what a different experience that had been with Marc. She endured, but when the show ended, she couldn't get out fast enough. Rob must have noticed something was wrong. They walked home in awkward silence. She tensed when he tried to put his arms around her. If only he were Marc.

"This isn't working between us," said Robert, the next time they met in the cafeteria. He sighed. "Your heart's clearly not in this."

Laura started to speak but stopped herself. She knew he was right.

Rob continued. "I know we haven't dated long, but I feel as if I'm being compared to the South African guy. I'm uncomfortable with it."

"I'm sorry," said Laura. "It's my fault. I really like you."

"But not as a boyfriend," Rob said almost inaudibly.

Laura was silent as Rob held her hand for a moment before standing up.

"It's better this way," he said. "I'll still see you in school. Hopefully we can be friends."

"I hope so," said Laura, thinking of some person's stupidity in coming up with the phrase 'out of sight, out of mind'.

She decided to hold off on dating and focus on her studies.

For a long while Laura kept her promise to herself. She made friends easily in college, but although she was regularly asked out on dates, she declined. Given the choice of writing a paper and getting a good grade, or enduring a long awkward evening with a stranger, she chose the former. Her attention to her undergraduate studies paid off and she graduated with honors. At the ceremony, Laura thought of her high school graduation four years earlier. Now she had her mother for support, but there was something missing. She wondered how Marc was doing. She imagined he was still in medical school. She wished she had a friend to talk to, someone she could tell how she really felt, and with whom she could discuss the many nights she stayed awake thinking of him. She missed Amber. She had her own problems, but she was a true friend.

TWENTY-SEVEN

Cape Town, January 1984

Soon after he graduated, Marc was surprised to get a phone call from his friend Ben, who understandably didn't trust telephone communications. Nonetheless he called and told Marc about a clinical opportunity on Robben Island, where he himself held a medical position.

"It's a part-time government post to be a doctor to prisoners and staff on the Island," explained Ben. "It isn't pediatrics, but it's a start."

Marc was keen to start practicing medicine. He would also have the chance to work alongside his friend and now colleague. Ben explained the responsibilities in some detail and reassured him that he would have support from him.

"I accept," said Marc. Still not sure of his medical residency plans, he had to work for at least a year. May as well be there. There was one nagging thought in the back of his mind, however. It related to the unusual conversation with Ben about the ANC and its plans. He wouldn't think about that now. Although working on Robben Island was not the dream job Marc had in mind when he pursued medical school, he rationalized that he would gain quick experience, which could only help when he applied for an internship and residency program later.

On the seven mile island ferry ride, Marc was anxious about embarking on this new phase in his life. As a physician away from the mainland he would carry responsibility for other people's health without the luxury of a major teaching hospital close by. He reflected upon the history of Robben Island. It had been the graveyard for many ships, several of which fell victim to its offshore reefs and were beaten to pieces. Even its lighthouse fought a losing battle against the elements. Marc had read that the island was home to a leper colony in 1845 and later a maximum security prison. Much later, in 1961 the jail was used for political persons convicted of crimes against the apartheid state just across the narrow strait. This history gave Marc pause, but he took the assignment anyway.

On his first day of work, when he alighted the ferry at the tiny Murray's Bay Harbor, he observed a group of penguins strutting, in what looked like tuxedoes, along the quayside in single file. He opened the brown paper bag which contained his cheese and tomato sandwich for lunch, and broke off a chunk. He approached the lead bird and offered the bread. The penguin flapped its wings and bit Marc.

Shaken and now clasping his bleeding hand, Marc made for the prison some two hundred yards away. In the clinic, he cleaned his hand and covered the puncture wound with a bandage. Then he went to meet his first patient. A middle-aged Coloured man was sitting on a wooden examining table with only a thin paper sheet covering his naked torso.

"Good morning Dr. Sennet," the man said, as Marc approached him.

Marc looked around for a moment before it sank in. Doctor Sennet. This was what he had wanted for a long time. After his graduation in December with a medical degree, an MB.ChB., he and his fellow grads had partied until late into the night. Now, only a month later, the reality of the profession was setting in.

"Good morning sir," he said.

That night, after completing his evaluation and progress notes for the day, Marc looked into the bathroom mirror. His temples showed signs of hair loss. I'm aging, he thought. If I ever meet Laura again, what would she think of me, old and bald? And wearing specs to read. He found it impossible to follow Ben's advice. He couldn't simply 'accept' and move on. Still, he tried to put thoughts of Laura in the back of his mind and instead focus on his priorities for the next day.

Soon after Marc became the island physician, he got a call from Schalk. Schalk Fouche was a no-nonsense prison warden. As he put it, he had to be. Over the years he had 'clever criminals' under his watch, some prominent, in his words, 'like the Mandela guy.'

"Doc, I need blood, pronto," Schalk instructed Marc early one morning.

"What's up?" asked Marc.

"I've got this convict passing blood like you cannot believe. I think he's anemic, about to peg out. Can you get over here quickly and give him a transfusion?"

This was the first time Marc had dealt with anything this serious without supervision. His boss, Dr. Murphy, was off the island, on duty in Cape Town for the week.

"Be right there," he said.

He gathered some equipment and left his home for the water taxi service to Robben Island. He looked at the ocean. The sea was choppy as usual with waves of about four feet. Not bad for a big vessel. Bad for a small boat. In the forty-five minutes to the prison quayside, Marc was seasick. He felt so bad he was tempted to cancel the consultation. But he knew the warden would not have overstated a life and death situation. He retched over the side of the taxi and persevered.

When Marc met Albie Mekoza, it was one look only to know Albie was at death's door. He examined a stool of his and found it to be a sticky black guck. His immediate diagnosis: Albie had a bleeding peptic ulcer which, as the warden had suggested, required medication and an immediate blood transfusion. To transport the patient to the mainland, then admit him to Groote Schuur Hospital, would take a day, what with the logistics and form-filling. He could die. Marc wished the one-room clinic on the island had more facilities. The equipment he had brought was hardly sufficient to do what was required. But he had no choice. He walked over to where Schalk had retrieved the inmate's papers. He ascertained that Albie's blood was Type "O positive", the same as Marc's. To his dismay, he found there was no match in the clinic's stored blood.

"Forget about it then," said Schalk, taking a big bite of a salami sandwich.

"I could donate the blood," said Marc.

The warden looked up, visibly shocked. "No, we have limited resources here. There's only so much we can do. If he dies, he dies."

"There is something I can do," asserted Marc.

"But Dr. Sennet, do you understand," said Schalk, "that your blood will be going into the body of a convict?"

The doctor didn't waver. "I'm aware. I'll need a nurse to help me set up as soon as possible." He motioned Schalk to call for assistance.

Marc and the aide readied two stretchers, each covered with a single white sheet. They set out antiseptic wipes, needles, syringes, intravenous tubing and bags, as well as emergency medications and an oxygen tank.

Marc approached the patient. "Mr. Mekoza," he said. "I'm Dr. Sennet. As you may know you've had a lot of blood loss from your ulcer. If you don't have a transfusion very soon, I'm afraid you may die."

The patient remained silent, so Marc continued. "We don't have the blood products we need on the island right now. The only option is for me to donate my own blood."

Albie's face was gaunt and he stared at Marc with expressionless eyes.

"Do you give permission, Mr. Mekoza? I need to know if you agree to that. If you can't talk, just move your fingers if you do."

Soon, the patient, now mumbling incoherently, and Marc were lying side by side, separated only by a flimsy curtain. Marc held out a steady arm as his life-saving blood flowed from his blood vessel into that of Albie Mekoza.

As Schalk looked on in shock, Marc wondered what his father would say if he found out what he had done. His own son's blood in the veins of a black man. Marc didn't care what he thought. He had rescued a man on the brink of death.

As was his usual habit, Marc roamed around the island whenever he had a break. He avoided the penguins. He had no company except for rabbits whose population without predators multiplied from year to year, and a lone tortoise that meandered across his path. In the distance he could see laborers hard at work in the quarry, pounding rocks. Was this forced labor? Perhaps that's what Ben was referring to. He would try to find out more. He found it hard to come to terms with the rugged terrain, the prison cells and barbed wire on the island, when just a short distance away was bright blue water, a bustling city, and freedom. As he walked past a patch of wild flowers, he thought of Laura and the shop they encountered on their walk together. He wondered what Laura would think of his work on the island and whether she was following her dream of becoming a teacher. It seemed she didn't want him to know.

Out of character, the Cape of Good Hope was experiencing a bad winter. The South Easter seemed to be howling all the way from Antarctica. With it came a dreaded influenza epidemic spreading like a wildfire across the Cape Flats. Marc was well aware that the Robben Island inmates were vulnerable to the disease. In close quarters, if one was afflicted, all would go down. It was essential that every prisoner get a flu shot. Only with forceful persuasion to the District Commandant was he granted permission to obtain the costly vaccines, so he arranged with Schalk Fouche to protect every inhabitant on a given day.

Jakobus Goosen was the person responsible for preparing food for the islanders. He was no chef. At best the cook was capable of making mielie-pap, the porridge staple made from white maize grits.

The warden's instruction to him was simple. "Boil the maize, add salt. Kaffirs like salt."

Marc was walking across the quad one morning as Goosen served the one and only breakfast course through the steel cell bars. To his surprise, it was rejected by every prisoner and flung on the floor of the central passage.

Goosen rushed to the nearby cottage to wake his boss, the warden. Marc heard him shouting. "Sir, the black bastards are going on strike. They refuse to eat the pap. I think you better see what's going on with them."

After only a few minutes, the two Afrikaners marched back to the prison, near to where Marc was standing in the central passage between the steel cages housing the convicts. He noticed the Smith & Wesson in Fouche's holster. The warden was in a combative mood.

"Tambo," he roared. "What the fuck are you up to? You want to be punished?"

Esiah Tambo was an imposing man and a natural leader. Fluent in several languages, including Xhosa, English and Afrikaans, he was midway to becoming a lawyer when he was arrested and sent to Robben Island for ten years. There he became the voice of the incarcerated.

There was silence until Esiah answered. He stood tall and spoke loudly in Queen's English. Every prisoner paid attention.

"Mr. Warden, Mr. Fouche, your government has locked us up. Locked us up because you can. You have guns, we do not. And you thump the bible as you turn the key. Does your bible not speak of kindness? Does your bible not say "do unto others..."?

You have deprived us of our families, our homes, and our dignity. Now you want to pierce our bodies with God knows what. Do not pursue this, for if you do, we will respond. Every one of the forty-seven men behind these bars has pledged to fast, rather than be injected. We will go on a hunger strike to the bitter end."

Schalk looked shocked, embarrassed. He did not answer immediately. When he finally spoke, he warned, "You will pay for this," as he pulled Marc to the side for a private conversation. "Doc," he said. "There will have to be consequences for this revolt. Bring your medical stuff. We are vaccinating today. Tambo, the ringleader, will be the first to get a shot."

While Marc was thinking what he could do to ease the situation, the warden added, "If necessary, by force."

The following day a guard, armed with a rifle, was stationed at each corner of the cell block. The warden, the cook and Marc walked down the central passage.

"Now Mr. Tambo, what have you got to say?" taunted Fouche.

"The same thing I said before. No poison in our veins!"

A quiet stalemate of twenty long seconds ensued before Marc stepped forward and addressed the inmates.

"My name is Doctor Marc Sennet. I'm here to help you. I suggested the vaccination. No one else. It is a prevention of illness. Without the injection in your arm, you are at risk of getting the flu. And with one of you getting flu, it is likely that all of you will get flu." There was silence and he continued. "The symptoms can be bad. You may get a high temperature, severe aching, and fatigue which can persist for weeks on end. Flu may even cause death."

He turned to face Esiah Tambo whose mouth seemed fixed in a mocking smile.

"I respectfully ask you, Mr. Tambo, to inject me with the vaccine to show everyone it is safe. It is not a poison. We are not trying to harm you. We are trying to help you."

With that, Marc took a syringe, filled it with vaccine and approached him. Reluctantly the prisoner took hold of the device and was persuaded to pierce Marc's upper arm. The audience looked on wide-eyed.

Marc let out a loud cry and buckled over in pretended pain. The prisoners gasped. Then the doctor bounced back, arms uplifted, and did a mock Zulu war dance, complete with wide stance and high kicks. Spontaneous laughter and cheers erupted. The tension was broken and everyone relaxed. Both sides in the standoff sighed with relief.

Now Marc went again to Tambo. "What's good for me is good for you, okay?"

Esiah Tambo paused, then let out a soft "Yes." He was the first convict to get his flu shot. The others followed diligently.

Marc left the prison that night feeling good, believing he was the most popular man on Robben Island. On the way home, he was oblivious to the ferry bobbing like a cork on surf.

He was off the next day and networked informally on the university campus with some of his medical colleagues, including Ben. He had a story to tell them about the flu vaccine. Afterwards they attended a lecture on tuberculosis at Groote Schuur Hospital.

"Good presentation," said Marc, feeling inspired, as they exited the auditorium.

"I agree. He's a good speaker," said Ben. "Pity he's emigrating. Leaving for the United States next month."

"It seems like we're losing our top professors."

Ben nodded. "A 'brain drain', they call it."

A colleague, Dr. Reardon, weighed in. "But I've heard that those who made the move have been happy with their decision. What about you two? Tell us about Robben Island."

"It's not anything like working in the posh suburbs of Cape Town, that's for sure," said Marc. "It sickens me to see the poor conditions there. But we do the best we can."

"I have my work cut out for me in Kenilworth too," said Reardon. "I never know who's going to come into my office. One hour I'm seeing a two-year-old, then the next hour I'm seeing a ninety-year-old. It's quite a challenge. And I get called all hours of the night. My patients' expectations are very high."

"On Robben Island, sadly, there are few or no expectations," said Ben. "Too many prisoners have had the stamina knocked out of them."

"How do the authorities get away with that?"

"Last year an island doc tried to fight the system," said Ben. "Refused to report for duty until the prisoners were given a more balanced diet and improved sleeping conditions."

"What happened?"

"He's still locked up."

July Jakobi was referred to Marc after several over-the-counter ointments did not heal the large wound from an accident in the island quarry.

July spoke no English and Marc no Xhosa. He did not need a translator, Marc thought.

"Hold out your left arm, please." Marc motioned to the patient to show his arm.

The festering on the arm of the black man was obvious. An immediate antibiotic was the answer, decided the doctor. He prescribed an oral Penicillin and expected a favorable response within a short time. Before the patient left, Marc made arrangements for follow-up three days later.

A day after, Marc was called to Schalk Fouche's office. As soon as Marc saw the expression on the warden's face, he knew something bad had happened.

"You did it. You killed a patient." Schalk's voice was matter-of-fact.

Marc felt his legs get weak. "I, I don't understand."

"Jakobi. Turns out he's allergic to Penicillin. Should have checked that before, shouldn't you? Don't they teach you that in medical school?"

Marc, devastated, could hardly speak.

"His family?" Marc eventually uttered.

"Don't worry about that," said Schalk. "No one close enough to notify. But from now on I'll be watching you, Sennet." Marc remembered the time he had heard a similar threat, from a prison guard, no less. He waited to hear his fate. But Schalk had nothing else to say. Marc understood it was because of the race of the victim that the inquiry into the fatality and his own punishment were both minimal.

After his catastrophic mistake, Marc lost his self-confidence and thought of giving up medicine. He was heartbroken after the loss of his patient and no longer sure he had what it took to be a good physician. All his ambitions were crushed because of one instance of poor judgment. He did not want to face his friends or his colleagues. Ben offered counsel.

"I know it's devastating, Marc. We are physicians, but we are still human. I am sure you have learned from this error. You've got to accept it and then put it behind you."

Marc shook his head.

"Marc, don't give up on medicine. You're a great doctor. Think about the good you have done. Please don't lose sight of that."

All Marc could think about was that he needed to get away. Away from apartheid and his father and reminders of his negligence. Far away from South Africa.

For months Marc reflected on what had happened and thought about his future, as he continued working on Robben Island. Ben agreed to be available for back-up if needed until Marc felt more secure.

Ben paid Marc a visit at his home one evening. "Don't make an impulsive decision," he cautioned.

"I'll think it through carefully," promised Marc.

Ben studied Marc's face before he said, "I have something to tell you. I trust you will understand this is strictly confidential."

Marc nodded and Ben continued. "I also had to choose, between accepting the evils of apartheid or engaging and fighting the regime. I decided to start in a small way with the latter. My job on the island gave me an opportunity."

Marc was worried about what might come next, but he motioned for Ben to carry on.

"I began by smuggling letters in and out between the ANC and the prisoners," said Ben. "Then dried meat to bolster the protein needs of the inmates." Marc stared, open-mouthed, as he remembered the suspicious parcels and the cover-up.

"There's more," said Ben. He gave Marc a look as if to ascertain whether he could be trusted.

"Go on," said Marc.

Ben's voice lowered to a whisper when he said, "More recently, I brought in two grenades."

Marc felt his hands become clammy. Involuntarily, he looked behind him. "Why?" he asked Ben. "Why on earth?"

Ben pulled his chair closer. "To be used by the prisoners in a planned break-out." Marc gasped as Ben continued, almost inaudibly. "I had a narrow escape when I was almost discovered." There was a long silence, and Ben added. "I'm no longer involved in these activities. Well, not for the moment." He rose from his seat and came up to within inches of Marc. Marc could feel Ben's breath on his neck.

"Marc," asked Ben in his low voice. "Would you consider getting involved if we needed you in the future?"

Marc felt his muscles tense. He stood up and took a few steps toward the door. "No, Ben, no. That's crossing the line."

Ben blocked him. "Stop, don't leave. I get it, Marc. I would never force my ideology on anyone else. There was never any intention of hurting anyone."

"Ben," said Marc. "You're lucky you haven't been caught. Very lucky you're still alive. I beg of you. Give this up before it's too late."

Ben tried to reassure Marc, who left feeling very uneasy about the situation and about his friend.

As time went on and Marc's confidence in medicine returned, he thought about his plans for the future and more immediately where he wanted to pursue his specialty training. He flinched as he thought about the conversation with Ben and the shocking revelation. Things were becoming more dangerous by the minute. It could get very ugly in this country and there wasn't a whole lot Marc could do to turn it around. There was no choice. He had to leave. He made the decision to look for a position in the U.S.A.

Within a few weeks Marc completed the American entrance examinations for foreign medical graduates and applied to several pediatric programs. He attempted to re-establish contact with his old friend, Brent Barlow, the medical director of Mount Sinai Hospital in New York. Marc wanted to let Brent know that he had inspired Marc to pursue a career in pediatrics. When he didn't receive a written response, Marc called Mount Sinai and was saddened to hear that the doctor had passed away. He thought back to the enlightening day with him in the neonatal intensive care unit and how willingly Barlow had shared information and given of his precious time. He would always consider him a mentor. When Marc received an offer of residency at the George Washington University Hospital in Washington, D.C., he readily accepted.

TWENTY-EIGHT

Pennsylvania, 1985

"Laura," said her mother, as she helped her daughter fold laundry. "When you were focused on your Master's, I understood you had no time to go out. And now, I see how dedicated you are to your work. But even teachers must take time off."

A Bachelor of Arts hadn't satisfied Laura, the perpetual student. She continued studying, completing her Master's, and accepted a teaching position at Harrison Elementary School in Walnutport, Pennsylvania, close to home.

"Mom, I can take care of myself," she said.

"I only want you to be happy," said her mother.

Laura occupied an apartment about a block away from Naomi and visited her regularly over weekends. Naomi repeatedly expressed unhappiness that Laura was not involved in a stable relationship.

"I know, Mom, and I appreciate your interest. Really. But I assure you I'm happy. I love what I do." She finished ironing a shirt and handed it to her mother.

Content she was, up to a point. Life was not fair. Earlier she was concerned with unprotected sex. Now, she thought back, she should have gone the whole way with Marc, sans protection. Fate would have given them a much-sought-after child before her hysterectomy.

"Just think about what I said," pressed Naomi.

Laura tapped her fingers on the ironing board. "I will," she said.

Yes, life was not fair. She, Laura, infertile. Her friend, Amber, at a young age with an unwanted pregnancy, now happily married to a farmer with three children, two boys by him. Ironic how Laura had incorrectly pigeonholed her friend for a bleak future.

Weeks later Laura still had no plans to enter the social scene, let alone date. That's when she met Neville by accident. She bumped into him-literally, at an art gallery exhibition. It was a fancy cocktail event which she might not have attended, but for the fact it featured several oil paintings by a friend. A guitarist played classical music while crowds congregated around the various works. Laura sipped pink champagne as she examined an unusual abstract in vibrant shades of red, orange and purple. Good for my living room, she thought, but as she looked more closely, she made out several bodies, entwined. Oh no, too risqué for my liking.

Just then, "Laura, thanks for coming," said a tall, voluptuous woman in a white off-the-shoulder dress. "I see you checking out my latest work. You approve?"

"Holly, it's really something. Congratulations on your show!"

Laura, glass in hand, turned around to hug the artist, but instead knocked into a Roger Moore look-alike.

"Neville, Neville Davis. Pleased to meet you." Without missing a beat, the handsome man in a tux wiped the champagne off his jacket with a napkin and extended his hand.

Laura blushed. "I'm Laura. So sorry. How embarrassing."

His smile was disarming. "Don't even think about it. Want to take in the rest of the exhibition with me? I'm safe. Holly can vouch for me."

The artist had already left, and Laura found herself following a perfect stranger.

"How about another glass of bubbly?" Neville filled two glasses and handed her one.

They sipped as they discussed and critiqued. By the end of the evening Laura was giggling like a teenager on a first date. When they realized that everyone except Holly had gone, Neville took a card from his wallet and gave it to Laura. "Hope to meet you again."

Laura went home, giddy from champagne and infatuation.

A week passed, then two. She had hoped Neville would have tracked her down. In a situation like this she was accustomed to being the one pursued. She rationalized he couldn't find her. When she relocated to Pennsylvania, she chose to be incognito and was still unlisted. If she wished to see her handsome acquaintance, she'd have to make the next move. She did.

"Hello, Neville. Remember me? Laura Atkin. We met at the art show."

Laura recognized the charming voice at the other end of the line. "How could I forget the delightful Laura? How are you? What mischief are you up to?"

"I'm doing well, thanks. Busy with my school, as always." She hesitated, then took a deep breath and exhaled. "Are you free for dinner this week?"

"Sure. It will be my treat. What about my club on Saturday at seven? I'll pick you up fifteen before."

"That sounds intriguing."

At the arranged time, Neville pulled up to Laura's townhouse and stepped out of a convertible blue Mercedes Coupe. He cut a neat figure. Tall and well-proportioned, he was immaculately dressed. He wore silver-grey trousers, a striped shirt and a blue double-breasted blazer with a pocket handkerchief. His long dark-blonde hair topped a handsome face.

Neville greeted her, kissed her hand and took her elbow as he escorted her to his car. He opened the door and helped her into the low-slung vehicle. A gentleman to his fingertips, whose nails, she observed, were neatly manicured.

The valet staff at the Hampstead Club recognized Neville immediately.

"Mr. Davis, good evening. I'll park your car."

The maître d' guided Laura and her host to a corner table. "Mr. Davis, I saw you featured as most eligible bachelor in The Uppercrust Magazine. Congratulations."

The couple drew admiring glances. Laura was flattered to be seen with such a prominent man, although he seemed immune to the attention. Probably accustomed to the admiration, she reasoned. No sooner had they ordered wine, when a red-haired woman appeared, kissed Neville on the lips, looked at Laura and said, "And you are?"

Laura stared at her coldly without answering. Neville brushed her off, and the woman left. The four piece band struck up romantic French melodies and Neville suggested they dance. They took to the small floor, an area cleared of tables. He moved effortlessly and expertly, leading Laura against his lean torso. She noticed that all eyes were on them. She was breathless when they returned to their seats.

Her dinner escort turned out to be a great conversationalist and expressed genuine interest in Laura's family and her work. They took time ordering and enjoying the gourmet meal. Laura relaxed. This was turning out to be one of her best dates in recent years.

As they shared a strawberry crème brulee, Neville said, "May I ask you a very personal question?" The room felt suddenly hot and Laura wished she had worn fewer layers. Fanning herself with the menu, she nodded.

"How come a beautiful person like you didn't marry?"

She was caught off guard, but then responded, "I could ask the same of you."

He smiled. "Touche."

Neville continued. "My parents are unaware that I'm gay. I don't think they'd…" He stopped when he noticed the stunned look on Laura's face. "You didn't know? Oh, I'm sorry. I thought Holly told you."

"Nope, haven't had a chance to speak to her since the art event."

After a moment of silence, they both burst out laughing.

Neville held up a glass of Merlot. "To friendship, then?"

"To friends."

TWENTY-NINE

"I'd like to propose something to you," said Laura to a school committee of teachers, parents and Harrison's principal. "As you are probably aware, there are several poor students who come to class hungry every day. I know it affects their concentration and ultimately their work and grades."

The eyes of the committee were fixed on her. "What can we do about it?" a teacher asked.

"It sounds very simple," Laura said, "but I believe it will work. What I'd like to do is provide each student in my class every morning with some nourishment in the form of a whole-wheat peanut butter and strawberry jam sandwich. The poorer children won't feel singled out."

When the teachers didn't respond, she added, "I'll fund it myself."

The principal looked around and when no-one objected she said, "I'm not going to stop you, Laura, but I can't see it working. Will the parents go for this? Who will make the sandwiches?"

"I've thought this through," said Laura. "Will you agree to give me a chance?"

The skeptical group agreed that she could go ahead, although they had little hope that Laura's unconventional project would be a success.

Years before Laura applied for admission to college, her middle school guidance counselor asked her the standard question namely, what she would like to be when she grew up. Without a moment's hesitation she responded that she wanted to be a teacher. Now, a long time later, armed with a B.A. and Masters, her answer would be the same. She loved teaching. Not that there weren't problems in the Pennsylvania school system. Lack of respect was rife. She often wondered if the culture in Marc's home, South Africa, was different and if teachers were held in high esteem there. In the elementary school where she taught, there was a high prevalence of children from poverty-stricken, single-parent homes who were underperforming. There seemed to be no quick fix to raise the standard to state or national averages.

Laura organized an estate sale to raise money for students in need of textbooks, calculators and notepads. She reached her target amount, but realized this was not enough. She decided, therefore, to attack the problem in two other ways, the first involving an incentive in an attempt to win the cooperation of her students and so motivate them to uplift themselves.

She arranged to give each member of the class a subscription to the magazines Smithsonian, National Geographic and Time. On the day she distributed the first copies, there was raucous behavior in the classroom. The children ran around sharing magazine pictures, laughing and talking in high-pitched voices. Laura tapped her long wooden pointer on the desk until everyone quietened. "I'm glad you're excited," she said, "but we're got to show respect for each other. All sit down now, and in turn you may talk about what you've read."

All the students took their seats except one.

"Justine," Laura instructed. "Sit down please."

Justine skipped around the room one more time before slowly lowering herself into her desk chair while she looked to her fellow students for approval.

Laura focused on the class. "Would anyone like to share an article?"

A boy raised his hand and opened the National Geographic magazine to a full-page picture of a menacing grizzly bear. The rest of the students gasped and quickly turned to the page in their copies as the boy read aloud from the article.

"How about you next, Justine?" asked Laura, noticing that the student had finally settled down. "Did you find anything interesting?"

"No," said Justine holding her hand out to gesture 'leave me alone.' In doing so she knocked one of the magazines off her desk. It landed on the floor with a thud. There was muffled laughter in the back of the room, reminiscent of the experience Laura had as a novice teacher.

In spite of the initial disruption, Laura could tell, as the day went on, that most of her students were fascinated by the magazines. She agreed to forego the day's planned curriculum and allow them time to read and explore. She heard them discuss articles on Africa and Japan, new inventions and space travel. She was pleased with how things were going.

Laura's second plan involved the sandwiches. On day one, when the home-made breakfast was distributed first thing to the twenty-three children in her class, there were complaints. Some students weren't accustomed to whole-wheat, others didn't care for peanut butter. Laura persisted. By the second week, the mood of the students changed for the better. It took many months for the program to show significant benefits, but there was no doubt about its overall progress and eventual success. Grades in Miss Atkin's classes were up. Morale improved and the relationship between teacher and students strengthened.

Shortly after her experiment, Laura Atkin won the 'Teacher of the Year' award. Her professional recognition among her peers soared. In the Philadelphia News, under the caption entitled 'Popular Sandwich Teacher tries novel approach,' an article appeared featuring Laura. She became a household name in the education profession in Pennsylvania.

THIRTY

Washington D.C., 1985

In the USA again, Marc, for the umpteenth time, thought of Laura. How was she? Where was she? He yearned for her. He had not dated another girl since meeting her. He wondered whether she was pursuing the goals she had discussed with him when they were still teenagers. He wrote another letter to her old address, hoping it would be forwarded to her this time, but it was returned. He made several enquiries, all without success. There was no way to locate her. Again he imagined all sorts of scenarios, including the possibility that she may have passed away. With much reluctance, he felt compelled to drop the search. He had to accept it. She was probably married. Perhaps it was wrong to intervene and disrupt her life. But the longing remained.

Marc stayed in contact with the Drakes whenever time permitted and became their after-hours physician attending to their minor aches and pains, gratis. It was the least he could do after they had generously offered their home and their hearts to him years before. At dinner at their home one evening, Helene, Sid and Marc made small-talk.

He slipped in the burning question. "Have you heard any news about where Laura may be?" he asked.

Sid shook his head. "No idea. It's a mystery. Helene and I found a few other Atkins in the phone book. We called, but they're not related."

Marc's head dropped.

"I'm so sorry," said Helene. "I know she meant a lot to you."

Finally Marc let it go. As a pediatric resident he had to work late nights and assume much responsibility. He would immerse himself in his work and his studies.

1987

Half-way through his residency program Marc found to his delight that he had more free time to himself. The new interns helped enormously by writing notes, answering calls and doing initial work-ups on patients. He missed his old friends. He remembered the very first person he told about Laura. His high school friend, Jason, at the football game. Somehow the idea of connecting with him made him feel closer to her. He found Jason's phone number.

"You remember me? Marc, from Lincoln High."

"No kidding. Great to hear from you, my friend. What are you doing in the States?"

"I'm living here for now," explained Marc. "Doing my pediatric residency at GW. I'd love to see you some time."

The following week he met Jason after work, and over beer, exchanged the significant life events since they had last seen each other. He learned Jason was happily married and working as a sports agent.

"I guess my insights into the game of football really inspired you," said Marc.

Jason laughed. "Yes, it was definitely that. The fact that you had never watched a game before we met helped a lot. Hey, you didn't even know what the ball looked like!"

"That's true," agreed Marc. "By the way, as an agent, does your friend get a free pass to a game?"

"Of course. Even two."

Jason asked Marc if he remembered the girl with the ponytail who had snubbed him at the football game. Marc did. He told Marc of another incident he had recently endured. Jason was nominated to be the president of the local sports association. He knew he was the most qualified for the job. After being notified that he did not secure the position, he overheard members of the board discuss the reasons for his loss. The association would not welcome a man of color as president, they said. Marc was shocked and saddened to hear this. "Isn't this meant to be the land of the free?" he asked.

Jason shook his head. "Apparently not yet."

They chatted for a long time about their work and personal lives, and before Jason left, he said, "Come over to our house on Sunday night. We're having a party."

The penthouse was bustling with beautiful people, standing shoulder-to-shoulder, trying to make their voices heard above the loud music. After being shown around and introduced to several friends of the hosts, Jason and Joan, Marc was relieved to find a quiet spot to sit and enjoy a drink. In his mind he was going over his crammed schedule for the following day when he saw a pair of shapely bare legs in front of him. He looked up to see a tall attractive woman, with wavy blonde hair, blue eyes and porcelain skin. She had a flirtatious smile. She held out her hand to take his. "Pleased to meet you, Marc. I'm Nicole. They were right. South African men are better looking."

"Nice to meet you too," he said. "I like your accent. Australian?"

"That's right."

They chatted and Marc learned she was an advertising executive based in Frederick, Maryland, and supervised media campaigns for television and radio. He was impressed when he learned of some of her projects and told her so.

"Thank you, but no talk about work," said Nicole. Let's get a drink instead."

She took his arm in hers and led him to the bar. "Martini okay?" She didn't wait for an answer. "Two dirty martinis please," she instructed the bartender.

Nicole was charming. She also became more forward after she downed a couple of cocktails and a glass of wine. As they stood outside on the dimly-lit balcony, overlooking the D.C. city lights, she kissed him brazenly on the lips. Marc tasted strawberry lip-gloss.

When Nicole began unbuttoning his shirt, he gently extricated himself. She pouted. He decided, however, to pursue the relationship later. He called her the next day. They went out for dinner and returned to his home. She wasted no time. As their naked bodies touched, Marc compared her to Laura. He quickly reprimanded himself.

Marc saw Nicole the next week, then every free weekend thereafter. He found her a little too assertive at times, but she was intelligent, energetic, and fun to be around. It was lonely when he returned from work at night and she provided the companionship he craved.

He and Nicole availed themselves of Jason's free tickets to a football game at RFK stadium. This time the Redskins were playing the Denver Broncos. The home team was at its best.

"Touchdown," yelled Nicole, jumping up from her seat and pulling Marc with her. She slapped the palm of his hand exuberantly.

As Marc watched the rest of the play, he reflected on their relationship. Things were definitely moving along well. They were compatible both intellectually and physically. Perhaps they didn't share all philosophical views, but what were the odds of finding someone who did? He'd lost that chance. He made up his mind that he would ask Nicole to marry him.

Several months later Jason and his wife were witnesses at a small wedding ceremony in court. Marc was sad that neither of his parents was able to attend. The best they could do was send a congratulatory note. In contrast, Nicole expressed no regret at the absence of her mother and father. She informed Marc she had broken contact with them many years before. He didn't press for more information about her family.

THIRTY-ONE

Pennsylvania

There was a welcome silence in the classroom. No whistling or humming, no calling across the room to each other and no asking to go to the bathroom. Laura could only hear the soft sounds of shuffling in seats and pencils on paper. It was exam day. As her students, heads buried deep in their test papers, concentrated on their writing, Laura sorted through the pile of work on her own desk. She was relieved to have ninety minutes to catch up.

After marking dozens of papers, she stretched her arms and looked up at the class. The students seemed engrossed in their work. All, except one. Near the back of the class she noticed Justine straining her neck to peer over the shoulder and onto the work of the student directly in front of her. Laura waited a minute to make sure she was reading the situation correctly. Sure enough, Justine had positioned herself so that she had a clear view of her classmate's test paper.

The students knew that cheating was not tolerated. Quickly, Laura contemplated how best to handle this. There had to be a consequence, some punishment, but perhaps she could give her student an opportunity to do the right thing now before it went further.

Justine startled as Laura approached her.

"Please come to my desk for a moment," Laura said quietly. "I need to talk to you about something." To the class she said,

"Carry on, everyone. You're doing well. You still have twenty minutes to go. If you finish sooner, raise your hand and I'll collect your paper."

The students looked up as they tried to figure out what was going on and then returned to what they were doing.

Justine dragged her feet as she reluctantly followed Laura to her desk.

Laura spoke so that only Justine could hear her. "Tell me what happened," she said.

"Nothing happened, Miss."

"Justine, I saw you look at Sam's work. Tell me the truth, please."

The student lowered her head. "I looked," she said, "but I didn't write down any of the answers."

Laura took out a folder. "I'm going to give you another chance," she said. "If you can show me you've learned from this and it won't happen again, I'm going to let it go." Justine smiled and was about to return to her desk, when Laura stopped her. She removed a paper from the folder and handed it to her. You're going to have to take a different test. You don't need to copy someone else's work, Justine. I know you're smart enough to do this on your own. I want you to prove it to me and to yourself. Then we can put this behind us."

THIRTY-TWO

Soon after they were married and toward the end of Marc's residency, he and Nicole rented a colonial house on Porter Street, in Chevy Chase. After graduating from the George Washington residency program, Marc was asked to join a private pediatric practice in downtown D.C., a short distance from his home.

He was ecstatic when he received the phone call from Dr. Helman, the senior partner. "We've been watching you over the years," he said. "We'd be honored if you'd come on board."

Marc was aware that several medical groups were interested in him, but this was without a doubt his top choice. Within a month he became a junior partner.

To celebrate his new home and new job, he and Nicole invited Jason and his wife and six other friends to come over for a fun all-night event at their home. The only requirement stipulated by Nicole was to bring pajamas.

Before the guests arrived, Marc helped Nicole set the dining room table, an antique mahogany gem they had picked up at an estate sale. They tidied the large living room, and study, where his Bausch and Lomb microscope enjoyed a place of pride, and lit the outside deck with colorful globe string lights. Marc carefully collected the glass paperweights and fragile porcelain ornaments, all wedding gifts, and moved them out of the way to the bedroom. At seven, they were ready and plopped down on the sofa together. Marc looked at his beautiful new wife. She was dressed in a low-cut ivory cocktail dress. He couldn't wait. He unzipped the back of her dress, lifted her into his arms, and in spite of her playful protests, made his way up the stairs.

"Are you crazy?" asked Nicole, giggling. "They'll be here any minute."

"We've got sixty," said Marc. "I don't need more."

Two hours later the house was filled with people, talking, laughing and drinking. Soft music played in the background. The evening had the promise of a great party. Nicole, sipping on wine and champagne, offered hors d'oeuvres and made small talk, before inviting the guests to the buffet table for dinner. As she handed out plates and napkins, she knocked over a glass.

"Damn," she shouted. She banged her fist on the table.

"Nicole," are you alright?" asked Marc, startled at her outburst.

"Stupid glass," she said. Her breath smelled of alcohol. She swayed and Marc caught her.

"Nicole," said Marc quietly, as he led her away from the staring guests. "I think you've had enough to drink. I'm worried about you."

"Worry about yourself," she said. "I can handle it." She pushed him away and staggered to the bathroom. Marc was upset and embarrassed by his wife's behavior in public, but didn't pursue the matter.

"After dinner we'll put on a movie," Marc announced when he saw that Nicole had returned, somewhat composed.

"Let's all change into pajamas," suggested Nicole. "We'll be more comfortable while we watch. You're all welcome to stay overnight."

She pointed to sleeping bags and pillows. "Tomorrow morning we'll have a French toast and champagne breakfast."

Guests changed into pajamas and made themselves comfortable wherever they could find a spot. Marc noticed Nicole on a couch squeezed in between two of his male colleagues. She had an arm around each. They were obviously enjoying the attention.

The following day, after the guests left, Marc thought about what had happened. He was disappointed in his wife's behavior, but reasoned it was likely a one-time problem brought on by the festivity of house-warming. Still, he decided against hosting another party.

As a partner in the DC practice, he delved into his new responsibilities. He saw numerous children and teenagers in the private clinic, made regular trips to the hospital to visit patients and newborns, and attended late night meetings. With the stability of his new position and a more substantial salary, Marc was finally able to put a down-payment towards the purchase of their elegant Chevy Chase home.

"Nicole, this looks like our first wedding invitation," said Marc, eagerly opening a posh envelope addressed in hand-written black script. Not so. He read from the card.

"His Excellency, the Ambassador of France, Alain Francois Le Roux, cordially invites you to a dinner performance by the acclaimed pianist Claude le Granise, winner of the Young Artist's award, at the Residence."

He continued with details as to the address and the attire.

"You'll have to get a tux," commented Nicole.

"I don't want to buy one. I'll never wear one again."

"Then rent one, my dear. We're going."

Marc recalled that he was placed on the V.I.P. list of the French Cultural Attache after he and his team treated the Ambassador's twelve-year-old daughter who had been diagnosed with a rare medical condition. For the occasion Marc rented a well-fitting tuxedo which he wore cum ruffled shirt with French cuffs, the former adorned with a set of ruby shirt studs and the latter matching cufflinks. A maroon bow-tie completed his formal attire.

Nicole wore a designer long V-neck bright blue dress. In her two-inch heels, she almost matched Marc's height. Her necklace had graduated baroque cultured pearls with diamond rondelles.

"You make a handsome couple," said the Attache as he welcomed them in the line of visitors.

An aide ushered them to a circular table not far from a grand concert piano and pointed them to their seat cards. Two chairs awaited the arrival of other guests.

Nicole turned to Marc. "Why didn't you wear the other bow-tie?" she asked. "This one doesn't look right."

"Not now, Nicole," said Marc.

Madame Henriette le Roux, the hostess of the event, made her appearance accompanied by a dignified middle-aged couple, introduced as the Duke and Duchess of Luxembourg, Willem and Marga.

"Do you know where Luxenbourg is?" whispered Nicole.

"In Europe," said Marc, "but I don't know where exactly."

The royal couple were friendly and spoke English well.

"Is this your first visit to our city?" asked Marc.

"No, we were here once before, many years back," replied the Duchess. "I must confess when your name was mentioned, Marc, I hoped that your wife's name would be Laura."

Marc and Nicole, who was aware of Marc's teenage romance, both froze.

"The strangest event occurred," said Marga, and she related a personal story from many years before.

She and her husband were sailing on an ex-presidential yacht. They had been going through a difficult time. After many medical consultations in Europe, they were without an heir to the sovereign monarchy. They believed that a royal baby was the answer to the political unrest at home. It would be rejoiced and would squash the call for abolition of the throne and its accompanying trappings. After enduring numerous tests, Marga, frustrated, had decided to give up trying and announced that to her husband as they sailed. He implored her to reconsider. Later, Marga paged through books she had retrieved from the Sequoia's mini-library. She was surprised to find an old visitors' book among other volumes. Its pages were dated and filled with names and notations. Her interest was piqued when she came upon a particular passage.

The ink was smudged but the message was legible and crystal clear. *". . . and bless our lives with many children."*

Superstitious, the royal couple believed this was a message of hope, love and optimism from someone they did not know. It was a letter from God, asking them to persevere and be patient. That's what they did.

"Our son, the prince, is now ten years old," Marga added, beaming.

Marc and Nicole were speechless. Everything around him went hazy as Marc tried to process this unforeseen connection with his past.

The first course was served. Marc had no appetite. He picked at his food, listened to the classical pianist and made polite conversation. He could tell Nicole was angry. She hardly blinked. They hadn't been married one year and already there were too many arguments.

Back at home, he went right to bed. He avoided any discussion of the Duchess and her story. And of Laura.

Over the following weeks, Marc avoided Nicole when he could. He stayed at work late, went to bed before she did, and woke early, so that he was dressed and ready to leave the house when she got up. Nonetheless, the weeks were rather uneventful until Marc heard the disturbing news about his wife.

THIRTY-THREE

Nicole had locked herself in the bathroom.

"Open up," called Marc. "We need to talk."

"I'm not coming out," she yelled.

Marc knocked on the door loudly. "You were engaged when we met?" he shouted in disbelief. When were you going to tell me?"

"I didn't think you needed to know," answered Nicole defiantly. "It doesn't affect us."

"You'd rather I found out from a stranger?"

Marc had attended an office meeting with his partners and Rick, an accountant, to go over their annual financials. Before they got started the Rick greeted Marc with "My wife's told me a lot about you. Her cousin Ron is Nicole's ex-fiance. Small world, isn't it?"

Mortified, Marc was at a loss for words. His face turned red. His partners, sensing a problem, tried to change the subject.

Rick pressed on. "Nicole broke up with Ron after she began dating Marc," he told the partners. "I heard Ron was pretty bummed out."

Somehow Marc made it through the meeting, and when he got home he found Nicole reading a magazine in the living room and confronted her. Her reaction was to go into the bathroom and lock the door.

"Open up," Marc called again.

With no response, he added, "Nicole, there's nothing you can really say to make this right. I need time to think." He left the house, shutting the front door loudly.

Outside, Marc thought about the romantic walk he took along the Potomac River with Laura soon after they first met. He remembered looking at the Protea flowers through the shop window and hinting at a wedding. He recalled imagining their bright future together. How mistaken he was. How different his life turned out to be.

THIRTY-FOUR

Pennsylvania, 1990

Laura worked hard to prove herself in her field. She became known to be an innovative, fair and respected teacher. To that end she was offered, in 1989, the role of principal at Harrisons, an honor she gladly accepted. Always a teacher at heart, she continued with several of her classes, including History and English, in addition to her administrative duties. On this particular day Laura was finishing up her last class when she asked for her students' full attention.

"I'll go over this one more time," she said. The topic of the essay is 'Someone who inspires me.' It is due no later than Friday the 20th. That's the week before your mid-terms."

She heard a moan from the class.

"Oh, don't be negative," she said. "You're good writers. I think you'll have fun with this one. And remember, it contributes toward the grade by twenty percent. You will not be graded if it's late. Does everyone understand the deadline?"

The students' hands shot up. "We do," they answered in unison.

As a teacher Laura prided herself in being strict but fair. She did not tolerate laziness or tardiness. She saw potential in her students and motivated them to push themselves to achieve what they did not dream possible.

"I'm happy to announce," she said, "that someone in this class has just had a poem published in the Monthly Gazette." A student rose and Laura walked over and shook her hand. "Congratulations to you. And there were also several honorable mentions. All stand please."

Laura's eyes glowed with pride as four students stood up. She felt rewarded when anyone in her fold received recognition and especially when she learned that her teaching had inspired them.

On the day of the deadline, her briefcase full of papers, Laura drove home, anticipating a very busy weekend. She had made it clear again that those who didn't turn their work in on time paid the price in terms of their grades.

There were two such, Sandra and Justine, who defaulted. Laura was disappointed. She wanted all her students to excel. She contemplated giving them another chance, but knew it would be unfair to give a deadline and then not enforce consequences. She graded the papers, noting the two missing ones provisionally as 'no grade'. She would make the scores final if there was no plausible explanation. There was not. At school the following Monday, she met with each of the two students individually. Both said they planned to get to it later. Justine added, "It's no big deal."

Two weeks later, Laura was summoned to appear in the school's administrative office. Apprehensive, she walked in to face a committee of school officials. She was asked to be seated, then handed a certified letter from an attorney representing Justine and her parents. They claimed Laura discriminated against the student based on her minority status. Laura could not believe that Justine and her family had taken such action and was particularly shocked when she read the words 'Because Justine is black, the teacher

187

refused to give her another chance and therefore her grades suffered.'

Laura clutched onto the arms of her chair. She looked around the room, certain this was a mistake. They couldn't be writing about her. The assertion couldn't be further from the truth. Not only was the second penalized student white, Laura's career clearly demonstrated her constant resolve to fight for equality. She felt dizzy and put her head down. A colleague brought her a glass of water. Then the school president spoke.

"Laura, we know this charge is unwarranted, but we have to take it very seriously and deal with it the best we can. So, let's see how we should handle this going forward."

Laura knew she was not guilty of any crime. She asked to speak to the family face-to-face. The committee tried to dissuade her, and recommended she take a legal route instead. Laura, wanting to stick to her principles, did not budge.

When she got home that evening, she felt disillusioned with teaching. She replayed the scenario of her meeting with the school officials over and over in her mind. To distract herself she put on soft classical music and poured herself a glass of red wine. She wondered why someone could do this to her when she had tried so hard to do the best for all her students. She couldn't come to terms with the charge. Even so she tried to put the ugly event behind her. She realized that she would have to contend with many difficult situations, particularly if she pursued a higher level position. As soon as she had a chance she would let Neville know what happened.

Two days later, it had been raining heavily and Laura was relieved to enter the coffee shop where she was to meet her confidant. She was a few minutes early, so she had time to dry off, buy a newspaper and order her warm signature drink. She waited in line. A man walked past and winked at her. "How ya doin, beautiful?" he asked. He made a kissing sound. Ughh, Laura hated that. So sexist. Would a woman treat a man that way?

"The usual?" asked the cashier when it was her turn.

"Yes, what can I say," said Laura. "When I find something I like, I stick to it."

As she sipped her single shot skim milk dry cappuccino, Neville pulled up a chair.

She told him about the unfair accusation against her and how close she came to giving up the profession.

"I don't believe they'll press forward with charges," she said, "but that's not the point. I've devoted my life to teaching, and I made many personal sacrifices. Perhaps I should have chosen a different path."

Neville took her by surprise when out of the blue he said, "You think about Marc a lot, don't you?"

"Where did that come from?" asked Laura. "How on earth did you connect this case to Marc?"

She was amazed at how well Neville knew her. Her eyes moistened. She nodded. "You're right, I suppose. For many years I haven't been able to admit this, but I think I'll always be in love with him."

"Oh Laura, I didn't mean to make you sad. Could it just be infatuation? You were very young."

"No, Neville. There was something more. His thoughts, his ideals, his passions, all aligned with mine. But you're right that it was a long time ago. We have separate lives now."

Neville didn't give advice and she appreciated it. Right now she needed someone to listen. He did that as Laura poured her heart out to him.

THIRTY-FIVE

Sibley Hospital D.C.

"Congratulations," said the nurse. "You have a healthy baby boy." Marc stood by, beaming, as the nurse wrapped the ruddy, eight-pound baby in a blue and white blanket and placed him on Nicole's abdomen. As the reality of fatherhood dawned on him, he thought about the challenges he and Nicole had faced in their three-year marriage. Time taught him that she was spoiled and over-impressed by money and status. She became loud and boisterous after a few drinks. But the breaking point was when she failed to tell him about her prior engagement. After days of not talking to his wife and watching her sulk, he sat down with her and they decided to patch things up. She vowed to be more transparent and considerate. He promised to be patient with her.

Now, much later, in the private labor-and-delivery room, Marc was emotional as he took in the sight of his wife and his son Derek. He put out his hand and touched the baby's delicate head with its fine hair. Then he took Nicole's hand in his. "He's beautiful, isn't he?"

She squeezed his hand. She had just gone through nine months of pregnancy and hours of labor, yet her face glowed and she looked lovelier than she had ever looked before. Marc lifted the baby gently, and cradled him in his arms. Then, upon Nicole's request, he held him close to her so she could get to see him better. After allowing the three to spend about an hour without interruption, the nurse returned to the room. Time for feeding," she said.

Nicole and Derek were discharged from the hospital on the third day. Nicole remained home and nursed for six weeks and then hired a babysitter to take over from nine to five when she returned to work. Marc tried to spend as much time at home as he could. Motherhood didn't come easily to Nicole. She was a career woman, uncomfortable at 'mommy and baby' classes and children's birthday parties. She didn't relate well to the other mothers. Although she loved Derek, she disliked changing diapers, doing housework and cooking. Marc took up the slack.

Over the years, he felt his relationship with Nicole deteriorate and verbal flare-ups became more frequent. She resented the fact that in ranking of priorities she seemed to come below her husband's job and their child. Even in precious spare time, Marc preferred going it alone walking or biking.

On her side, beyond advertising work, her preference was the social scene. She attended, mostly on her own, numerous embassy events and regularly reminded her husband that there were more than a hundred international agencies in D.C., each in need of her presence. Much of Marc's hard-earned money was spent on evening gowns and diamond jewelry. Yet the acquisition of these trappings of wealth brought her no lasting happiness.

At times, particularly after he had argued with Nicole, Marc thought about what a wonderful mother Laura would have made. He knew it from her interactions with children when they played cricket together, and by the way she spoke of her mentoring and her aspirations to teach. One night he dreamed he had a child with her, a little girl. Pushing their daughter in a stroller, they walked to the park together, and played on the swings and the slide. When he woke from sleep it took a while to process the fact that he was the father to a baby boy, with Nicole.

THIRTY-SIX

Pennsylvania, 1990

The banquet hall was decorated in soft greens and whites. Twenty round tables with glass and floral centerpieces added to the adornment. A few couples swayed on the dance floor to the five-piece band playing 'Wind Beneath My Wings.' Entering the function, Laura was impressed. She had accepted an invitation to chair the annual gala to raise much-needed funds for her school. Without this charity event, Harrison Elementary could not fund the ambitious technology project which she had initiated. Parents and teachers helped with the planning and execution of the ball with great enthusiasm.

Laura and Neville took their place cards and made their way to Table Six where four people were already seated. She was pleased to see the familiar face of Colin, a teacher, and sat alongside him as he made introductions.

"Laura and Neville, please meet Gavin, Rosemary and Bill. Laura is my colleague and is principal at Harrison. Neville is a connoisseur, I hear."

Colin extended his hand to Neville and winked at Laura. She was tempted to state they were not a couple, but refrained.

There was a pause in the music and Laura was escorted to the stage and handed a microphone.

"Ladies and gentlemen," she announced. "Welcome to the tenth annual charity celebration of Harrison Elementary. Thank you for participating in our fundraiser. We still have some work to do as we approach our goal of raising one hundred thousand dollars for a new technology center. I urge every one of you to contribute to the best of your ability. You'll be investing in the future of our children."

There was loud clapping and cheering. She continued. "There is a wonderful evening planned for you tonight, including a delicious dinner, great music and a live auction. Enjoy!"

The band took off with a lively number as Laura was congratulated by her table companions. When everyone was seated, Gavin addressed Laura. "Exciting event for a great cause."

"Yes, thank you. How did you come to Harrison?"

"A close friend is married to one of your trustees," said Gavin. "I'm impressed with the school's achievements and happy to contribute."

They all chatted while dinner was served, starting with a pear and field green salad, followed by a cold gazpacho soup, and tender Filet Mignon.

After a Baked Alaska dessert, the band played a drumroll to introduce the auctioneer.

"Good evening," he announced. "My name is Len, of Len Auctioneers. I have a question for this wonderful audience. Are you ready for some fun?"

"Yes," roared the attendees in unison.

"Let's get started then. Everyone participating in the auction should have a bidding paddle. Use it! Remember, our charity has no overhead expenses. Every tax-deductible dollar goes to the school."

An attendant displayed the first item, a colorful Tarkay painting of two women.

"Who will start us off at one thousand dollars?"

A woman raised her bidding paddle.

"Thank you, I have one thousand dollars," Len staccatoed. "I'm looking for eleven hundred for this magnificent masterpiece. Thank you, sir. I have eleven. Who will offer twelve? I'm looking for twelve hundred dollars." After two more offers, he knocked it down to the original bidder for fifteen hundred dollars.

"Good start," he announced. Thank you, madam."

He continued with varied items such as an antique cash register, a music box and a Tiffany diamond ring. Laura was shocked to witness how thousands of dollars were being paid so freely for objects d'art. By contrast, her school was often pressed for a few hundred.

The auctioneer continued. "Now for number 22, the feature of tonight's sale. This is an original owner's bequeathment to his alma mater. We are proud to offer at a reserve price of ten thousand dollars, a rare 18 karat yellow-gold Patek Philippe Geneve wristwatch, circa 1920. It is a perpetual calendar model. This watch is appraised for seventy thousand and has its original box and papers. Ladies and gentlemen, you are witness to the sale of a rarity. Who will offer me ten thousand?"

Two paddles shot up and the competition soon drove up the price to forty thousand dollars, where there was a lull.

"This is still way below comparable market," said Len. "Who will clinch the deal for this great timepiece at a round fifty thousand?"

Until then Neville had displayed casual interest in the auction. Now he seemed alert. He slowly raised his paddle. The auctioneer made eye contact and asked, "Sir, is that a bid of fifty thousand for the Patek?"

"It is," said Neville.

"Going once, twice, three times, sold."

The auctioneer appeared to take the sale in his stride. "Thank you," was all he said.

The crowd, focusing their attention on Neville, clapped loudly. Laura, open-mouthed, turned to her partner. "What on earth have you done? It's a fortune."

"What's the problem?" asked Neville. "I just made myself twenty grand. It's a win-win."

"You constantly surprise me," said Laura, as guests vied with one another to shake the connoisseur's hand.

Laura thought about the children who had so few resources, yet such big aspirations. "That money will go a long way toward helping the students," she added.

The event was coming to a close. A woman took the mike. "Everyone up on the dance floor now. Last few songs before the closing speech."

"Care to dance?" Neville asked Laura.

"Sure." She was glad to get up and stretch.

Neville was well-trained and the band was at its best. Laura enjoyed moving to the music with him, following his bold rhythmic steps. During a slow dance he pulled her close to him, and she closed her eyes and imagined she was with Marc. When the music ended, she was disappointed with the reality.

After Neville dropped her off at home, Laura felt lonelier than she had in a long time. She did what she always did when she felt that way. She picked up a book and immersed herself in the comfort of its fantasy.

THIRTY-SEVEN

Laura had made her position clear. If a student's family was making an unfair charge against her, they would have to do it to her face. After much debate, Justine's parents agreed to a meeting on condition it included their attorney. Within a few days, Laura, apprehensive, and carrying files of relevant documents, arrived at the appointed legal office without personal representation. Justine, her parents and their lawyer were already seated at a round table. Laura took her place next to the student's mother. The attorney introduced everyone formally, after which time there was a pause while he and the family reviewed their files and consulted with each other quietly.

When they were ready to begin, the attorney restated the family's charge of discrimination. His voice became louder and louder as he stared directly at Laura. For what felt like a long time she listened to the raised voices and unfounded accusations. Every word felt like a stab, but she remained composed.

Then she spoke softly with determination. She explained her policy of fairness and equality and how she had made the students fully aware of the consequences. She tried to prove that Justine had not been singled out by showing them evidence of her commitment to her students and their success. She looked around the room so that she came face-to-face with each one, including her student to whom Laura had shown patience in class in spite of her disruptive behavior. She remembered how she had tried not to embarrass her in front of her peers when she had cheated and how she had offered to give her another chance. To her surprise, Justine, who had remained silent until then, stood up unexpectedly and spoke.

"Ms. Atkin has always been fair to us," she said. "I told my mom and dad it was my fault."

The mother looked at the attorney, who shrugged his shoulders.

Justine continued. "We all knew we wouldn't be graded if we didn't hand the assignment in on time." Justine's mother held a hand over her daughter's mouth.

The attorney stiffened and remained silent. Laura thanked the student for her honesty. There was a lengthy discussion during which the other side attempted to minimize the student's testimony and threaten Laura with further proceedings. She would not be subdued. "Justine's comments speak for themselves," she said.

Finally, they adjourned. Before the meeting ended, the lawyer promised a follow-up letter to lay out his client's position. They all looked to Laura. She nodded in agreement. She was confident Justine's support had confirmed her innocence.

THIRTY-EIGHT

Marc handed his son, one at a time, blue and red wooden blocks, which Derek stacked one on top of the other. "Look," Derek said proudly.

Marc hugged him. "I see that. It's a beautiful castle, with princes and dragons. Big."

Derek threw up his arms to mimic his father. "Big," he repeated.

Marc had arrived home from work this evening to find Amy, the twenty-year-old babysitter, with his son.

"Where's Nicole?" he asked when he saw her. "Wasn't she meant to be home by now?"

"She called to say she'd be a bit late, but would probably be here by seven," Amy explained. "I made macaroni and cheese for Derek."

Marc thanked her for staying late and joined his son on the carpeted floor. Together they built a car and a house before tackling the castle. Within a few minutes, Derek appeared bored. As Marc began constructing a door of sorts, his son picked up a block and threw it against the wall. Marc collected all the blocks, placed them in a box and handed his son a coloring book with markers to distract him.

Marc flipped through the mail on the kitchen table. He began to worry. His wife had been getting home later recently, but never this late. Now, without explanation.

The phone rang. It was Nicole.

"I'm in a meeting with a couple of colleagues," Marc heard voices and music in the background. "We're working on a deadline. I'll be home by about ten. Is Derek okay?"

"He's fine. Let me know next time. You scared me."

By the time Nicole returned, Derek had fallen asleep on the couch. Marc carried him to bed and tucked him in. He returned to find his wife and her silent treatment. This was the point of no return. He did not have the will to question or fight, although he knew he was staring at the face of marital failure.

It took only a short while for him to realize that his wife was having an affair with a former lover from Australia, and he made up his mind right then he would file for divorce. Lying in the sofa bed alone that night, he recalled his experience with his first patient. After the rescue of Albie Mekoza he was prompted to think he could save the world. Now he couldn't even save his marriage.

THIRTY-NINE

Maryland, 1992

"Please talk to me, Derek," Marc pleaded again. His son remained silent. Marc knew the divorce and animosity between his parents had taken a heavy toll on their child.

After an arduous legal battle, Marc had moved to a small condo in suburban Bethesda, and two-and-a-half year old Derek shared time between his parents. Marc engaged his son by teaching him the rudiments of chess, and soon Derek was able to identify each piece and articulate how it moved. Marc assured him that both parents still loved him and, with infinite patience, answered numerous questions about the separation from Nicole. Try as Marc did, however, the parental tension had rubbed off on his son who became irritable and easily frustrated. For days he hardly spoke.

Now, as Marc watched Derek sitting on the living room carpet, he observed that he was intrigued by a book on the coffee table, 'Portraits of Jazz Musicians'. Marc saw an opportunity to break through.

"Want me to show you the pictures, Derek?" He opened the book. "Let's take a look together."

Derek was quiet, but as his father slowly turned page after page, he seemed to study each photograph at length.

"Want to live with daddy," said Derek unexpectedly. Marc was thrilled to hear his son's love for him being voiced.

He fought his instinct to say "I understand. Your mother's an adulterer, a cheater."

Rather, he said, as he gestured with his hands, "I also want to spend more time with you, Derek, but now you live sometimes with your mommy and sometimes with me." Derek pushed the book away and lay his head down on the glass table.

Marc felt deep regret that his son had to pay the price for his father's poor choice of a partner. Yet he reminded himself that it was Nicole who gave birth to Derek. He was also thankful the outcome of the divorce had not been worse. Although Nicole had filed for full custody, child support, sole ownership of their house, and full legal reimbursement, the judge had ruled for Marc on all matters, the most important of which was shared custody of their child and fifty percent on property division. Marc found he was physically and mentally exhausted and almost $100,000 poorer by the time the eight-month legal dispute was over. That was it. He vowed he would not marry again.

Marc put his arms around his son and Derek rested his head on Marc's shoulder.

"I love you very much," said Marc. "I promise everything will be okay." He prayed that he was right.

Months later Marc waited at the front door while Nicole kissed Derek goodbye. It had been almost a year since the divorce was finalized and she still exhibited her characteristic sulkiness. She drove off in a huff without acknowledging her ex-husband. Marc wondered how it could have come to this. He hugged his son and knew that whatever he had endured, it was worthwhile.

"I have a surprise for you, Derek," said Marc. "What do you like to do more than anything else in the world?" Derek shrugged and Marc persisted. "Play with my microscope?"

Derek shook his head. He dropped his backpack on the floor and climbed onto a cushioned chair.

"What then?" asked Marc. "Take photographs?"

When Marc had seen how his son was drawn to photographs of musicians, he explained how cameras captured pictures. Now he had Derek's attention. The boy nodded. Marc handed him a 35mm Voigtlander camera and six rolls of Kodacolor film. Excited, Derek examined the camera while Marc read from the maker's manual with the boy in rapt attention.

"This is yours," said Marc. "You should know how it works. Let me show you how to thread the film."

As he demonstrated with patience, Marc noticed how quickly Derek caught on.

"Let's open the camera again," said Marc. "We'll put in a roll of film. Then we'll tuck the film on the side and wind it a little. Now you close and lock the camera door."

Derek took the instrument from his father and repeated the steps he was shown.

"Congratulations, son," said Marc after Derek mastered the basic technique. I'm proud of you. You could become a great photographer one day!"

FORTY

1992

After a while, Laura settled back into the comfortable rhythm of teaching, having pushed the legal case into a far corner of her mind. She surprised herself after work one day when, rummaging through unpacked boxes from her move, she found her 1972 acoustic guitar. She was tuning the guitar when she heard the doorbell ring. Her mother entered the unlocked door, kissed her daughter on the cheek, and switched the kettle on for tea. Laura played an A chord, then an E, and to Naomi's delight, went into a full rendition of 'Hey Jude'. As she performed one of her favorite Beatles melodies, memories of Marc became so vivid that she put the instrument down before she finished the song.

"I'm glad you've taken up the guitar again," said Naomi. "You haven't played for years. Actually, you're not doing any of the things you used to love to do. It's all work."

Laura ran her thumbnail across the strings which caused a loud reverberation. "I'm fine," she said over the echo.

"I have an idea," said Naomi. "I'd like to take you to the Kennedy Center in D.C. to see a show. You used to enjoy theater."

Laura shook her head. "You know it's hard for me to get away from work."

Naomi persisted. "You need to take time off. It'll do you good."

"I'll think about it. Anyway, what's showing?"

"Your favorite, 'The King and I', with none other than Marie Osmond."

Laura thought back to how much she and Marc had enjoyed watching the movie together. She hesitated for a moment, then said, "Okay, you've convinced me. Yes, I'd like that."

A few weeks later, at the Kennedy, Laura sat in a balcony seat next to her mother, taking in every moment of the award-winning show. At intermission she offered to go downstairs to buy drinks. As she waited in line at the concession stand, she noticed a tall, broad-shouldered man in the front. From the back she could tell he had a hint of grey in his dark brown hair. He approached the stand and as soon as he spoke, Laura recognized the accent.

"May I have a water please?" he asked.

"Coming up," said the cashier. "Where're you from?"

"I was born in South Africa. Been here a while."

Laura gasped. She had imagined this scenario many times. After so many years apart, Marc Sennet, only a few feet from her now. She wanted to push through the queue and throw her arms around him. No, better that she wait until he made his way back. Then they would hold each other tight and kiss, and all would be as it once was. Heart racing, she watched in anticipation as the man paid for his drink. Then he turned around and his eyes met hers. Laura saw a stranger. She felt a sudden deep loss, as if she had separated from Marc all over again.

Laura sat through the second half of the show, but her mind and heart were elsewhere. For years she had resisted dwelling on her loneliness, and feeling the pain of separation from the only man she loved. She felt it now. Perhaps it was all her fault. Back at home after the show she looked at her nude body in the full-length bathroom mirror. She realized her once trim waist had thickened. Turning, she winced at the big cut in her abdomen with the ugly scar tissue. She was repelled by her own body. Good that Marc could not see her now. She was a failure as a woman.

That night she could not sleep. She remembered how she and Marc had met, their prom night, their shared love of music, their goals, and how much they wanted children. She remembered why their relationship ended.

Like The King and I, the encounter with the South African was 'make-believe', a mirage, imagination theater.

FORTY-ONE

Driving in heavy snow under suboptimal conditions, Marc was relieved that Derek was home safely with Nicole and not out in this weather. His son was adjusting better to the shared custody arrangement and Marc noticed that he seemed happier.

As Marc turned on the front window defroster, he thought what he would only give to have the warm, low-humidity Cape Town weather right now. Ben had called from Cape Town the previous day. He tried to smooth the path after their unnerving previous meeting. He stressed to Marc, mostly in code, that he was not involved in any of his previous activities. Marc understood his reluctance to talk openly. Whenever they met he reminded Marc that one never knew who was listening. He updated Marc on conditions in South Africa. They discussed the referendum the prior year which resulted in white South Africans voting to put an end to apartheid. Things seemed to be moving in the right direction, Ben said, although there was still a lot of concern about potential violence and riots.

Now Marc focused on the road. The snow was coming down fast and visibility was very poor. He turned on the radio for an updated weather report, and was shocked to hear the news item of the day.

Having grown up in the mild South African climate without icy roads or heavy snowfalls, he was never comfortable with winter excursions in the U.S. When his friends went snowboarding or cross country skiing, he opted out. But it was ice that was his number one enemy. He saw so many victims of accidents in hospitals due to slippery conditions, he became obsessively careful. When he was invited to give a talk the previous evening to fellow physicians across the river in Virginia, he checked the forecast. He heard that snow and ice were on the way. Taking a cautious approach, he decided to spend the night at the Marriott hotel in Arlington, Virginia, the venue for the meeting, hoping for warmer conditions the next morning. Before the talk, he joined several colleagues for dinner.

"Smart move, staying overnight," said his partner, Dr. Helman. "I detest driving in this weather."

"I'm worried about how my sister's going to make it to the airport tomorrow morning," said another, identified by his name tag as Dr. Singer. "Her kid's flying to see his dad in Ohio."

"Your sister's not going?" asked Marc.

"She's got to stay for work. The airline is instructing a crew member to keep an eye on Sean."

Dr. Helman peered out of the window. "Okay, you all convinced me. I'm checking in to the hotel right now. There's nothing so urgent that can't wait for tomorrow."

After chatting for a short while longer, Marc excused himself to run through his presentation one more time. The lecture was well-received, and after a good night's rest, he decided to brave the weather and make an early start home this morning.

Now the radio announcement told of a tragedy that had occurred minutes before, when a plane, just after take-off from nearby Washington National Airport on its way to Cleveland, Ohio, crashed into the Interstate Bridge. The supposition was that formation of ice precluded the wing flaps from giving the aircraft the lift it needed. People were trapped in the freezing Potomac River, only two miles from the White House. Rescue was difficult. An appeal was made for medical personnel to help at the riverside and at local hospitals, while recovery efforts were underway.

The report described a scene of the damaged plane disappearing into the water and a few desperate survivors struggling to get ashore. Marc knew exactly where the plane had come down. It was only a few streets away. He had driven past the location the previous night. Without further thought, he drove through the sleet, to the scene of the accident.

On arrival there, the picture was chaotic. Police were gathered in groups, but no one seemed to be in control of rescue efforts. The smell of jet fuel was everywhere. He shoved his way through a crowd of onlookers to the river bank and peered over the low retaining wall.

He almost cried when he saw several people struggling for life. A woman, her flight attendant's uniform just visible, succumbed and drowned. No one was able to help. There was no adequate equipment. Makeshift lifelines from belts proved ineffective. No one dared venture onto the ice to afford a bridge to the stranded passengers. Swimming seemed impossible. No more than 100 yards from shore, there were cries for a rope, a life jacket.

One sound from the ice floes was particularly tragic. Marc, the pediatrician, identified it as the voice of a young boy crying for help. Marc searched the surface and saw the victim floating on a part of the plane. Without thinking, he tore off his coat, jacket and shoes and made for the river bank, hoping the ice would support him so that he could save the youngster. The drifting ice did not. He was soon flaying in the water, battling in the cold to stay alive. This was not swimming in Clifton Bay. The current under the ice was strong and he found he was being pushed away from the shore toward the kid. He called out and made eye contact. He yelled, "I'm coming." Miraculously he inched closer until he touched the frigid boy as he slipped down, about to sink.

Marc's bravery, as some onlookers described his action, or stupidity, as the cynics referred to it, did not go unnoticed. Television crews documented his every move and soon millions of viewers throughout the U.S. were following this live drama.

Meanwhile a police officer had brought to the bank a gun used in docking ships. It fired a braided linen cord. He aimed it just beyond the drowning victims and pulled the trigger. His shot cut through the air and the string landed nearby where Marc was struggling to hold the boy. Marc reached for the line. He tugged at it and a voice over a bullhorn instructed him to reel in. With great difficulty he pulled and to his relief he saw that a life ring attached to the cord was slowly bouncing his way. For the first time in this catastrophic episode, there was hope.

Marc knew the potential risks of subzero temperature exposure to him and the boy.

The cold had surely inflicted more than superficial damage to the child's skin. Probably severe, third degree frostbite. He himself was feeling intense pain and numbness. He battled to grab the life-saving device. He wondered if the boy who had gone silent would survive this horrendous ordeal. They were close to the end when he somehow slid into the life preserve.

Meanwhile a helicopter appeared above and hovered noisily, as the police rescue team on the ground remained alert to every movement Marc made.

The boy appeared lifeless. When an officer saw Marc don the life jacket, he radioed an order to the pilot to "drop the lift". Somehow, with maximum effort, made more difficult by the helicopter blades churning the water, Marc managed to secure the child into the lowered harness. The youngster was airlifted into the helicopter, paramedic on board, and flown to George Washington Hospital to receive emergency attention. Volunteers on the river bank grabbed the lifeline to Marc and hauled him toward the shore. He ploughed, slid and bumped through ice and water to the safety of waiting medical personnel.

Pennsylvania

"Come quickly!" Naomi Atkin called.

Laura rushed into the living room, concerned about the urgency in her mother's voice. Naomi was staring at the television set, glued to the unfolding drama on the Potomac River.

"Look," she motioned with her hand. "It's him. Your prom date!"

True enough, on the screen, large as life, was Marc, Laura's first love, quite a bit older, stuttering and shivering and wrapped in a blanket, being approached by a reporter on national news. In the background were crowds of people, cheering loudly for him. Laura could barely get a word out. Feeling dizzy, she sat down.

"What's going on?" she whispered. The reporter continued.

"...without regard for his own safety. Dr. Marc Sennet risked his life. He is a real hero. Good news has just been received. We have word from the hospital that the child, Sean, is stable. His mother announced that she will be eternally grateful to the person who saved his life. Dr. Sennet, tell our viewers what was going through your mind when you approached the scene and decided to dive in."

Marc was too weak to respond. The interview ended abruptly.

Laura could barely process what she had seen and heard. Long after the news report concluded, she sat on the sofa staring into space.

"Speak to me, Laura," said her mother. "What are you thinking?"

"I feel as if I want to call him now. With all my heart I want to see him again. But he could be married with his own children. And even if he's not with another woman, we know it was his wish, the dream of his life, to have a family. I can't provide what he wants. Nothing's changed." She hid her face as she burst into tears.

Naomi put her arm around her daughter's shoulders and tried to comfort her.

"I'm so sorry, dear. I wish things could be different. If you want to reach out to him, I'll support you, you know that."

"No mom, I'll try to put this behind me."

But Laura could not forget.

FORTY-TWO

Five days after the traumatic plucking of the boy from the icy Potomac, a pretty brunette woman arrived at Marc's office in downtown Washington D.C. on the corner of L and 22nd Streets. She introduced herself to the receptionist as Natalie Peterson, the mother of the child rescued after the plane crash.

Marc, wan, with a stethoscope dangling around his neck, approached her in the waiting area.

"Mrs. Peterson?"

"Yes, doctor," she said. "I'm Sean's mom. You saved my son's life. I will always be indebted to you."

"Just doing my duty," said Marc.

"How can I repay you for your willingness to put your life in jeopardy to save a stranger?" she persisted.

"You owe me nothing," said Marc. "I am thrilled that Sean is out of danger. I've been monitoring his progress."

"Doctor Sennet…."

"Please call me Marc."

"Marc, can I ask a personal favor of you?"

"Sure."

"May I give you a hug, please?"

Marc wasn't prepared for this unusual request, but before him stood a mother who had endured a terrifying experience and almost lost her child. "Of course," he said.

As Natalie came close to him, he was intrigued to see dimples on her smooth cheeks, a feature he had not seen in a woman for decades. They wrapped arms around each other in an emotional embrace as the receptionist viewed this intrusion into her territory with rolled eyes.

"Will you come for dinner next week when they discharge Sean?" asked Natalie.

Marc hesitated, then, seeing her disappointment said, "Sure, that will be nice."

"Do you eat everything?"

"No meat," he replied.

On the evening of the invitation, Marc picked up a box of Godiva chocolates and a bouquet of fresh flowers and drove several miles to the apartment complex where Natalie and Sean lived. As he rode the elevator to the sixth floor, he had a nagging moment of self-doubt and wondered whether what he was doing was appropriate. He considered calling the whole thing off. This is the mother of a patient, he thought, then corrected himself. Not a patient. A survivor. In any case, it was just a thank-you dinner.

He rang the doorbell and was greeted enthusiastically by Natalie, who was dressed in a black cocktail dress. She wore a fine gold chain around her neck.

"Come on in and make yourself at home," she said, as she escorted him to the living room. "What will you have to drink?"

"Just a sparkling water for now," said Marc, wanting to play it safe.

Natalie filled a glass for each. "I'm glad you agreed to come for dinner. I'll let Sean know you're here. He still tires easily, but I'm sure he'd love to see you."

She left and Marc looked around the modern room. There were two grey leather couches, a three and a two-seater, at right angles to each other. Between them stood a low glass and metal coffee table. The walls were covered in abstract art. Marc was impressed.

After a few minutes, Natalie returned with the young boy in his pajamas. Sean's trauma had left its mark. He was pale, and he walked slowly, almost shuffling. In his arms he held a small brown teddy bear. He communicated only upon the prompting of his mother. Marc found the situation particularly poignant, especially as he thought of his own son, and how traumatic this experience would be for any parent.

His mind flashed back, as it too often did, to the newspaper article of the horrific event, including the transcript of the plane's black-box recording. The report read that Washington National Airport had been temporarily closed due to severe snow and ice. When it was reopened, the plane was de-iced with chemical antifreeze. Captain Scotty McLaughlin had reminded his copilot, Greg, that he was about to make the 2000 flying hours mark.

"We shouldn't fly in this fucking weather," Greg had warned.

"I've seen worse," said Scotty.

They went through the checklist and approved the flight for take-off. Apparently the plane had difficulty moving away from its gate due to the ice. When it eventually made it to the only usable runway, it was forced to wait an hour for take-off clearance. Again Greg recommended they abort the flight, and again Scotty dismissed the recommendation. During the wait ice accumulated on the plane's wings so that when it finally took off, it failed to reach a sufficient altitude, and veered wildly off course. The news report documented the ominous conversation in the cockpit and the panic that ensued.

"We're going down," shouted Greg.

"I know," replied Scotty.

They both died in the crash.

Reliving the scene of the accident again, Marc was both stunned and thankful that the boy had survived and was recovering as expected. His heart went out to Natalie.

She addressed her son. "Sean, say hello to Dr. Sennet. He saved you in the ice. He helped you get lifted into the helicopter."

"Hello, Doctor," Sean whispered.

"Hi Sean," said Marc. "I see you're getting stronger. You're a tough guy."

Natalie bent and kissed her son on the head.

"Sit with us if you like or you can rest in your room if you prefer."

Sean mumbled "Good night," and returned to his bedroom.

Marc looked at Natalie. "It takes a while. I have a son a little younger than Sean."

"I'd like to meet him one day," said Natalie.

Natalie had prepared what she thought of as a safe three-course dinner for a vegetarian: lentil soup, pasta with vegetables and apple crumble.

Marc enjoyed the food and complimented his hostess on her cooking. "The lentil soup has an extra kick. Curry?"

"That's right. I prepared the soup and entree but I must confess I bought the dessert from a pastry shop. I'm glad you liked it. Now tell me about you."

Marc told her a little about his upbringing and professional life without going into a lot of detail. He reminded himself of the nature of this relationship and decided to keep it at arms-length and business-like.

"Let's move to the living room," said Natalie, before he could plan his strategy.

She sat alongside Marc on the smaller sofa and took his hand. "You are a gift from God," she said as she kissed his palm.

Marc was shocked at the intimacy. But he found Natalie attractive and reminiscent of a passionate relationship a long time back. After moving close, there was a quick progression of events. Marc kissed Natalie on her cheek and she turned to meet his lips. He didn't resist. He cupped her breast over her bra and blouse and she wrapped her legs around his hips. He picked her up and carried her to her bedroom.

The following morning Marc was in a deep sleep back in his own bed when he was awakened by a phone call. He jumped up to answer.

"Hi honey," said Natalie in a husky voice.

Honey? It took Marc a few seconds to orient himself and remember what had happened the previous night. As soon as he did, he realized what a big mistake it had been. She knew just how to play him and he had allowed himself to be enticed against his better judgment. His heart was elsewhere. He had to set the record straight as soon as possible.

"Come over for breakfast?" she asked. "I have champagne."

"Sorry Natalie, I can't today," he replied.

"Dinner tomorrow then? I'll get a babysitter."

He agreed to meet her at a nearby restaurant the following evening after work. That way, in a public setting, he could quash the idea of any ongoing relationship. Rather not meet at her home. He couldn't predict how she would react in private.

Sitting opposite each other at the table, Marc took her hands in his. "Natalie," he said. "We've been through a lot, but I must be honest with you now."

"What are you trying to tell me?" she asked.

Marc cleared his throat as he searched for the right words. "I think we rushed into this," he said. "Your feelings for me may have been confused with gratitude after I rescued Sean. It's my fault, because I should have recognized that."

As he expected, Natalie didn't make it easy. He gave her time to vent her disappointment.

When she finished speaking he said, "I wish the very best for you and Sean. I'm so sorry it came to this."

She jabbed her fork into her half-eaten entrée and stormed out of the restaurant, leaving the other patrons staring at Marc. He had tried to be respectful, but there was no walking back from the fact that she had idealized him and he had slept with her. He should have known better, but it was too late now. Hopefully she would forgive him in time. Marc left the restaurant feeling bad, knowing he had caused her deep hurt in being truthful to himself.

FORTY-THREE

Pennsylvania

Laura read the attorney's letter in disbelief. She was convinced they had dismissed the case. Instead, more than two years later, Justine's family was demanding $100,000 for the alleged discrimination, to make up for 'hardship and humiliation.' So much for the friendly student's testimony. She met with the school president who was already aware the case was continuing. Before Laura broke the news to her mother, she phoned Neville to get a third party perspective.

"Even if your insurance company suggests it," he said, "I wouldn't settle if I were you, Laura. You have done nothing wrong."

"I agree. I'll fight it. If the school won't support me, I'll hire an attorney."

Neville had come into her life just when she needed a friend the most. Laura felt close to Amber too, but she was far away and busy with her own family. In contrast, he was here for her and she was grateful for his friendship and support. Still, she imagined how much better it would have been with a life partner by her side. Now, as had happened before, painful thoughts surfaced about whether she had made the right decision in breaking from Marc. As she always did, she pushed them out of her mind.

After several meetings with the school board, Laura consulted a prominent legal firm. The partners were willing to take her case on a pro bono basis. They even suggested she counter-sue.

Laura entered the attorney's office with trepidation. Her future was riding on one person, about whom she knew almost nothing. A woman of about forty greeted her.

"Ms. Atkin, I'm Marcia. I've been assigned to your case. I've heard a lot about you, more than you can imagine."

"I hope it's nothing bad," said Laura, concerned.

Marcia had a soft voice and a gentle demeanor. "Don't worry, you're fine," she said, smiling.

Laura scanned the small office. Several framed photographs hung on the wall. There was a desk, two chairs, a computer, and a bookshelf with textbooks and journals. Obviously the workplace of a busy lawyer, with files and stacks of papers. On the desk, a wooden plaque with gold letters read Marcia T. Bryan, Esq. The name looked familiar.

Marcia must have read her thoughts. She asked, "Do you recognize my name?"

Laura nodded. "Bryan. I knew someone with that name. Oh, now I remember. Decades ago I mentored this student, Tharisa. The nicest student with the same last name." She looked at Marcia's expression. "No, she said. You're related?"

"My younger sister."

"You knew about the connection?" asked Laura, caught off guard, but overjoyed to hear mention of her first mentee. "How is your sister doing?"

"Doing well," said Marcia. "She's spoken of you often. She told me you inspired her to pursue a career in literature and creative writing. While many of the poor black children in her neighborhood felt hopeless about their futures, she believed, because of you, she could achieve a promising future."

"I hope that came to fruition," said Laura. "She was very talented."

"She's a teacher and has had several of her short stories published."

"I'd love to read them," said Laura.

"When our senior partners told us about your case," continued Marcia, "and asked which of us would be willing to take it, I recognized your name and volunteered. I want to thank you personally for all you have done."

"What are your thoughts?" asked Laura. "Should I be optimistic?"

"The other side has a strong team," said Marcia, "but so do we. They'll try and dig up any dirt they can find." She smiled. "Going by what I've heard from my sister, you'll come out squeaky clean."

Scanning the photographs, Laura pointed to one of a woman about her own age.

"Yes, that's her," Marcia said. "She lives in Chicago."

Laura scrutinized the face. Yes, the picture revealed a woman who looked to be in her early thirties, but with the same expression in her eyes, the same posture, and the same smile. "Please give her my best," said Laura. "She has a special place in my heart. My very first mentee."

The next few weeks took its toll on Laura. She spent painful hours poring over legal documents, while continuing with her teaching and administrative duties. Ms. Bryan went far above the call of duty and devoted a great deal of time and energy to Laura's legal situation. Six weeks later, after two depositions, Marcia called Laura back to her office. "They're willing to settle out of court for half the amount," she said.

"Absolutely not," said Laura.

Marcia looked surprised. "You're not going to negotiate?"

"Why should I? I'm innocent. I won't pay a price for that."

"If that's your decision," said Marcia, "I respect it."

It took another month until Laura heard the good news that the case had been dismissed. There would be no court hearing. Marcia asked if she wanted to pursue a counter-suit, but Laura decided against it. Although the long legal ordeal was finally over, she was drained emotionally. She felt the need to re-prioritize her commitments. She had devoted so much of her adult life to her students and her work. Now was the phase in her life to find balance and focus more on family.

FORTY-FOUR

Allentown Pennsylvania, 1993

Laura paged through a family magazine as she waited her turn for a haircut at the local hair salon. She watched an interaction between a mother and her young daughter who had just had her hair braided for a wedding. Laura thought, as she often did, how different things would have been if she hadn't had the surgery.

An article caught her attention. It featured a middle-aged couple with an adopted child. The story included in-depth personal interviews with the parents and the girl, now eighteen, and a behind-the-scenes look at a 'week in the life' of the family. They spoke about the blessings and challenges of adoption, but most of all about how united the family had become.

At thirty-four years old, Laura accepted her status as a never-married woman. She didn't wed, "because, after Marc, at no time did I find the right person," she reasoned. But her strong maternal instinct remained. She scanned the article for a list of resources and jotted down the name of two adoption agencies. That night, pulse racing, she did her research, and found that Paramount Adoptions, a local agency, was hosting an informational session the following week.

At the event her eyes were opened to the large numbers of babies and children waiting for homes. She learned that the adoption process would not be easy. There would be tedious paperwork to fill out, documents to produce, and intrusive home visits to endure. She worried that her advanced age relative to other applicants and her single status could be barriers.

After detailed exploration, Laura was not deterred and made a life-changing decision to take the next big step. She completed and mailed an application form together with supporting documents, and waited. For many weeks, she barely slept. Finally one morning she received a letter from the agency. She opened it with excitement, only to find she had been rejected without explanation.

She was heartbroken, but decided she would not give up. She wrote a letter detailing her circumstances, support structure and strong motivation to have a child.

Soon thereafter she received a phone call inviting her to a preliminary interview. The enormity of the situation registered. She remembered the infant who was abandoned by its mother and for a moment relived the guilt she felt as a student volunteer when she had not been able to do more. Was she ready to take on full responsibility now? She believed she was. She was grateful her mother supported her lifetime commitment, as she had with all of Laura's choices.

The interview was conducted by a middle-aged man wearing thick glasses and a bow-tie. His face betrayed no expression. Laura was disappointed and anticipated another rejection. She wondered if the man had children and whether he would be understanding of her situation.

"What makes you believe that you, a single woman, will make a good parent?" he asked, even before she could collect her thoughts.

Laura tried not to become defensive. "I believe that I have a lot to offer a child, in terms of love, education and support," she answered. "As a teacher I've spent many years advocating for children and although, as you pointed out, I am not married, I have the resources available to provide for a child."

He stared at her. "You said you teach. Who will look after the child when you are at work?"

"My mother is available whenever I am not," said Laura. "She is very supportive of the adoption."

"I see," he said. "We'll have to speak to your mother too."

The questioning continued for about half an hour, and then he asked, "What happens if you have a second child? Do you plan to become pregnant in the future?"

She composed herself, then responded with restraint. "I prefer not to answer that question, if you don't mind." She was sure he had crossed a line and even more certain she had failed the test.

"Very well," he said, standing up, and leading her to the door. "We'll get back to you shortly."

After the ill-fated interview and two lengthy, uncomfortable home visits, Laura hoped she had convinced the committee members she would be a good parent.

Within a month she received a photograph and the medical history of an eligible baby. She scanned the report. Anonymous single mother, seventeen years old. Unknown father. The infant was born by normal vaginal delivery at thirty-eight weeks gestation and weighed six pounds and ten ounces. Everything seemed fine to Laura until she read the line 'maternal history of substance abuse.'

She was concerned about the implications. Had the addiction affected the infant and would the baby be at risk in the future? Her baby. She was restless that night. At two a.m. she turned on the lights and re-read the report from the agency. She contemplated calling a meeting and discussing potential problems. Then she thought about how long she had waited for this opportunity. She didn't want to miss her chance at motherhood. She called the agency the following morning. She was ready to meet the infant, and if all went well, sign the contract.

Laura entered the clinic in anticipation. There was no turning back now. The place smelled of curdled milk and diaper cream. There were several portable cribs. A nurse wearing a white starched hat led her to one of them in which lay a thin, ruddy, swaddled infant, whose blue eyes fixed on hers. Seeking approval before she lifted her, Laura looked to Betty, the aide, who nodded. "Go ahead."

"Hello little girl," said Laura, as she carefully picked up the squirmy, blanketed infant. "Hello little Ruby."

She held the baby close to her and swayed back and forth, as Betty looked on with encouragement. Laura cautiously held out her pinkie and the infant grasped it. When she began to fuss, Laura put the bottle to the corner of her mouth and Ruby latched on hungrily.

"I was going to teach you, but you're a natural," said Betty.

It felt that way to Laura, as if she were always meant to be a mother. From that day forth, Ruby became her child.

Naomi was waiting when Laura arrived home with her baby in a car-seat.

"She's beautiful," she said, wide-eyed, staring at her newly-acquired granddaughter as if she were a most unexpected, precious gift. She turned to Laura. "And you look so happy."

Carrying Ruby, Laura followed her mother into the decorated room, with 'Winnie the Pooh' wallpaper, crib, changing table and rocking chair.

"We've got a lot to do," said Laura. "I have only two sets of clothes and one bag of diapers for her. We've got to go shopping."

"We could use another lamp, a diaper bin and a musical mobile," said Naomi. "We'll go to the baby shop tomorrow."

The next few weeks were extremely busy. Laura and her mother, accompanied by Ruby in her stroller, assembled a layette for a princess. Wherever they went, they were stopped by well-intentioned people asking to see the new baby. "She's so cute," "Is she yours?" or "Is it a girl or a boy?"

Laura, believing she still had a lot to learn, signed up for weekly parent-to-be classes. Naomi accompanied her to several of these, in which they were taught about infant safety and given valuable tips for new parents.

"What a wonderful mother you are," said Naomi to her daughter one evening, while she watched as Laura sang a lullaby to Ruby, who, much to their delight, produced a smile.

"I had no idea one could love a child this much," answered Laura.

"Let me look after her for a bit," offered Naomi. "I know you've got work. I'll put her to bed, don't worry." She took the baby from Laura. "We'll be in the living room if you need us."

Laura kissed her child. "I miss you already."

Reluctantly she went into the study and moved a stack of folders from a filing cabinet onto her desk. She opened the first, labeled 'Substitute Teacher Protocols,' and began reviewing and editing. Soon she was on to the next folder, 'Meeting Minutes', thereafter the rest, one by one.

Laura was surprised at the late hour. It was already 10:00 pm. She cleared her desk and went to the nursery, where Ruby was sleeping peacefully. As she watched her baby she felt a wave of sadness thinking about her daughter growing up with no father, much like she had done. There were times she still felt lonely. Although she appreciated her mother's companionship and derived much joy from her adopted daughter, neither was a substitute for a life partner. With this on her mind she doubted she could fall asleep. She returned to her study, tempted to continue working, but decided against it, knowing she had a seven o'clock meeting the next morning.

FORTY-FIVE

Maryland, 1994

It was almost midnight by the time Marc got to bed. This was the second Friday he had missed his favorite detective show on television. His on-call shift had ended at 9:00 pm, but at 8:45 he got a dreaded phone call from Mrs. B. Although the partners didn't publicize their schedules, she somehow managed to track him down again. He couldn't call her bluff, because he never knew if this was a legitimate problem. What if her three-year-old was truly ill this time? He agreed to meet mother and son at the clinic. Marc made sure he reached his office before she did. That way he could turn on the lights and radio, and pretend he was not alone. When they arrived, he examined the child.

Marc removed the thermometer from the child's armpit. "98.1 degrees," he said. "Normal."

"I don't understand," said Mrs. B, gazing at him with wide eyes. She had long legs and wore a short skirt and low-cut pink sweater. Marc tried not to notice.

"His temperature was much higher when I took it," she added. "Must have come down after the bath."

Marc checked the boy thoroughly and reassured his mother that he appeared healthy.

"Just tired," said Marc. "He should probably get to bed. It's late."

She was not in a hurry. "Thank you for coming out in the evening once again," she said.

"No problem," said Marc, as politely as he could, despite the fact that this was becoming a nuisance.

His partners often teased him. "I guess that's the price you pay for being the good-looking one," they said.

"May I ask where you live, Doctor Sennett?" Mrs. B persisted.

Marc shrugged off the question and led the two to the door. Once he saw they were safely in their car, he filed his notes, locked up and headed home as quickly as possible. Women flirted with Marc regularly, and it surprised him. Other than not wearing a wedding ring, he gave no indication that he was available or interested. After Laura, his experiences with women had been disappointing. He would not put himself in that position again. He was exhausted and frustrated by the time he got home, but thankful he had no appointments the following day.

It was not often that Marc could sleep in on a Saturday morning. At four years of age, Derek was a handful. Marc had two days off of work and his son was spending the weekend with Nicole. He decided to take full advantage of this opportunity to be free of commitment. In the kitchen he brewed a pot of fresh coffee and, still in his pajamas and robe, savored his hot beverage while paging through The Cape Times, a South African newspaper delivered to his home monthly. Marc read the headlines.

"Mandela becomes South Africa's new president. Peaceful transition."

The man who had been imprisoned on Robben Island for so many years, now without violence, the country's leader. What an historic milestone. Marc thought back to his months treating prisoners. He remembered the ferry rides back and forth, and the steep learning curve from medical school to becoming a practicing physician. And then the tragic event of his life: how a patient died because of his carelessness. He had failed. He could never forgive himself. He tossed the paper into the trash-bin, poured his coffee down the drain and went upstairs to dress. He would drive somewhere, shop for groceries, and do chores, anything to take his mind off Robben Island.

When he returned home late that afternoon, he wrote a letter to Ben Murphy.

Dear Ben,

I thought of you when I read the news of Mandela. You must be proud. As for me, I can't complain. I'm a partner in a well-established medical practice and have a wonderful son, Derek. I am very busy, so there's not much time to think about the past, but I am still burdened by the death on Robben Island, trying to learn from it and then put it behind me. Talking to you was very helpful, but still, it's not easy to forget. As far as Laura is concerned, I've heard nothing. You were right, I'm sure, when you told me to move on, but sometimes I still dream of what could have been. Please let me know what you're up to.

Your friend,

Marc.

Writing the letter was cathartic, because he felt much better when it was done. After a dinner of left-overs, he called to hear his son's voice and wish him good night. Then, more relaxed, he fell into a deep sleep.

FORTY-SIX

"Dad, can we play Battleships?" Derek pleaded. "We hardly get to do fun stuff together anymore."

Marc had the weekend off. Since one of his biggest regrets was not being able to spend more time with his son, he vowed that when he did have the opportunity, he would make it count.

"Sure," he said. "Give me five minutes to get ready."

He put down his briefcase and pager, and pushed aside the mail on the kitchen table. He took out two pencils and two sheets of paper. On each page he drew numerous small squares, a vertical column on the left marked with the letters A through J, and a horizontal column on top marked from 1 to 10. He then plotted the location of his fleet, by boldly outlining groups of squares to represent battleships, cruisers, destroyers and submarines.

He handed a page to Derek. "You fill in yours. Tell me when you're ready."

After a few minutes, Derek jumped up. "Ready," he shouted, holding up his piece of paper.

"Good. You start," said Marc.

They played several sets. Between each, his son hopped up and down with excitement. The game ended as a draw. Marc gathered the papers and stood up.

"One more," said Derek. "One more, please." He tugged on Marc's shirt.

"Okay, last one. Your call."

"B3, D6 and G7."

Marc looked at his fleet. "Destroyed a Sub at D6."

Then it was Marc's turn to call out. "A3, 4 and 5."

"Deep Blue Sea," chuckled Derek. "You hit nothing!" This was his favorite game.

After they tidied up Marc noticed that Derek had brought his camera.

"Have you been taking photographs?" Marc asked.

"Yes, want to see?"

"Of course," said Marc.

His son laid out several photographs of musical instruments, a photo of a young man playing the drums and lastly, one of a formally-dressed Nicole, next to a greying man in a suit and tie.

Marc tried not to verbalize his surprise. "You did a good job," he said. Tell me about the pictures."

"Mommy took me to an outdoors concert," said Derek. "I met the musicians."

"And?"

"They let me photograph them."

"I see that." He waited.

Marc was not going to get the information he wanted. He decided to let it go. If Nicole was happy, it was better for him. She never questioned him about his relationships with other women. Other than Natalie, whom he no longer saw, he wouldn't have anything to report anyway.

FORTY-SEVEN

Pennsylvania, 1999

Laura looked forward to her periodic get-togethers with Neville at the Espresso Café in Bethlehem. It was an opportunity to relax and let off steam. Most importantly, she felt safe talking to her confidant about anything. A month after the charity auction, she entered the coffee shop with Ruby and sat on a bench alongside Neville. He gave each a hug and ordered a cappuccino for Laura and a hot chocolate with vanilla marshmallows for Ruby. Laura noticed he was wearing the Patek Phillipe watch.

"I'm glad you didn't sell it," she said, as she sipped her coffee.

"Reminds me of my glorious evening with you," said Neville.

Laura, usually responsive to his teasing, did not react. Neville sensed her downbeat mood. He handed Ruby a paper and crayons and drew his chair closer to Laura.

"Laura darling, I know you'll meet someone and fall head over heels in love again," predicted Neville.

"At this stage of my life, I don't know," whispered Laura. "My daughter is my priority. She starts first grade next week."

"Well until you do meet Mr. Right, you have me, like it or not." He grinned. "On that note, why don't we go to The Barns Friday night? They have great music and dancing every weekend. It's open to all."

Laura was unenthusiastic. "That's exactly why I won't go," she said. "I don't dance with sweaty strangers."

Neville laughed, but persisted. "Well then you'll dance with me. Come on, be adventurous for a change." He put his arm around her and she lay her head on his shoulder.

"I'll do it for you, Neville," she said. "You know I love you."

"I know you do."

Ruby's drawing was taking form. She had drawn a stick-figure girl with long yellow hair, smudgy pink cheeks and blue eyes. On either side of her were figures wearing long dresses. One had shoulder-length brown hair, while the other had grey hair. She pointed to herself in the middle of the picture as she explained to Neville that the grownups were her mother and Granny Naomi.

"There's no daddy," said Ruby in a matter-of-fact tone. "I'm adopted."

Laura gave Ruby a hug. "What did mommy tell to you about that?"

Ruby continued drawing. "You chose me to be your baby," she said.

FORTY-EIGHT

2000

Marc would have liked to see his parents more often. He also
wanted his ten-year-old son to get to know his grandparents, but for
now they would have to communicate by phone or mail. Nicole
refused permission to allow her son to leave the country without her,
so Marc had traveled alone to visit Molly and Stan the previous
year. If Derek wanted to see his South African grandparents, Nicole
said, they would have to come here. To date there was no such plan.
Marc was understanding, because he knew that the long trip to
America would not be easy for his parents. Also, although he didn't
know their financial situation, he imagined the expensive overseas
flights would impose a significant financial burden.

Marc made a point of writing to them frequently and sending
pictures. For the last few years, Derek also contributed at least a
sentence or two.

Marc sat down and wrote.

Dear Mom and Dad,
I can't believe it's been a year since we last saw each other.
You probably won't recognize Derek in the picture, he's
grown so tall. The photograph I enclosed was taken last
week, at his tenth birthday party. He wanted a music theme,
as you can see. Now that he's older, he's asking about you
often. Let's try to talk by phone every week if we can.

In your last letter you asked about Nicole. We find it's best to communicate by mail. When we speak it inevitably results in a fight. This way things stay calm. Unfortunately she still does not approve of Derek traveling abroad without her. Hopefully that will change in the near future, so that I can bring him to see his grandparents and their home.

Mom, have you read any good books lately? I've been reading only textbooks and journals. I miss having a librarian in the house. These days I have to go to the library myself. Dad, I hope you've stopped smoking. I know it's difficult to do, but I've seen patients who succeed after trying multiple times.

As far as I'm doing, I can't complain. I have a good career, a great kid and many friends. I still keep in touch with the Drakes, of course. They've been very supportive, as has my friend Jason, whom I first met as an exchange student.

I read about the political situation in South Africa and it appears as if things are better. I'd like to hear it from you, so please write soon.

Love, Marc

Derek added the following, with some editing help from his father:

Dear Granny and Grandpa,

"I hope everyone in South Africa can live peacefully together now. When you visit, will you bring me an ostrich egg?
I love you,
Derek. "

FORTY-NINE

2003

It was almost December, Laura's favorite time of year, when she, Naomi and Ruby put up their tree, baked and iced Santa cookies, and shared stories and gifts. The town of Bethlehem, Pennsylvania exceeded expectations with abundant Christmas decorations and holiday spirit. Laura was excited to share the season's festivities with her ten-year-old daughter.

"Laura, how about joining Craig and me for dinner at the 'Fig Tree' tonight," said her friend Wendy. "Please say yes."

Laura, accompanied by Ruby, was shopping for winter clothes. Ruby had favored a bright purple coat for herself, thankfully on sale. Teachers' salaries did not allow room for limitless discretionary spending.

"Wendy, how can I?" said Laura. "I've got to make dinner, then get my daughter to bed. You know how it is."

"I'm sure your mother would be happy to babysit. It's time you had some fun. You always say no." She nudged Laura. "Oh, come on."

Laura succumbed. "Okay, I'll ask my mom."

At the restaurant that evening, Laura was surprised to find her friends seated with a stranger, whom Craig introduced. "Keith is an old high school friend of mine."

Keith shook Laura's hand. "Pleased to meet you."

"Nice to meet you too." Laura threw a questioning look at Wendy, who shrugged her shoulders.

Craig went on. "Keith and I haven't seen each other in ages. He moved back into town from Los Angeles a few weeks ago."

The four took their seats. A waiter filled their glasses with water and put a basket of assorted breads with the signature fig preserve on the table. They ordered a bottle of Argentinian Malbec.

Laura assessed Keith as good-looking with dark hair, strong cheekbones and soft brown eyes. He turned to look at her and she felt herself blush. She couldn't remember the last time that had happened. She visualized what it would be like to go out with him, but quickly pulled herself together. I don't know this guy, she concluded.

"Wendy told me a little about your career," said Keith. "Heard all about the sandwich queen. Impressive."

Laura hadn't prepared for a date. She would have washed and blow-dried her hair, put on more make-up, changed her shoes.

"Not a big deal," she said. "What do you do?"

"I direct TV commercials," said Keith. "I spend too much time on the west coast. Now I'm ready to be back home. Miss the change of seasons. I want some time to travel, take it easier."

"Oh, yes, poor Keith," said Wendy. "So rough to live on the sunny west coast."

Keith laughed.

After a glass of wine, Laura relaxed. Keith pulled his chair closer and his arm brushed against hers. She enjoyed the sensual feeling. She hadn't desired a man in a long while. They chatted for some time, despite the noise around them. Abruptly she was surprised to find that it was already time to relieve her mother of her responsibility as a nanny.

"I've got to get going," said Laura. "I have an early start tomorrow." She stood up. "It was a wonderful evening. Thank you."

"I'll drive you home," offered Keith, helping her with her coat.

She shook her head. "Thank you, but I have a ride." She looked pleadingly at Craig, but there was no response from him. "Craig?" she asked.

"It's alright," he said. "Go along with Keith. It's on his way."

Laura couldn't argue. En route home, Keith asked if she would accompany him to a theater performance of Evita that weekend. After a hesitation, she accepted, deciding she had to 'get a life' and would work out the logistics later. Keith learned then that Laura had a ten-year old daughter.

"Really? Craig didn't tell me."

There was an awkward silence, during which Laura internalized from his tone that he regarded her loving child as baggage. He probably read her expression and added, "I was thinking it must be hard to cope, with a full-time job and the responsibilities of a young kid."

"It's not a problem," assured Laura. "My mother enjoys having time with Ruby."

Laura told him about her move to Pennsylvania and the adoption. She left out any mention of her first love and the reason for leaving Maryland.

"Ruby's a sweet child. She loves music and performing. She's also been a good companion to my mother."

"Still, must be tough to be a single mom with a career, and have time for other things in life," he said.

Laura nodded. "I'm working on it."

He walked Laura to her front door, took her face in his hands and kissed her on the lips. He was a good kisser. She had only experienced a reaction like this with one other person, but that was way in the past. Now she felt guilty about dating when her daughter was so young.

As soon as he left, she called her confidant.

"Neville, I'm sorry I'm calling so late."

"What's up, Laura?"

"There's this guy."

"Oh, I see. Two-timing me already, are you?"

Laura laughed. "Never. You'll always be my favorite. Keith and I only met tonight. He asked me out and I accepted. I probably shouldn't have. I'm not ready for anything yet."

"You've got to forget the past, Laura. You've got to move on."

"But Ruby…"

"She'll be okay. She's better off with a mom who's happy."

"Somehow you always know what to say. Thanks, Nev. I'll try not to wake you up next time I need a consult."

"You know you will, kiddo. But I'll still love you. This chap had better be good to you."

Laura was familiar with the music of Evita the stage show, but had never attended a live performance. She enjoyed it so much she vowed to go to the theater more often. Keith was a donor to the company, so after the show they were invited backstage, where they met the director and several actors. They laughed and chatted and drank champagne. The stage manager asked the couple to stay for an after-party, but although Laura was tempted, she declined. "It's late. I should probably get back to Ruby."

Keith tried to persuade her. "Come on," he said. "Be a sport. Learn to have fun."

He didn't succeed. She noticed his disappointment as he drove her home.

Two weeks later Laura took Keith to the Espresso Café to meet Neville. Keith was hesitant at first, but agreed to go along. Laura had tried to evaluate her relationship with him. If she wasn't falling in love, she was certainly infatuated by his charm, wit and sense of humor. She wanted her best friend's approval, however. Neville, hard to miss, wearing a grey vest and bright red scarf, was waiting at his usual table.

He kissed Laura on the cheek. "Well hello. Good afternoon, Keith, is it?"

They shook hands and Neville pulled up two more chairs. The three made polite conversation until Keith appeared distracted. A young boy was making airplanes out of paper napkins and flicking straws across the table next to them. His parents were patient and engaged him as best they could. Keith leaned over to them.

"A coffee shop is not a playground," he said. "Is it?"

They didn't reply, but looked embarrassed.

"Oh, it's fine, don't worry," said Laura to them, trying to mitigate the damage. "He's just a child. He's probably bored by all the grownup talk. He isn't bothering us."

She could feel Neville was not impressed with Keith. And she herself couldn't help comparing him to Marc, who would never have spoken about a youngster that way.

They spent an awkward half-hour and then Neville got up. "Got to go," he said. "Talk to you soon, Laura."

The incident at the Espresso Cafe gave Laura pause. After a heart-to-heart with Neville by phone the following morning, she made up her mind to end the relationship with Keith. She called him and arranged to meet. He suggested dinner that evening. At the restaurant, Laura found she had no appetite.

"It's not going to work between us, "she said, even before they were due to order appetizers.

"I know," he said. He looked relieved. "We have different goals. Different priorities in life."

Laura took a big sip of wine. "I'm really sorry."

"Don't be," he said. "I understand. It's good we realize it now."

That night Laura resolved to give up dating. Her self-esteem had never been more fragile. Finding the right man and getting married were no longer on the cards. It seemed life had other plans for her. She had a wonderful child and an important job. Once more, she resolved to focus her energy on those.

And she did.

FIFTY

Bethesda, 2007

"Dad, I got into Maryland," shrieked Derek, jumping up and down.

"I'm very happy for you," said Marc. "I know it was your first choice."

Derek had considered attending an out-of-state college and Marc decided to go with any decision his son made. When he made the choice to stay near home, Marc was relieved. His son was interested in studying business, with a possible minor in photography, and preferred a larger school. He hoped to join a band in his spare time. The University of Maryland fulfilled all those needs. Being an in-state school, it would also save Marc a lot of money.

"Derek," said Marc. Let's celebrate by going out for dinner tonight, just you and me. What do you say?"

"Dad, I'd like to, but I'm due to meet the guys this evening. Can we make it tomorrow night?"

Marc hid his disappointment. "Tomorrow's perfect. I'll make a reservation at Skyros."

Derek enjoyed the company of his friends, and Marc understood. He, as an exchange student, was only seventeen when he got wings and flew overseas on his own. Now he had no evening plans. Jason had asked him to go to a jazz club with several friends and the invitation was still open. Marc considered it, but after the experience with Natalie, he was cautious about meeting women. He decided against joining the boys. It was seldom that he had a free night at home to catch up on reading and television. He would do that now. Whenever he had time alone, his thoughts turned to his first love. He retrieved a photo album from the bookshelf. The label on the cover read '1976-77, Exchange Scholarship'. He opened it to the first page, then, overcome with emotion, closed the album and replaced it among his collection of books.

Marc was about to get into bed when the ring of the phone made him jump. He wasn't expecting a call at this time of the night. He was aware of his heart beating as he lifted the receiver. It was his mother.

"Marc," she said, "I'm sorry to let you know that your father's been ill."

"What is it?" asked Marc.

"We've known your dad had lung cancer for a while," she said, "but he now has an infection which has complicated matters."

Marc listened in disbelief as he struggled to make sense of what he heard. He felt angry that he had not been told about the illness sooner, and at the same time he felt sad for what his father had to endure. "I'm so sorry," he said, his voice croaky. "So very sorry."

Molly updated Marc on the details of the illness and the hospital where he had been admitted and Marc promised that he would fly there as soon as he could. She told him it wasn't necessary, but he could hear the relief in her voice when he insisted.

"I didn't want to trouble you, Marc," she said. "You have a lot of responsibility there. I didn't tell you sooner, because I didn't want you to worry."

FIFTY-ONE

Ruby swirled into the living room in a navy strapless prom dress, which accentuated her fair skin and svelte figure. Her blonde hair was piled up high, with loose strands framing her heart-shaped face. Around her neck she wore a strand of pearls. Laura was emotional as she scrutinized her teenage daughter.

"Mom, why are you crying?"

"I'm happy for you, my darling. These are tears of joy."

The years had passed so quickly. Laura thought back to the time Ruby had celebrated her fifth birthday party with a Cinderella cake. The day after, she made a dramatic appearance in the family room of their home, draped in Laura's blue dress, wearing grandma's heirloom sapphire necklace and clip-on earrings. Her lips and face were smeared with bright red lipstick. Laura gasped.

"I'm having a tea party with my dolls," said Ruby, holding up the bottom of the long gown and trying not to trip. "I'm Cinderella."

"Oh, that explains it," said Laura.

Ruby led her mother to the playroom where she had set a small table with miniature plates and cups. Two porcelain dolls were seated on chairs at the table, and Laura and Ruby took their places next to them and pretended to sip on tea and eat cookies. Laura remembered what a wonderful time that was. It seemed like yesterday.

Over the years Ruby had asked about her adoption. Laura anticipated the questions. She made sure Ruby knew that although it was a closed adoption, she would support her if she ever wanted to open the file and try to track her biological parents. Ruby did not.

Laura was brought back to the present when her teenage daughter nudged her.

"Mom, tell me about your school prom. What was it like? Who did you go with?"

Laura told her about the blind date and the short, intense relationship, saying "I have no idea whether he would even remember me." She omitted seeing him on TV.

"You spend far too much time alone," said Ruby. "You really should start dating again. Let me look up this guy. Maybe he's available. What's his name?"

Laura laughed. "No way. Absolutely not. Your date will be here any minute. You don't want to be late for your prom, do you?"

Ruby hugged her mom. "I love you," she said. "I guess you're right."

"I love you too, more than you can imagine."

While they waited, Laura thought about her own mother, Naomi, and how proud she would have been to see Ruby today. Naomi had been a doting grandmother and she, Laura and Ruby had shared numerous fun occasions together. Sadly, when Ruby was eleven years old, Naomi succumbed to breast cancer and passed away. It took a long time for Laura to accept the reality of the loss of her mother. She attended weekly therapy sessions for a few months and found those to be somewhat helpful, but she knew only time would heal the trauma.

Laura was brought back to the present when the doorbell rang and Ruby jumped up to answer.

"It's Austin," she called. "Bye mom, we're leaving. You okay?"

"Of course I am."

Laura followed her daughter outside. Ruby's date, looking handsome in his tuxedo, greeted her politely. Memories of the prom more than three decades ago flooded back.

As the young couple walked to the car, Laura called out, "Have a wonderful time, both of you. Remember, no later than midnight!"

After they left, she tried to busy herself by sorting laundry items, unpacking the dishwasher, and cleaning the fridge. She tried to push old images from her mind, but failed. She climbed the rickety steps to the attic. On a shelf she found a black and white prom photo and the painting of a young couple on the beach. Then she retrieved a wooden box, which was safely tucked in a corner. She took out the letters, and read them again. 'I wish more than anything that you were with me...' Laura closed her eyes. How she wished that too, but her journey was different now. Perhaps she had erred with her bold decision. She studied an old photograph of Marc as a teenager in South Africa. He was leaning against the railings on the Sea Point beachfront. You could see the ocean in the background. He had an air of confidence and his eyes hinted of mischief. She compared it to the image of the doctor featured in the newspaper report of the D.C. plane crash. Handsome, no doubt, but Marc had aged, as she had. He was still the most wonderful man she had ever known. What she would give to be back in his arms.

After months of friendly banter, Ruby convinced her mother to give her the name of her long-ago date. Ruby went to the Internet and typed in "Marc Sennet". Three Marc Sennets popped up. She reviewed their bios, and one excerpt stood out. She read, 'Pediatrician, born in South Africa, former international exchange student, now a physician in Washington, D.C. Hero of the Potomac plane disaster....' Bingo! Clearly a match. But in spite of her daughter's persistence, that was as far as Laura would go.

A week later, Laura mulled it over again. She experienced the yearning, the familiar pain deep in the pit of her stomach. The feeling she had spent years trying to suppress, only to have it come flooding back at the thought of 'What if?' 'What if she could see him again?' There was nothing she could lose by trying to contact Marc. She had lost it already. All that was left was her pride. She logged into the computer, entered his email address and typed.

Dear Marc,

I think about you often, the way you entered my life so unexpectedly. I remember our philosophical discussions, watching movies and dancing with you, and of course, how you supported me when I was ill.

A lot has happened since then, far too much to write about
now. I'm sure much has changed in your life too. I hope you
are doing well.
Laura.

She stared at the computer for a long time, deleting and re-writing her words, before she finally pushed 'send.'

It was too late to retract.

After she sent the message, she waited, believing that she had made a terrible mistake. Before, she didn't know how Marc felt about her. Now, if he didn't reply, she would learn.

Marc returned home from work late, as was often the case. He opened the fridge, found a dish of penne parmesan with marinara sauce, popped it in the microwave for a few minutes, then carried it to his desk to eat while he checked his emails. His inbox was flooded, with a combination of spam mail, invitations and work-related messages. He methodically went through each, answering emails, and deleting as necessary, while eating the day-old pasta.

A caption caught his attention. 'Hello from Laura'.

He opened the email and stared at the screen in disbelief. A tidal wave of nostalgia engulfed him. Laura. Laura Atkin. The girl from yesteryear, who swore loyalty to him, had appeared. She was alive.

Thinking this could not be real, he got up, and paced around the room. He had gone to bed at one in the morning and was overtired. Perhaps he wasn't thinking clearly. It was probably spam mail. He made some coffee, took a few sips and returned to the computer. The words were still there as clear as they could be.

He re-read the message, then breathless, and not wanting to waste another second, he began typing. He needed to know whether or not she was married. A second chance with the only woman he truly loved would be a rare and precious gift.

For several hours Laura wondered whether Marc had received her message. At ten pm she went to her desktop computer. With trepidation, she logged in. Her inbox was empty. She sighed, shut down the computer and went to bed. On her alarm clock, she watched the time change from eleven to twelve and then to one o'clock. The following day, with little hope, she checked again, and there a reply was waiting.

"I have not forgotten you for one moment, Laura. It's been a long, long time, and there's much to catch up on. I've been living in the Washington D.C. area for the past twenty-five years. My number is below. Please call me. I have so many questions. Marc."

Laura had only one. Was it possible to rekindle a school romance 35 years later?

FIFTY-TWO

February 2011

The February day in New York was windy and cold. Marc arrived at the Sofitel Hotel in Manhattan at 5:45 pm. He and Laura had agreed to meet in the lobby at 6:00 pm on Valentine's Day. They planned an overnight stay to get re-acquainted. Marc wondered if he dare hope for more. Uncharacteristically nervous when finalizing their arrangement, Marc had asked: "Two rooms or one?"

"One," she answered.

It was difficult for Marc to wait ten days for the reunion. His emotions fluctuated from longing to a mixture of anxiety and resentment. He could not fathom why Laura had made such a rash decision to leave him, nor what he had done to deserve such treatment.

Still, when February 14th came, as he clutched a bouquet of red roses, the anticipation of seeing her within a few moments was exciting beyond anything he could have imagined.

Marc looked around the lobby of the hotel. A man was checking in at the front desk. A woman sat with her back to him. She had wavy blonde hair and was wearing a fur coat. Laura? Would he recognize her? Unlikely she would wear fur and the hair color was different. He tried to catch a side glimpse. Still uncertain as he contemplated approaching the stranger, he felt a gentle touch on his arm.

He turned and looked into the familiar face. How could he ever forget those lovely green eyes and the delightful dimples? One look ignited the feelings he had tried to suppress for so many years.

She reached up and touched his cheek lightly.

"I've waited for this so long," said Marc.

A bellboy took their suitcases as Marc stood mesmerized by the beautiful woman, a person he had thought he knew so well, yet hardly knew at all. He led her to an adjacent lounge, where they sat in a private corner and he presented her with the flowers. He opened his mouth to talk, but couldn't. Instead, he gazed at her for a long time, trying to read the expression in her eyes, hoping she would speak and tell him what he wanted to hear.

"I've never forgotten you," she said.

Marc, choked up, nodded. In barely a whisper he asked, "Would you like something to eat or drink?"

Laura shook her head.

She followed as he led her to their room. The door had just closed when he took her in his arms. He held her gently but firmly, as though he was determined that she would not get away from him again. As their lips met, he felt a desire unlike he'd ever felt before. Hardly a word was spoken between them as they embraced.

"My Laura," whispered Marc, as he slipped off her cashmere sweater. "I've always loved you."

Within seconds they were in bed, reliving their sensual connection, undeterred by time, until exhausted, they succumbed to sleep.

Hours later Marc woke to the loud noise of a passing ambulance. It took him a while to orient himself. He looked at Laura sleeping peacefully, and for a moment everything was as it should be. Then it hit him that this was the woman who had broken his heart and left him doubting whether there was such a thing as a soulmate. He heard her relaxed breathing. He glanced at the clock. 11:45 pm. He should let her sleep, but he had too many questions. The room was warm and his mouth felt dry. He got a drink of water, then climbed back into bed and peeled off one of the blankets. He touched Laura's shoulder lightly. She rolled onto her side.

"Laura," he called, then a little louder, "Laura."

She sat up quickly. "Is everything alright? What happened?"

"I cried for you, Laura," he said. "Why did you give up on us?"

She rubbed her eyes. Her golden-brown hair was tousled. Even half asleep, she was still lovely. She tried to focus as she woke.

Marc continued. "And then you left town with no forwarding address. You knew I wouldn't find you."

"I couldn't give you what you wanted, Marc."

"What are you talking about? What do you mean?"

Laura, fully alert now, sat up. She reached for her nightdress and slipped it over her head.

"When I was told I couldn't have children, that we could not have a biological family, I was devastated. You told me over and over it was your dream to have many kids. You remember?"

"But why couldn't you discuss it with me? Being with you was more important to me than anything. I thought you knew that."

"You would have felt obligated to commit. I didn't want you to be with me out of pity. But I've never fallen out of love with you. When Ruby convinced me to look you up…"

"Ruby?"

"My eighteen-year-old daughter."

Marc's face turned ashen. "But…"

"No, no, Ruby is adopted. I never married. Marc, the important thing is that I'm unable to conceive."

There was a long period of silence.

Then the two filled each other in with their respective histories. With pride, they shared stories of their children and Marc elaborated on the circumstances of his divorce resulting in joint-custody of Derek.

"From early on in our marriage," he said, "my wife proved not to be loyal."

"I'm so sorry," said Laura.

Marc opened up with anecdotes of his dating history. "I was always looking for you," he said, as he told of Natalie's infatuation and the fact that he could not commit to a relationship.

"Are you sure you don't have feelings for her?" asked Laura.

"One hundred percent sure."

Laura sighed. "I apologize for what I did," she said. "I made a mistake."

Marc looked away. He remembered that many years back Jason asked him what he was looking for in a girlfriend. He said, she 'must be loyal'. When he first dated Laura she appeared to be. Now, things were different.

"You're right," said Marc. "A mistake. A big one."

Laura closed her eyes and nodded.

Marc switched on the overhead light and unlocked the minibar. "Can I get you anything to eat?" he asked.

He removed drinks and a selection of nuts, cheese-crackers and chocolates. As they munched on their midnight snack, Laura turned to him.

"I brought a package with me. Guess what's in it?"

"No idea," said Marc.

She opened a small inlaid wooden box and revealed Marc's letters written from South Africa decades before. He gasped with surprise.

"Good grief, its 35 years later!"

"I kept every one," said Laura. "Occasionally I went back to them, always praying we would meet again."

They barely slept that night. There was so much catching up to do. They tried to remember every detail of their teenage romance. Marc had packed a CD in his case. He placed it in a player and the familiar tune brought Laura back into the cinema on the night of one of their first dates. Marc reached for her hand. She stood up, then leaned against him as they swayed slowly to the music, in the Manhattan skyscraper, enjoying the nostalgia of their past. The Bee Gees were at their best.

"I know your eyes in the morning sun.

I feel you touch me in the pouring rain.

And the moment you wander far from me

I want to feel you in my arms again."

In bed, Marc lifted Laura's nightgown, exposing the surgical scar on her abdomen. He tenderly caressed the scar and kissed the area. Then he rolled over onto his back and brought Laura on top of him. She nestled her head on his chest and, just as it had in the past, the rise and fall of his breathing calmed her.

When they parted from the hotel the following day, to different commitments, Marc promised to stay in touch and meet again soon. He realized he was still in love. He also knew they were not the same people they once were.

Two weeks later Marc was in the audience at Laura's school in Pennsylvania with admiration as she addressed the crowded assembly of students and parents about new school initiatives and programs.

From his front row seat he watched her closely. In command as principal, she was focused and in control. She had a pleasant lilt to her speech and her insightful comments captured the attention of her audience. Marc remembered the day when she, a teenager, pledged to become a teacher and empower students. She had now lived up to her promise. After they left the auditorium, he stood back as he watched parents line up eagerly to speak to Laura. She looked to him and he convinced her to take her time.

Much later, on their way out, Laura thanked him for driving the long distance to hear her speak.

"I wouldn't have missed it for anything," said Marc. "I've always admired you, but I've never witnessed this other side."

"What side is that?"

"Bold, commanding."

Later, at her home, Marc met a vivacious Ruby. She was playing the piano and singing without inhibition, but stopped abruptly as they entered. Marc introduced himself.

"Please carry on," he said. "I don't know the tune, but it's beautiful."

"My own composition," said Ruby, obviously flattered. "I like to dabble in song-writing."

"My son is quite musical too," said Marc. "Like your Mom, he plays the guitar. You should meet Derek. Perhaps you can sing in his group."

Ruby showed no interest. "Maybe some time," she said.

While Laura prepared a light supper, Marc tried to get to know Ruby. "Do you attend college nearby?"

"Yes, Cedar Crest. I'm studying English and History."

"Not your mother's alma mater?"

Ruby gave a mischievous smile. "I thought I'd forge my own career path."

She was precocious, more brazen than Laura, Marc thought, but also witty and articulate.

"I've no doubt you'll be successful," he said. "I can tell you're very independent."

When they sat down to eat, Ruby went for the jugular. "And now I want to hear all about how you met my mother."

"Some things are private," replied Marc, as he winked at Laura.

FIFTY-THREE

Laura suggested and Marc readily agreed to take two weeks off work and spend the time together, getting to know each other after their long separation. They planned to turn the clock back thirty-five years, retrace their steps and relive the blessed few weeks of their teenage romance. Perhaps, after the nostalgia, they would take up where they left off in life. Marc, the planner, prepared a schedule for each day's activities in Washington D.C., a tourist mecca. The Smithsonian came first: its East Wing art, the Air and Space Museum's Wright Flyer and its National History Museum's Hope Diamond, were must-see stops. Marc was intrigued by the diamond and told Laura about how it had been on exhibit in South Africa at one time.

Early the following morning they took a bus to the crowded National Zoo on Connecticut Avenue. Marc had mixed feelings about the excursion. He enjoyed seeing and learning about the various animals and he could tell they were well taken care of. Still, he didn't like the fact that they were caged when he was so used to seeing them in their natural habitat at home. After taking a formal tour, they spent most of the remainder of the time watching the pandas. Laura was so taken by the adorable animals that Marc bought her an enamel and gold panda charm at the gift shop before they left.

That night they went to Blues Alley to have a glass of wine and take in some jazz. As they listened to the gifted musicians Marc enquired whether Laura was still playing the guitar. He made her promise she would play for him again one day.

The following evening they dressed up for dinner at The Prime Rib in Washington D.C.

"It opened the year I first arrived in the U.S.," said Marc. "I've always wanted to bring you here."

Laura laughed into her napkin at the waiter's surprise when Marc ordered vegetarian at the famous steakhouse.

Finally on the tour, they visited the National Arboretum, a botanical research center not far from the Capitol, with magnificent trees, shrubs and tropical plants. As Marc parked his car, he faced a pond with two stately swans gliding in tandem across the water. It felt peaceful watching them.

"You know swans are monogamous," said Laura.

"Yes?"

"Oh yes. They form bonds for life. In fact, the image of a pair of swans with their necks intertwined in the shape of a heart is a symbol of love throughout the world."

"You're really fascinated by them, aren't you?"

"They're loyal creatures."

They sat in silence for several minutes.

"What are you thinking about?" asked Laura, taking Marc's hand in hers.

"Wondering about home in South Africa. My dad's not doing well."

"I didn't know that."

"He was diagnosed with cancer a few years ago."

"That's rough. I'm sorry."

"I've visited a couple of times. He was doing better with treatment, but his condition has deteriorated recently."

"What will you do?"

"I've decided to go. We've never had a good relationship, but he's my father. And I want to be there for my mom, of course. Also, I have unfinished business in South Africa."

"What do you mean?" asked Laura, surprised.

"I have to face my demons," said Marc. "Go back to Robben Island. There was a tragic event I've tried for years to forget, but it's probably best to deal with it now."

"I won't press for details," said Laura. "You'll tell me when you're ready."

Marc hugged Laura tightly, then continued. "I also have a close friend there, Dr. Ben Murphy. I told you about him. He remained in Cape Town, doing what he can to help build the new South Africa. I hope to meet with him."

"Seems like you're wrestling with a lot," said Laura.

Marc spoke quietly, "I've witnessed some of the evils of racist policies firsthand. I've seen black people locked up for no good reason, I've seen segregation and humiliation and people treated like second class citizens." He paused before continuing. "On the one hand, I didn't want to condone it by living there while enjoying my privileges. On the other I didn't want to run from my duty to fight the system in even a tiny way."

When Laura didn't speak, Marc continued. "So I find myself in this dilemma, not knowing if I should stay here or go back."

"Marc, don't be so hard on yourself," said Laura. "Look what you've done already. You made your voice heard in government protests at great personal risk, you treated everyone with respect and most important, as a doctor, you saved lives, here and in South Africa."

Her last statement struck a nerve with Marc. There was one life he didn't save. In spite of his achievements, he could not forget his error on Robben Island.

Marc planned his next move. The uncomfortable relationship with his father needed attention. They had to talk. He would return to his country of birth, where he had unfinished business. The very next morning, before he changed his mind, he booked a flight to South Africa leaving in ten days.

In the interim, prior to his overseas trip, Marc took a weekend off to spend at Laura's home in Allentown. They embarked on their usual routine strolling the streets and exploring quaint shops, restaurants and art galleries in nearby Bethlehem. On previous shopping expeditions they had bought a couple of glass paperweights and prints, a handbag for Laura, and a sweater from an Irish wool shop for Marc.

On this sunny Saturday morning as they browsed through antique stores in Old Town, he tried to enjoy the beautiful day, but failed. He couldn't help thinking of his forthcoming visit to Cape

Town and the tension of making contact with his father after many years of separation. He remembered how his dad reacted with anger when he heard Marc's plan to leave the country. Stan made it clear that if his son were to emigrate it would be tantamount to treason and he would be disowned. The large estate would no longer be left to him. Marc realized how little his father knew of him. He was not one to care about inherited wealth.

Reliving these memories and feeling anxious, Marc looked to Laura for support. She was on the phone, dealing with work-related issues.

"Laura," he whispered. "Will you be long?"

She motioned with her hand for him to wait. He walked on, next to her, but felt alone. It hurt. To him it seemed obvious her career came first.

Late that night as they were in bed, just before turning off the lights, Marc asked, "What are your three priorities in life?"

Laura appeared surprised by the question, but he begged that she indulge him.

"Ruby,…you, …and my work," she answered sleepily.

"Are you sure items two and three are not reversed?"

"Stop it," she said, yawning. "You're being silly. Good night."

Marc checked his phone and switched off the bedside lamp. "I'm leaving for South Africa next week," he said. "Don't forget me." He waited for reassurance from Laura, but she had already fallen asleep.

FIFTY-FOUR

South Africa

One week later Marc entered the intensive care unit in Paarl Memorial Hospital, afraid of what he might encounter. It had been almost a year since he last saw his father. He was warned that he might not recognize his dad. Although the resuscitation equipment, noisy environment and stench of bodily fluids were familiar to Marc the doctor, it was very different from the perspective of Marc the family member. As he approached the hospital bed with trepidation, he saw an emaciated man with an oxygen tank by his side. The smell of death permeated the room.

The old man acknowledged him with a nod. His voice was hoarse as he tried to formulate the words "Hello, son."

Looking at his frail father beside him, Marc was overcome with a combination of grief, regret and compassion. He felt animosity for the bigot who so readily condoned discrimination, yet deep compassion for the person, his flesh and blood, who was suffering beside him.

When Marc learned his dad had been diagnosed with lung cancer, he felt the urge to shout at him 'I told you to stop smoking!' Now, instead, he lowered the bed rails, held his dad's hand gently and gave him comfort.

His father spoke very softly. "Come close to me, Marc, so you can hear what I say."

Marc moved his chair till it touched the bed, and leaned forward.

His father continued, one slow word at a time. "I'm glad you came." He paused to catch his breath, then with difficulty said, "I regret my past behavior. I'm sorry I hurt you."

"It's okay, dad. Please don't worry about that. Just think about getting better."

His father winced in pain and a black male nurse gave him his medication and adjusted his neck-rest.

"Thank you," said Stan. "That feels more comfortable. Meet my son. Marc, this is my friend, Jehovah."

Marc found it ironic that his father's main source of solace was now coming from someone he would have looked down upon in the past. The patient closed his eyes and for a long time Marc held Stan's hand while his father slept.

Marc jumped when he heard his name. "Marc Sennet?" A female nurse peered in from behind the screen. "Your mother wanted me to check that everything was okay."

Marc locked the bed railing into position and joined his mother sitting alone in the waiting room. She too had aged. One could tell by her facial bone structure and features that she used to be pretty. Now her once thick dark hair was thin with streaks of white, and she sat with her shoulders hunched.

He put his arms around her. "I'm sorry I haven't been here for you, mom."

"You've been with me in spirit," she said, as she motioned for him to take the seat next to her. "But I'm glad you're here now."

Marc squeezed her hand.

"Have you noticed?" asked Molly, forcing an upbeat tone. "Your dad has changed. He's become more reasonable, less harsh."

Marc did not reply. If she was in denial, this wasn't the moment to discuss it. He lost count of time as they sat in silence. He contemplated the human condition and the dependence on doctors at times like this. He remembered how he got started in the field. Perhaps it was Murray, with his shock of white hair, and who practiced at this very institution, who inspired him with the microscope. If he were alive, he would have been 114 years old today.

Before Marc left the hospital, he looked in on his sleeping father. Observing his vulnerability saddened Marc.

Jehovah must have read his expression, because he said, "I will try to keep him comfortable, Mr. Marc. I promise you."

The following day, Marc had lunch with Ben Murphy. Ben filled him in on the country's political situation and the ANC, which had won most of the popular vote.

"The government and governmental officials have faced multiple allegations," he said. "We still have a volatile situation in this country. Even post-apartheid."

Marc in turn told him of his own struggle and how he was torn between making his home in the States or in South Africa.

"Only you can decide," counseled Ben. "We each do what we feel is right."

They spent over an hour catching up on news and then Marc looked at his watch.

"I'd better leave now, Ben. Got to check on my dad."

"I'll be thinking of you, Marc."

On the way to the hospital, his mother called. "Get here as soon as you can, dear."

Marc arrived at the hospital too late. His mother's face said it all.

"No, no!" cried Marc."

"He's gone," said his mother. "He passed away peacefully about half an hour ago. He just couldn't fight any longer."

Marc didn't like to reveal his emotions. But now, he could not hold back. It was as if a gate had been unlocked, allowing all the disappointment, sadness and regret to escape. He wept without embarrassment and when he had no more strength to cry, he focused on practicalities.

After urgent arrangements were made, he left the ICU with his mother. He walked along the narrow corridor to the lobby, as he had many times before. The numerous gold plaques on the walls spoke of patients' appreciation and dedication to the medical community. The last plaque caught Marc's attention. In bold letters, it read, 'In Support of our Future Physicians and Healthcare Personnel. With Gratitude, Stanley Sennet.'

Marc could barely comprehend what he had seen. He gestured to Molly to take a look.

She nodded knowingly. "He was a complicated man, Marc." She took his arm. "Come, we should go home now. I'm really tired. I'm sure you must be too."

In a short while, Molly's house was filled with flowers, food and cards from caring neighbors. Marc was grateful to see that his mother had such support. He called Laura, told her about his father's passing and listened as she tried to comfort him.

The funeral service was held in an Anglican church not far from the family home. Dressed in a dark suit, Marc stood at the chapel door while one by one, friends and family offered condolences. So lost in grief, he hardly heard what they said. How he wished Laura could have been by his side.

There were many changes – some good, some bad, in the new South Africa, but it did not take Marc long to realize he didn't feel as close to his place of birth as he did before. That night a definitive decision came to him. This was a different country. He would go back to live in the United States. That would be his permanent home.

FIFTY-FIVE

USA

The green card issued to Marc by the Federal Government was not green. That didn't matter. It gave him authority to live and work permanently in the United States with the immigration status of 'lawful permanent residency.' He was a resident alien with no voting rights. Like other holders, he was obligated to carry the physical card wherever he went.

Conversion to citizenship involved an application for Naturalization and an interview after a minimum residency of five years. Laura studied the test booklet with Marc and then quizzed him to make sure he was prepared. "How many U.S. senators?" she asked. "When was the Declaration of Independence adopted? Who was the first President of the United States?"

The immigration office was located in Baltimore and there Marc answered questions about his application and background and passed English and Civics tests.

A month later he attended a ceremony where he took the Oath of Allegiance to the United States of America supporting its constitution and renouncing all allegiance to any foreign entity. The judicial ceremony for Naturalization took place in a large assembly room of the District Court in D.C. where he and fifty other applicants from countries across the world returned their permanent resident cards in exchange for certificates of naturalization. While people were rejoicing around him, Marc had mixed feelings. He had lost his old identity. He would no longer be a citizen of South Africa. He hoped he had done the right thing.

Marc's colleagues decided on a private after-party to celebrate the important milestone. His partners hired a room at the Four Seasons Hotel where a lavish dinner was served. American flags and balloons adorned the room and a DJ provided lively country music. Thirty family members and friends, including the Drakes, enjoyed the evening. Marc gave an emotional speech as Laura, Ruby and Derek stood by his side.

"Family, friends and colleagues,

What an honor this is to stand before you as a naturalized citizen. Those close to me know I have spent many years soul searching, deciding on the best path to take and where to live the rest of my life. Choosing to leave my place of birth was not easy, but I was fortunate to be given the opportunity to come to this country, this United States that I now call my home. I made the choice to become a citizen of the United States of America and I hope to do my part to make our nation even better. I'm sorry my parents can't be with us this evening. Laura, Derek, Ruby, Sid and Helene, thank you for your love and support."

After the function they returned to Marc's home, where Laura had planned to stay overnight.

Lying in bed next to him, she yawned, and reached to switch off the light.

Marc shifted restlessly. "Don't, I'm not sure I'm ready to sleep just yet."

She sat up. "How does it feel? I mean, do you feel different as an American citizen?"

"I do," he said. "I've imagined this day, but the gravity just hit me. I don't take it lightly."

Laura snuggled up close to Marc. "I know you don't. It was a special experience and I'm glad our kids could share it with us."

When he didn't speak, she nudged him playfully. "What's wrong?" she asked. "It's understandable if you're a bit stressed. You've gone through a lot. While you were in South Africa, were you able to confront the demons you spoke of?"

He didn't answer.

"Talk to me, please," said Laura.

Marc took a deep breath, then recounted the experience of his patient who passed away on Robben Island, for the first time sharing with someone close the extent of his guilt, sorrow and remorse.

Laura listened carefully without interruption and after he had finished speaking she said, "It's time to forgive yourself, Marc."

He shook his head. "I'm not sure if I can."

"You owe it to your current and future patients," she asserted.

Marc stared at the ceiling, then at his white coat, ironed and ready for work the following day. He thought about the many patients under his care, the children and families who depended on him. "I know," he said. "Of course I know."

Having shared his secret with Laura, Marc felt relieved. His colleagues said they noticed a change in him, a lighter mood. He eagerly attended a charity event and was the winner of two tickets to see the Rolling Stones in concert in downtown Washington D.C. Because of a work conflict, he offered the tickets to Derek and suggested he take Ruby, who had expressed her wish to see the band perform.

Derek was hesitant. "I feel weird asking her out. I hardly know her."

"It doesn't have to be a date," said Marc. "You both love music. She'll appreciate the offer."

After a short back-and-forth, Derek was convinced. "I'll give her a call."

"That's my son," said Marc. He gave Derek a pat on the back.

Laura drove her daughter from Pennsylvania to Marc's apartment. On the way, Ruby asked about Derek.

"He's polite and clever," said Laura. "And very talented musically." She continued. "He's a little shy, so go easy on him."

"Must have been hard for him after his parents divorced," said Ruby. Laura flinched, as her daughter went on. "Is he in contact with his mother?"

"I believe he is," said Laura, but I don't know how close they are. Marc doesn't say much about Derek's mother."

"I can understand that."

They parked in front of a tall building. "This is where Marc lives," said Laura. "He's on the second floor. Not a bad trip, was it?"

"Of course not," agreed Ruby. "You had me for company."

She walked around to the driver's side of the car, gave her mom a high five and took the suitcase from her. They entered the building and let themselves into the condo with a spare key Marc had provided. They freshened up, had coffee, and were joined by Derek from his nearby studio apartment. After engaging in polite conversation, Ruby doing most of the talking, the young couple took a cab to the concert.

While Laura waited for Marc's return from a medical meeting, she prepared a candlelight dinner. She had brought with her fresh rigatoni noodles. She found several ripe heirloom tomatoes in a bowl on the kitchen table, and simmered them with basil and spices to create a rich and fragrant sauce.

When Marc returned, he was happily surprised. "What's cooking?" he asked.

"One of your favorites," she said.

He followed her to the dining room, where the table was set for two, with elegant glassware, cloth napkins and silver candlesticks.

After dinner, Laura brought a cozy blanket, they made themselves comfortable, and watched 'You've Got Mail' starring Meg Ryan and Tom Hanks.

"I've seen this three times," said Laura when the movie ended, "and it still makes me cry."

"I think it's the dog," said Marc. "If you want a tearjerker, bring in a pet."

Laura laughed. "It's just so romantic. The ending, when they get together after all that time, just finishes me."

"Are you crying again?" asked Marc. He took a tissue and gently wiped her cheek, as he held her close.

"Our children are so different," said Laura, changing the subject. "I hope they get along."

"I'm sure they will. Derek is easy-going. And at least they have music in common."

"Ruby's a fireball, not as laid back as Derek, as you well know, but she's a lot of fun. I think they'll have a good time."

Well after midnight the teenagers returned, exhilarated.

Ruby hugged her mom and shook Marc's hand. "We had a great time! Thank you Dr. Sennet."

"Call me Marc. You're welcome. And you, Derek? Did you like the show?"

"It was awesome."

Ruby studied the photographs on the wall.

"These are fascinating," she said. "Who took them?"

"I did," said Derek. "They're images of jazz musicians in Harlem. I interviewed several of them."

"That must have been some experience."

"It was," agreed Derek. "Their stories were very inspirational."

"Derek wouldn't tell you," said Marc, "but he won an award for his photographs."

Derek appeared embarrassed by the attention, changed the subject and motioned Ruby toward the kitchen, from where Laura and Marc could hear them talking and giggling.

"Something to eat?" asked Derek. He opened the fridge door. "Want pancakes?"

"Sure," said Ruby. "You have pancakes in there?"

"No, but my dad's fridge is always well-stocked. We'll make them."

"You don't know how to make them, do you?" she asked.

"Nope. Do you?"

Ruby laughed. "Men, men. Okay, you've got the eggs and milk. I'll need vanilla, oil, and a pan. Oh, and flour."

There was silence from the kitchen, then cries of laughter.

"Pancake landed on the floor!" shouted Ruby.

"Sure sounds like they're having fun," Laura said. "I'm glad they have something in common."

"I thought they'd be okay," said Marc

"Thanks for letting her stay over," said Laura. "We'll probably head home early tomorrow."

"Whatever works best," he said. He retrieved a bath towel and soap and handed them to Laura to give to Ruby. "You two stay as long as you want."

Laura heard the children still chatting when she woke to get a drink of water at two in the morning.

She and Marc slept late the following day. She slipped on a robe, and went into the kitchen to make coffee, then brought a mug to Marc, still in bed.

"It's quiet. The kids must still be asleep," she said.

"Put down the coffee," said Marc. He pulled her back into bed playfully. "Don't wake them yet. Stay a little longer. Please. It's Sunday." He drew her toward him and kissed her on the neck and then on the lips.

"I want to stay right here," said Laura, catching her breath.

"I wish you could."

"How does next week look for you?" she asked.

"It's a busy week, and I'm on call next weekend."

She sighed. "I guess that's the downside of dating a doctor."

Years before when Marc told his parents that he was considering emigration to America, his father was angry and vocal. "Abandoning South Africa in its time of need is unpatriotic," he said. If you proceed with this madness, you'll be out of my will."

When Stan passed away Marc assumed the proceeds of the estate would go entirely to his mother. He knew his dad had money, but Marc never sought to quantify the worth. He was therefore surprised to learn that he was a fifty percent beneficiary and that his share was very substantial. Another pleasant shock was the bequeathment to Jehovah of ten thousand rand. He was relieved that his mother would have no financial burden for the rest of her life.

He discussed his endowment with Derek and Laura. It took time for Marc to accept the reality of his wealth, but he finally came to the conclusion, as did Laura, that he would not feel comfortable if he did not make a sizable charitable contribution. After donating a significant percentage of the money, paying off his mortgage and loan debt, and putting some into a savings account, he would still have a sufficient amount of capital which could be income producing. This opened a gateway of opportunity to change his life for the better. Prior to this he was unable to consider long distance travel plans. Now he was free to do so.

Pennsylvania

While Marc was doing hospital rounds in D.C one Saturday, Laura walked into the Espresso Café and spotted Neville in his usual corner seat, reading the newspaper. She pulled up a chair.

He smiled. "And I thought I would have peace this morning."

"Hey!"

"No, you know I'm happy to have the company, kiddo."

"Marc sends regards," said Laura. "I'd love you two to meet some time."

"I'd like that. You've never really told me the details of how you met."

"You could say I've known him since I was seventeen. It's a long story."

Neville took off his jacket and leaned back in his chair. "I've got all day. Start at the beginning."

Laura recounted the story of how she and Marc had gone on a blind date and fallen in love, only to have him leave to return to South Africa. She told Neville that Marc had returned to support her through the surgery, which had meant so much to her, but when she discovered that she could never bear children, she distanced herself from him.

Laura noticed Neville's look of surprise. "I did it for him," she explained. "Marc desperately wanted children of his own. I didn't want him to stay with me out of pity."

"So you forfeited your love?"

"No! Yes, you're right. I wasted many years, meeting the wrong people, yearning for him. He moved to the States, married, had a son, and then divorced. My adopted daughter encouraged me to look him up after all these years."

Neville looked thoughtful. "A second chance. Not everyone gets the opportunity. Don't mess it up."

"I love him so much," said Laura, "but we don't get to spend a lot of time together. My position is very demanding, and he has a busy on-call schedule."

"If you want it to work," said Neville, "you should make a plan. You could move closer to each other, for a start."

"What about my career?" she asked. "The students and staff depend on me."

"What's more important? Think about your priorities." He shook his head. "Don't find yourself in a position you'll regret later."

Laura was quiet.

"Laura," said Neville. "You won't get a third chance. Do you know what I'm saying?"

"I hear you," she replied.

FIFTY-SIX

2013

Lehigh University was on spring break for a week, so Laura suggested she and Ruby spend a long overdue day together, going for a morning run, then clothes' shopping and a late lunch. Ruby showed up in sweats, and Laura drove to a nearby park, from which they began their run. Jogging alongside her fit daughter, she was proud that at her age, she was still able to keep up. After three miles they returned back to the same spot, panting and sweating. To their delight they found a wedding ceremony being held in a gazebo in the midst of the rose garden. Ruby's eyes were fixated on the bridal couple taking their vows in the beautiful public venue. When they felt they might be intruding, they went home to change clothes, before embarking on a shopping spree and lunch.

In the afternoon Laura and Ruby discussed a wide range of topics from school to relationships. Out of the blue Ruby raised the matter of her adoption.

"Do you know the name of my egg donor?" she asked.

"You mean your biological mother," said Laura. Ruby was aware that she was a single mother.

Ruby shook her head. "I don't see her as my mother," she said. "She abandoned me."

Laura realized she had underestimated the psychological effect of the adoption on her daughter. She was disappointed in herself for not recognizing this sooner.

"There are many reasons mothers and fathers place their babies for adoption," she explained. "Sometimes they can't manage financially and they want to make sure their child will have a good life. Sometimes they have medical or other problems and believe they are not capable of raising a child. The fact that your biological mother gave you up does not mean she didn't love you, Ruby."

Ruby was silent as Laura replaced a pair of shoes back in their box.

"I didn't answer your question," said Laura. "No, I don't know her name. But if you would like to find out and meet her, we may be able to arrange it through the agency." She held her breath.

Ruby didn't comment.

"Would you like to meet her?" asked Laura, afraid of the answer.

There was a long pause before Ruby said, "No, you're my mom. I'm happy as we are. Also, I'm scared of what I may find out."

"I'm sure she loved you," said Laura. "And if you ever change your mind about wanting to meet her, let me know and we'll explore this together. Alright?"

"Okay," said Ruby.

Laura bought Ruby a pair of silver evening shoes after which they decided to forego the rest of their shopping. Over a lunch of green salads and mushroom quiche they made light conversation.

"I'm glad we could talk about your adoption," said Laura, as they got into the car. "You know you can speak to me about anything."

That night Laura called Marc and told him about the conversation with Ruby. "I dodged a bullet," she said.

Laura woke early the next morning. She had a busy schedule ahead of her. An eight o'clock morning assembly, two classes and a staff meeting, all before midday. She was conducting the meeting and troubleshooting a dispute when an announcement came that there was an important call for her. Excusing herself, she went to the phone and was surprised to hear Ruby's voice.

"Everything okay?" asked Laura.

"I thought about it again," said Ruby. "I want to meet my birth mother."

"What are you going to do?" Marc asked Laura that evening when he heard of Ruby's change of heart.

"I'll contact the agency tomorrow. See what the options are."

The following morning Laura was on the phone to Paramount Adoption Agency as soon as they opened. She gave them her case number and waited as they retrieved the file. When she expressed the desire to contact Ruby's birth mother, she was told there was a procedure that Ruby, no longer a minor, would need to follow. They would mail the instructions and forms to Ruby. That night Laura asked her daughter whether she'd changed her mind. "It'll be a very emotional process," cautioned Laura. "We don't know where she is, or even if she'll respond."

"I understand," said Ruby, gripping Laura's hand, "but I have to find out."

A week later and with trepidation, Laura dropped the envelope into the mailbox. There, it was done. Ruby had written a poignant note, answered several personal questions and signed to indicate that she understood the potential consequences.

Every day Laura checked the mailbox. Nothing came. A delay was not unexpected. They had been warned that birthparents, for whatever reason, might not have interest in reconnecting with their adult children.

After three months of hearing nothing from the agency, Laura closed the mailbox and let out a breath of relief. She didn't think a reconnection at this stage would be beneficial for her or Ruby.

FIFTY-SEVEN

October 2013

On an excursion, Marc and Laura traveled to Traverse City, Michigan where they left their car in a parking garage. It was a bright autumn day. Marc and Laura rented bicycles. Soon they were pedaling through the red, orange and yellow leaves alongside a shallow stream, wriggling with trout. As Marc passed Laura, she called "wait for me!" and raced to catch up. They laughed all the way amidst the beautiful scenery. In the distance between the hills, they caught sight of the remote country inn where they planned to spend the weekend. Their agenda included fly-fishing, cooking classes and relaxing.

Once inside the gate of the inn, they parked their bikes and unhooked their backpacks. They walked up the cobbled path through the main entrance to check in at the front desk. The lobby was quaint, with walnut floors and an antique rug. The walls were covered with beautiful landscape paintings. Through a screen, Laura could see a dining room with lace curtains, and several tables set with linen cloths.

A friendly-faced woman with a grey bun greeted them. "Good afternoon. Dr. and Mrs. Sennet."

Laura blushed. "Yes, good afternoon."

"Your room is ready. I think you'll enjoy it here. The weather has been beautiful all week." She handed them a key.

"Room 204. Second floor to your right. The steps are straight ahead."

The room didn't disappoint. A handmade quilt covered the large four-poster bed, and the walls were covered in Laura Ashley paper.

"They must have known I was coming," said Laura. She inspected the rest of the suite. A small sitting room with a comfortable couch and chairs led off the main bedroom.

Marc sat down and put his feet up.

"Don't get too comfortable," said Laura. "We have a cooking class at five. Then we get to eat what we made."

"Oh no," said Marc. "I thought we came to rest."

Laura threw a pillow at him playfully. "It'll be fun. We're learning how to make eggplant parmesan."

At 5:00 p.m., Marc and Laura were joined by four culinary students in the inn's spacious kitchen. The instructor handed each an apron and a chef's hat. Marc felt silly, but decided to be a good sport. They started off learning knife skills and a few basic kitchen techniques. Laura practiced slicing an onion. Her eyes watered profusely.

"No, no," cautioned the instructor, taking the knife from her. "You'll cut yourself that way. Let me show you." Marc threw her a teasing look.

By 7:00 p.m., after mastering peeling, cutting and dicing, they flopped onto their stools, exhausted, laughing and covered in flour. Every student agreed the home-made dinner that followed was delicious.

Back in their room, Marc opened the complimentary bottle of iced Riesling and poured a glass for each. They clinked them against each other. "Cheers," Marc said, before taking a long sip. He told Laura about the Paarl vineyards, the plump yellow grapes and his favorite Cape Riesling. They found a radio station with music and sat together, enjoying the wine and reminiscing. Marc gave Laura a neck and back massage, knowing it was her favorite for relaxing.

While she showered, he waited for her under the covers. For an inn, the amenities were above average. Soft bath towels, Egyptian cotton sheets and fluffy down pillows. Marc looked up as Laura entered the bedroom wearing only a delicate white negligee. Through the lace he could see every curve of her glorious body. He took her in his arms and was swept away by her softness and her signature perfume. They slept deeply and woke late the following morning to the sound of chirping birds and chattering guests.

At breakfast Laura noticed Marc was not as talkative as he usually was. She tried to make conversation. "How do you feel when people refer to us as "Dr. and Mrs.?" she asked.

"I'm fine with that," Marc responded quietly, as he toyed with a silver napkin ring.

Laura waited for him to continue, but there was silence. She raised her eyebrows and pulled her chair closer. "Talk to me," she said.

"You know how much I care about you," said Marc.

Laura nodded. "But?"

"I'm worried," he continued. "I saw you as my soulmate and although you promised to love me always, you disappeared out of my life. Much later, when I gave marriage with someone else a chance.... Well, you know how that ended."

"I explained to you why I left," said Laura. "I thought you understood. That's now water under the bridge."

"We wasted so many years," said Marc. "We can never get them back. And even now we can't make up time because you're always working."

Laura glared at Marc. "Why do you say things like that? My decision was out of love for you. Do you know how hard it was? Don't you think I feel guilty enough?"

Marc, immediately regretting what he had said, reached over to Laura. She pulled away. They became aware of two waitresses hovering and whispering to each other. Marc motioned to Laura. They rose and excused themselves from breakfast. She, still angry, grabbed her purse and in doing so, knocked her plate off the table. A mess of waffles and syrup landed on the floor.

Marc, embarrassed, apologized to the staff.

"Let's take a walk and get some fresh air," he suggested.

Laura reluctantly followed him through the patio door and outside to the back garden, knowing this was an issue that would not be easily reconciled.

Two weeks after their Michigan trip, Marc, excited, handed a letter to Laura. "I'm being awarded an honor for my hospital service," he said. "We're invited to a gala celebration on the tenth."

Laura checked her calendar. "You should be very proud and I wish I could go with you, Marc," she said. "I really do. But I can't."

Marc showed his disappointment with a frown. "It's a special night for me. I'd really appreciate it if you could be there."

"I have a big presentation the following day," said Laura. "I can't let the teachers down. I'll make it up to you, I promise."

Marc let it go. He knew Laura. Once she made up her mind, there was no changing it.

"I understand," he said, with resignation.

He didn't really. Marc was well aware that Laura was devoted to her profession. Her recognition amongst her peers as she promoted educational excellence in her school and community was without question. The wall of her home office was decorated with citations honoring her successes in raising standards. Sometimes Laura questioned whether this was the life she wanted. She had underestimated the challenges and was left with little free time, but still, she concluded teaching was her calling. Marc noticed that she went far beyond meeting her professional responsibilities and no task asked of her was too big. He was afraid she was losing herself in her work. There were times he didn't recognize the fun-loving and charismatic person he was dating. He wondered whether what they once had together could still be salvaged.

FIFTY-EIGHT

Two years later

Since Stan passed away, Molly had more frequent contact with Marc. Previously, when she had suggested to Stan they take a trip to visit, she was met with the same negative responses from her husband. "Do you know how many rand it will take just to buy the airline tickets?" "Do you know how much money I'll lose by being away from my job for so long?" Now, no longer wanting to waste time, she visited Marc at least twice a year.

When the engagement was announced toward the end of 2015, Molly was determined to be there for the wedding celebration in April.

"I can't tell you how happy I am that you'll be here to celebrate," said Marc when his mother called to tell him. He was delighted when she visited.

"How's precious Ruby doing?" she asked. She had met Ruby on a previous trip and they had become regular pen-pals, which cemented a bond between them.

"She's doing really well," said Marc.

"And my grandson, Derek?"

"Very happy, mom. You'll see them all soon. They can't wait."

Pennsylvania, 2016

The chairs arranged on each side of the manicured lawn were separated by a white carpeted pathway lined with 'blushing brides.' Laura remembered becoming acquainted with those delicate flowers from South Africa on a riverside walk with Marc, years before. Now, two bridesmaids, in pale-blue silk dresses, walked solemnly along the path toward the bridal canopy. As Laura watched them from her front row chair, she noticed that Neville had arrived and discreetly taken a seat toward the back. She nodded to acknowledge his presence.

Marc's mother, sitting close by, on the other side, appeared overcome with happiness, and could no longer hold back tears. She was flattered she had been recruited by her granddaughter-in-law, as a wedding consultant. She turned around to look at the guests and caught the smiling face of someone she had just met, Amber, the schoolgirl without parental support when a young mother. She was sitting behind Laura, next to her husband and one of her sons.

Laura heard Amber say to Molly, "I wouldn't miss this occasion for the world. Laura was always there for me."

The week before the wedding had been a whirlwind as Molly helped finalize arrangements. The bridal gown needed last-minute alterations, bridesmaids' gifts needed selection, flowers chosen, menu planned, wedding cake designed. Molly had spent hours filling gold lace tulle with Jordan almond candies for wedding favors. Now the big day arrived and everything seemed perfect. Even the weather co-operated. Soon the couple would be on their honeymoon in the Holy Land. Molly was teary-eyed when she heard the question. "Do you take this bride…?"

The bride's ivory gown was studded with pearls. Her delicate veil revealed a glimpse of her honey-blonde hair. On her neck shone the star sapphire of her late grandmother. The groom stood confidently by her side in a navy suit and bowtie.

"Do you take this man to be your lawful wedded husband?" asked the minister.

Looking lovingly into Derek's eyes, Ruby replied, "I do."

The entire congregation cheered.

For Marc, sitting between his closest friends, Ben and Jason, the moment was bitter-sweet. His lips quivered. He wiped his eyes, and turned his gaze back to the bridal couple as they embraced with passion. He remembered how happy young love was. Jason nudged him in support. Marc was touched that his longtime friends had traveled such far distances to witness and join in the celebration. He was hurt that Derek's mother was not in attendance.

In the groom's party, Marc looked across the aisle and saw Laura very much alone. He had barely seen her over the past few months. Now his heart went out to her. Their eyes locked as they pondered on the historic moment in their lives. Marc blew a kiss to her. Then, with a resigned shrug of his shoulders, he opened his hands and mouthed, "It's the best we could do."

Immediately after the celebration Marc said his goodbyes to friends and family and accompanied his son to a blue Fiat spray-painted in white with the words 'Just Married'. An emotional Derek threw his arms around his father and thanked him for everything he had done. Nearby, Marc saw Laura kissing Ruby farewell. He hesitated, then with a heavy heart, started to walk away as the newlyweds drove off.

It began to drizzle and Marc quickened his step. An impulse made him stop and look back. Standing there, right where she had been, was a girl in a satin gown. For several moments they stood, looking at each other.

"I think about you all the time," he said, just loudly enough for her to hear.

Laura gave a big dimpled smile.

He saw his prom date all over again.

FIFTY-NINE

Allentown, Pennsylvania

Home early from school, Laura watched, in exasperation, the Teachers' Demonstration on National Television. The cameras panned to a close-up shot of Heloise Gutman, the Head of the U.S. Education Association. To describe Heloise as 'unattractive' would be kind to her. Short and heavy with a squarish jaw, she looked like 'a cross between a bulldog and a sumo wrestler' according to a member of the association. She was elected to high office of the largest labor union in the nation, not for her looks, but for her brain.

Laura heard that Heloise was a brilliant orator and to the benefit of her union, a rabble rouser par excellence. She had the ability to stir up a crowd, and to activate an audience to march, sit-in, strike or riot. She was a fearsome foe. Laura had the misfortune of crossing swords with Heloise.

For the many years of her career in education Laura was a loyal, dues-paying member of the U.S. Education Association, but she came to question its core policy after the findings of the Teacher Advancement Program. TAP recommended merit pay, stating 'performance-based compensation will stimulate a market for superior teachers'. She voiced her agreement and so came face to face with Heloise.

Merit pay was anathema to Heloise. Likewise the abolition of tenure. She initiated an aggressive campaign against Laura, arguing that she had a record of undermining public schools.

Heloise decided on a Teachers' March to the Capitol in Washington DC, singling out Principal Laura Atkin for criticism, and threatening a major strike if her demands were not met.

Glued to the television, Laura watched as dozens of marchers carried picket signs which made her wince, with captions varying from 'Send Laura Home' to 'Atkin Not Our Kin'.

On the steps of the House of Delegates, before a crowd of several hundred, Heloise bellowed, "My name is Heloise Gutman. I am here as the head of the U.S. Education Association, an organization with three million members. I represent public school teachers throughout the nation. They are our future.

"We are here today because of urgent problems. The quality of education and the public interest are at risk. We are fed up with the current policies in regard to teachers. There is a lean towards Performance Review and away from Tenure. The principal Laura Atkin and her cronies are to blame. They stand in the way of a better education system. We insist on her removal from office."

Laura gasped. She held onto the back of her chair for stability as Heloise continued.

"To make matters worse, Laura Atkin has had a charge of racism against her. We cannot trust our kids to her school. She must go!"

Laura felt sick to her core. She wanted to turn off the television to make the false, libelous remarks go away, but instead stood frozen as she heard her accuser's voice continue.

"Since 1920 Tenure has been a proven policy which gives stability to our profession.

"Our teachers have been very resilient in the face of budget cuts, longer school days and larger class size.

"Now is the time to say 'no more'! We demand recognition for the vital role of our teachers. And we demand the firing of the traitor, Laura Atkin, who does our profession a disservice."

Then Heloise paused, bent down and lifted a picket sign with an unflattering head and shoulders photo of Laura wearing super-imposed heavy spectacles and captioned 'Let Laura Go!'

She read the slogan twice and the crowd responded in a rhythmic 'Let Laura Go!'

"We intend to march to her school and demand that she resign," bellowed Heloise. "Do you agree?"

The crowd echoed its agreement with a resounding 'Yes!'

Laura, flushed from fury, was more convinced than ever that education should be about learning for children and not jobs for adults. Yet she was faced with a dilemma: acquiesce for the sake of peace, and quit, or fight for what she believed was best for students. She turned off the program and threw the remote onto the chair. She went to her bedroom, changed into pajamas and went to bed without dinner.

Ten days later Marc, having breakfast at home in Bethesda, was taken by surprise when he received a call from Neville.

"Marc, I've only met you once," began Neville, "but I hear of you often. I've heard enough to know how much you mean to Laura. For that reason I'm compelled to ask you to go to

Pennsylvania as soon as possible." There was urgency in Neville's voice.

Marc feared the worst. "What happened?"

"It's Laura. I called her about the school fundraiser and she didn't sound well. She spoke of a threatened strike. You may have read about it in the papers. I followed up with Ruby, who said her mother's not eating properly. She's lost weight and has become quite withdrawn."

"I had no idea," said Marc. "I feel terrible."

"I have a feeling Laura didn't want to burden you," said Neville, "but I think it's fitting that you're the one who goes to her. I know how much you care."

Marc felt a knot in his stomach. He knew Laura worked too hard, but she appeared to be so resilient. "I'll be there tonight, of course," said Marc. "A colleague will take calls for me. Has Laura seen a doctor? Was there a diagnosis?"

"Ruby told me they didn't find a physical cause," said Neville. "They think it's related to stress. This business of the strike took a big toll. And the fact that they called her reputation into question was just too much for her."

On the drive to Pennsylvania, Marc could barely focus on the road. Laura sounded depressed. He prayed that she would be alright. Worrying about her well-being, he realized his feelings for her were as strong if not stronger than they had been when they first fell in love. He would do whatever was needed to help. The invisible wall she had created around her, however, was hard to penetrate.

Laura was a loving person, but Marc was competing with the needs of thousands of schoolchildren.

SIXTY

Upon arrival at her home, Marc saw that Laura was pale, withdrawn and tense. He had never seen her so unsettled. He lifted her effortlessly into his arms and held her till he could feel her body begin to relax. He noticed a tremor in her hands as she said, "Gutman's attack on me has deteriorated to a diabolic personal level. She knows no bounds. No civility. Just crude psychological warfare. Education issues have become secondary with her." Trying to muster energy, Laura added, "I wish we could put her in her place. Gutman zealously defends tenure. She even opposes school choice. I am proud to be a teacher. But teachers' unions should exist to improve schooling, not benefit its members."

Marc understood the medical profession, but knew almost nothing about collective bargaining.

He paused before responding. "I'm sad you're hurting, Laura. Let's think about how to deal with her without sinking to her level. Explain to me what her rhetoric is all about."

Laura listed several common arguments against performance –based compensation. She patiently responded to each objection as she spelled out her responses.

"Most importantly," she added, "American children lag behind those of other nations in international tests."

Marc measured his words. "You have a strong case. Speak from your heart and people will believe you. No one can question your credentials."

"You really think I should take her on?"

"I do," said Marc. You're right to fight this. The Department of Education will support you and I'll support you. You should meet publicly with this woman and have the media present. Show her up. I know you'll win any debate."

Laura was too tired to argue. Marc continued. "Laura, I love you. Have confidence in your worth. Since you've become school principal, there's more accountability and you've created a sense of community. You've helped countless students who were going off track graduate."

Marc backed up his words with a devotion that surprised Laura. He arranged for his workload to be assumed by his partners as he and Laura prepared for battle with Gutman. For a week, Marc was there for her day and night as Laura wrote, re-wrote and practiced her speech. At first, she had so little energy, he had to help her take notes and remind her to eat. Within days, however, she began to regain her strength. Laura recounted her high school debate with her fierce opponent, Diane. She would have to do even better this time, she told Marc. When she finally said to him, with a glint in her eyes, "I'm ready!" he knew Laura the leader and advocate, was back. The girl who had big dreams and who once said to him, "I've always wanted to teach. That's my way of contributing, through empowering others."

Laura arranged for a Press Conference at which she and Heloise Gutman spoke, the latter shouting more than speaking. Her bullying attitude and threats to bring schools to a halt did not win support from her audience. She appeared desperate. Her aggressive behavior backfired and no teacher's strike took place. Although Laura emerged as the victor of the dispute, it took a tremendous emotional toll. This time, however, Marc was by her side.

That evening, after they had finished dinner, Marc sat down next to Laura. Gently he held her face in his hands.

"Look into my eyes," said Marc. The emerald green pierced deep into his soul. "Be with me," he continued, "and let your obligations go for a moment."

"I'm with you now, Marc," she whispered. "I'm with you."

"Laura, for a long time you've been distant. Tell me the truth, am I still the person you love?"

Laura tried to clear her mind of her worries. She took slow deep breaths. She recalled all the things they did together. She remembered the only times she ever felt whole was when Marc was in her life, close to her. She thought about how throughout her major challenges, whether surgery or professional difficulties, he had been there to provide unconditional love and loyal support.

Laura experienced Marc's presence as she hadn't for a long time. She felt his chest against hers and listened to his breathing. The soothing accented voice still made her heart flutter. She realized she was one of the few to be blessed so young with the discovery of a love so extraordinary. She had been given a second chance thirty-five years later. Laura would not risk losing it all again.

"Yes," she answered. "Always."

SIXTY-ONE

Pennsylvania

Laura was humming a tune as she sorted through a tall pile of letters at home. She froze when she saw the envelope addressed to Ruby from Paramount Adoption Agency. Part of her wished it would never come, but here it was and they would have to deal with it. Ruby wouldn't be home for another two hours and it took restraint for Laura to refrain from opening the private letter. She thought of the twenty years of parenting, and the possibility of sharing her daughter with a biological mother, a stranger who would intrude on their lives, causing heartache and confusion.

When she reached Ruby on the phone, Laura asked her to come over quickly.

"What's wrong, mom?"

"Nothing, just come. I have a letter for you."

Laura pressed the envelope into Ruby's hand as she entered the house. Ruby looked at it and shook her head. "You open it," she said. "Please. I can't."

"Ruby," are you okay with this?" asked Laura.

"Yes, mom," she answered.

Laura kissed her daughter on the forehead. "I'll be here to support you no matter what."

Laura held her breath as she pulled out the single-page letter. With difficulty, she read aloud, "Dear Ruby, Thank you for your interest in trying to find your birth mother, Rosalind Varo. We deeply regret to inform you that she passed away from a heart condition five years ago." Laura held Ruby as she continued. "We were instructed by her, in the event you contacted us for information after her passing, to inform you that she loved you deeply, but as a single mother could not afford to provide for a baby. She also wanted you to know that she was born in Barcelona, Spain and loved music. She hopes you will understand and forgive her."

Laura processed this as she tried to read her daughter's emotions.

Ruby stared with a blank expression. "I can't feel anything," she said. "Only emptiness. I must be a terrible person."

"It's a lot to digest," said Laura. It'll take time. It's a shock to both of us."

"She was Spanish," said Ruby.

"And she loved music, just as you do."

Ruby nodded. "Our names both begin with 'R'." Trembling, she took the letter from the agency, and folded it carefully.

As she turned to walk away, Laura saw tears flowing down her cheeks.

That evening Laura called to check on her daughter. Derek answered the phone. "She's doing okay," he said. "I stayed home with her to make sure."

Ruby came on the line. "I do forgive her," she said. "I feel I know something about her now. She's a real person, instead of a figment of my imagination."

Laura was thinking of the right words when Ruby added, "Thank you for doing this, Mom."

And at that moment Laura realized that everything between them was as it had been. Nothing had changed. She would always be Ruby's mother. Now, nobody could challenge that.

SIXTY-TWO

Marc felt nostalgic as he lay on Laura's bed listening to her play songs from the 70's on her acoustic guitar.

"I promised I'd play for you again," she said.

Afterwards he told her about his dream to visit Italy, in particular an area in Tuscany about which he had read. He begged her to consider a trip together during the next public school recess.

"I discovered a small house in Radda in Chianti, not far from Florence," he said. "You've always wanted to travel. What do you say?"

Laura hadn't taken time off from work for a long time. She had built up months of vacation credits. School breaks had been used to read, catch up on paperwork and review lesson protocols. She needed a vacation desperately. And Italy was high on her list. Yes, she would go. It would be a great opportunity for her to spend time with Marc, without work obligations.

Over the next few weeks Laura made arrangements to take time off from school. Marc, in turn, arranged for coverage at his practice, and spent hours a week planning every detail of the trip.

Laura called him on the phone one evening. "Tell me our schedule," she said. "It looks like you're doing all the planning."

"Leave it to me," said Marc. "You've always wanted to travel to Italy. I want to make it a surprise."

Tuscany

It was still dawn when Laura and Marc, tired after the international flight to Bologna, loaded their two suitcases into the rental car and headed toward Florence and their vacation home in the magnificent province of Siena. At times on the long drive Laura covered her eyes when she saw drivers weave in and out of traffic speeding and swerving on the winding roads and in dark tunnels. It took all her restraint to resist grabbing the wheel. She would need some time to feel rested.

The country house was situated at the bottom of a vineyard and required driving down a steep, narrow path to get to the front. Marc navigated the gravel road as best he could. To their relief the door key was waiting in the mailbox as promised in Italian by the landlady. As soon as she stepped out of the car and onto Tuscany soil, Laura felt more relaxed. The farmland setting was stunning. To the right she saw acres of land with hundreds of rows of grapevines meticulously spaced. On the left a large patch of colorful flowers grew wild amidst a few olive trees. Alongside the perimeter of the house was an herbal garden with a bed of blue bushes. No doubt rosemary, thought Laura. To their delight the house was spacious, boasted two bedrooms with pretty views, a large bathroom and a kitchen. In the back was a swimming pool and patio with table and chairs. The considerate hostess had left tourist guides and magazines in the foyer and essentials in the kitchen and bathroom.

After they cleaned up and changed, they decided to explore the neighborhood. As soon as they stepped outside, they heard the unexpected sound of opera emanating from the vocal chords of a man riding a tractor between the vines. "Figaro, Figaro," he bellowed as the operatic rendition echoed in the valley.

"It's another world," said Laura happily, as she plucked a handful of herbs.

"No, don't pick that," cautioned Marc. "It could be poisonous."

Laura laughed and put a twig in her mouth. "Don't be neurotic, Doctor Sennet. It's rosemary. Smell it."

Marc was skeptical but trusted she probably knew what she was doing.

In spite of being tired, they decided they would take a walk up the steep hill to the small town center to get their bearings. Scrutinizing a local map, Laura and Marc, in shorts, tees and sunglasses, made their way to the Internet Café. There travelers dropped by to meet locals, check their e-mails and savor the gelato. After checking their messages and making small talk with some of the locals, they roamed further through the town, marveling at the quaint narrow streets and the medieval stone buildings of Radda. They discovered a pottery shop where Laura bought a set of four handmade ceramic egg cups, then they tasted the local wine in an underground wine cellar. They walked back as the sun began to set and Marc took photographs of the red-roofed houses amidst the idyllic landscape.

For the first time in a long while Laura slept through the night. The following day, rested, they boarded a bus on a daytrip, the first stop being Castellina, where the group visited the historic fortress Rocca di Castellina. The afternoon was spent in medieval San Gimignano. After making their rounds at the tourist shops and attractions, they walked on their own for about a mile, and then stopped at a kiosk to quench their thirst, before heading back to the waiting bus.

"No diet soda," said the clerk. "Americans always want diet soda."

Marc and Laura settled for sparkling water.

That night they headed out to a small restaurant owned by a husband and wife team, both chefs and known for their hospitality.

The wife seated them outside, brought them food and wine menus and then addressed Laura. "You married?" she asked, using a combination of hand gestures and Italian, and pointing to the wedding ring on her own hand and then to Laura's bare fingers.

Laura glanced at Marc, then threw up her hands and said, "Sorry, don't speak Italiano."

Marc noticed that Laura was affected by the question, so he cheered her up by attempting a conversation with her in Italian. Their hosts were amused by their language as they struggled to place their orders with help from their pocket dictionary. On the outdoor terrace, amidst acres of trees, they dined on mozzarella and vine-ripened tomatoes, bruschetta, and the best eggplant pasta dish they had ever tasted.

Lying in their king size bed that night, windows open, feeling the fresh Chianti breeze, Laura felt more at peace than she had in a long time. "So, where's our next stop?" she asked.

"I told you," said Marc. "It's a surprise."

Sea Point, Cape Town, one week later

The weather report read seventy-eight degrees with low humidity. A perfect day for the beach. As Marc and Laura strolled down Worcester Road toward the ocean, Laura pointed to a building on the corner.

"It's the sculpture of the monkeys you spoke about," she said. "See no evil, hear no evil, do no evil. They're still there!"

Laura pulled Marc by the arm as she sprinted toward the sea.

"It's just as you described it. The waves crashing on the rocks. The seagulls and the salty air."

Marc was happy to be in familiar surroundings and relieved to see there were no longer signs mandating racial separation. Gone were the warnings 'Whites Only'.

"Some progress at last," he said.

Like teenagers, the two ran along the boardwalk, past the red and yellow swings and past the giant chess set. Out of breath, they made their way down the steps to the beach. In their bathing suits they lay nestled together on the soft sand. Laura felt the sun warm her body and the cool water tickle her feet as the waves broke gently on shore. It had taken her a long time to find true happiness and everlasting love, but it was worth the wait.

ABOUT THE AUTHORS

Tania Heller, M.D. is a physician and independent medical school admissions consultant. She completed her medical school training at the University of Cape Town and her pediatric residency training at the Georgetown University Medical Center. She is the author of the following books:

> *On Becoming a Doctor* (Sourcebooks); *You and Your Doctor*; *Eating Disorders: A Handbook for Teens, Families and Teachers*; *Pregnant! What Can I Do?* and *Overweight: A Handbook for Teens and Parents* (McFarland)

Izzy Heller was the CEO of a grain milling conglomerate in South Africa and the co-founder of Heller Jewelers in Chevy Chase, Maryland. He is the author of the following books:

> *Secrets of a Jeweler* and *Death in McMurdo,* and co-author of *Deadly Truth.* (AuthorHouse)

Izzy Heller and daughter Tania Heller immigrated to the United States from South Africa in 1980 and 1983 respectively. You can reach Tania at taniaheller@yahoo.com and Izzy at heller.antiques1@verizon.net.

71397672R00180

Made in the USA
San Bernardino, CA
16 March 2018